Uphill Battle

A ROMANTIC COMEDY

ALICE DUKE

Prologue

ADA

THERE'S some expression I've heard that goes, "Those whom the gods wish to destroy they first make mad." It seems like a lot of work for something you just plan to ruin. But what do I know? I don't ruin things. I make them and I make them gorgeous.

But I digress.

I'm pretty sure that there were some gods out for my cute behind because someone was definitely trying to make me mad and they'd put this insanity-inducing-nightmare into the most adorable package of tall, unshaven man I'd ever seen.

I'd been studying him from behind my aviator sunglasses for a few minutes before he came up to the car window and had to bend almost double to look in. That's the thing with chopped hotrods — they aren't meant for the tall men of this world, but they are picture perfect for someone short and slight but still a touch curvy —like me. Why do you think I built one? This one, to be precise.

She's my pride and joy from the period-correct headlight bars to the pearly tuck-and-roll interior. And she rumbles like she's craving cheesecake and can't keep it to herself. My kinda girl.

"Miss, can you direct me to your husband?" is the first thing he says to me. Not promising. Maybe he's not very bright.

I lift my left hand and wiggle the fingers. No ring. No husband.

He should have left then and let me enjoy watching him leave. And trust me, it would be worth the sight. Watching him arrive had already been a real tall glass of water on a sweltering day.

"Your boyfriend, then," he says coolly as if it makes no difference, and it doesn't, since I don't have one of those either. He's got an accent. I like it. It's not quite Russian, but close.

"If that's a pick-up line, I'm sure you can do better," I say lazily, taking off my aviators so I can study him while I chew my toothpick.

Hot days are the best because shirts stick to sweaty skin leaving nothing to the imagination. He's gone ahead and worn a black one, which is worse for him and better for me because I get to see all those nice lean muscles that this cute white boy is bringing to the table with all that sass.

"It's not a pick-up line," he says tightly, his unshaven jaw practically bristling.

That's a pretty face he's wearing. A bit pale for my taste, but his dark hair is thick, his brows even thicker, his nose straight, cheekbones defined, lips a little too full for his face, and those baby blues are priceless. Maybe I'll play with him a bit before I throw him back.

"No, it's not," I agree. "It's never going to get you anywhere."

I let myself smile slowly at him and I lean back and look him up and down, taking him in.

"Fine, where's your father, then?"

This game is getting old.

"Here's the thing, honey," I say smooth as butter. "We could pretend I'm Siri — who I'm pretty sure would be white if she were a person, so that's a poor fit — or you could stop asking me one-hundred-and-one irrelevant questions and go buy me a lemonade. What's it going to be?"

"I'm not here to buy you a lemonade," he says tersely. When he clenches his jaw like that, lines run down his cheeks perpendicular to his mouth and I've always liked lines like that. I want to run my tongue down them like an ice cream treat. Which I could also use right about now. Have I mentioned it's hot? Even for San Diego?

"And I'm not a white girl named Siri," I say, but I start my car because this is getting old and I don't know any other way to extricate myself without losing my cool-cat image.

"I don't think you should be driving that," he says, looking worried now. He glances around the crowd like he needs support — which he most certainly will if this is going to be a man v.s. car situation. I have a lead foot and I'm not afraid to use it.

I don't know what he thinks he'll see around him. It's a car show. It's mostly old white guys in polo shirts and shorts. There are a handful of Latinos over by the muscle cars and drifters. A few girls dressed like pin-ups or in poodle skirts. Some old ladies with too much makeup attempting to tailgate off a '54 Chevrolet truck. None of them care where my dad is or if I should be allowed to drive.

"Honey, I'm about to put my foot on the gas, and you won't want to be standing there when I do," I say, returning my aviators to my nose and then casually spitting my toothpick out the window. It sticks to his workboot. Guess he shouldn't have been standing there.

"Hot rods have a lot of throttle. You really should wait for your boyfriend to get back before you leave," he says nervously. "Or your father, or whoever. Here. When he gets here give him this."

He hands me his card.

Nicola Petrovic

Independent Journalist

"Nicola," I say. "That's a girl's name."

"It's a man's name," he says, bristling, but at least he isn't leaning into my window anymore.

I shake my head. "Ends in an 'a.' That makes it a girl's name. Like my name, 'Ada.'"

"It's a man's name." His accent is thicker when he's mad. I wonder if I could make it unintelligible if I pushed him hard enough. That might be fun.

"Well, honey, thanks for the card. I'll call you when me and the girls go out for two-for-one Ladies' Night."

"I want to feature this car in a freelance article I'm working on about San Diego hotrods and it's the best one I've seen at a show so far," he says testily, arms crossed over his chest. "But I could use some details about the car. "Can you just give the card to the owner of this hot rod?"

"Don't need to," I say, tossing the card on the seat beside me. I'm already slowly easing out of my space and he has to jog to keep up.

"Why's that?" he asks. Awfully dense, this one.

"Because you already have, Nicola." I draw his name out nice and slow and really enunciate the "a" before I step on the gas and peel out of there with a squeal of my tires and a slight shudder to the right. Yeah, she does that sometimes.

I love watching his face in my rearview mirror. It's priceless. Not exactly as good as watching him leave would have been, but hey, you can't have everything. And I'll take second place if the prize is good enough.

Chapter One

ADA

"WHILE PERFECTLY ACCEPTABLE — as all her work is — this particular piece lacked the verve of her past interiors," my cousin Jasmin reads before pausing to sip on her cherry cola. "I think this one is a bit nicer, Ada."

I huff loudly and try to uncurl my body from its current pretzel pose. If that's a yoga thing, then I so have it nailed, and if it's not then maybe I need a chiropractor. I'm trying to fit this headliner I made for a client's Ford Falcon and it's being belligerent.

"Fit!" I demand. "Just fit!"

It's gorgeous — seafoam green sparkle vinyl with tuck and roll seats and a matching headliner. It's not what I'd pick for the car, but it's pretty and bright and he'll look like he wants to go surfing every day, which I think is kind of his deal.

"Did you hear me?" Jasmin asks, tapping her high heel on the concrete floor. She's leaning over the workbench on one of my stools, glaring at her phone. "I don't think this is the hit piece you thought it would be."

"They're all hit pieces, Jasmin. All of them."

Jasmin scoots off the stool and sticks out a hip in a pose she perfected in middle school. She's in design school and she loves to show off her figure when she's wearing clothes she made herself. She's adorable, of course. She always is. She looks perfect with our vintage shop highlighting all her color and life.

My dad and I share a three-bay garage. It's way too small for us, but it's been in the family since the time of his father and our family has been building great hotrods since Pappy got back from the war in '46. Every old gas station sign and black and white picture pinned to the old tar-soaked wood walls is from that era. So are most of the hand tools, and my dad refuses to shift over to power impact drivers or drills, so that's almost every tool we have.

Thankfully, he didn't give me that restriction on my sewing machine, or he would have heard from me. I am *not* working a pedal-powered machine just to keep the vintage feel of the shop — though I admit that I do wear the cute vintage clothes Jasmin makes me because they look "hot rod" and right now the fitted red pedal-pushers and my black leather spaghetti-strap top are her adorable designs.

"I still don't get why he hates you," Jasmin says with a magnificent pout. No one can pout like Jasmin.

"He hassles her because she's a capable woman," my Pops says from down in the pit.

He's working on a roadster's exhaust system. Been at it all morning. My Pops is in his sixties, lanky and a bit worn-looking. Probably because he's been raising me as a single dad since my mom died in childbirth. Did you know that African American women are more likely to die in childbirth in the United States of America than any other race? I do. I know because that's how the love of my dad's life died. I bet she was pretty great. People always say I remind them of her, and I'm spectacular.

"He didn't know I was capable when he met me, Pops," I say, working to clip the headliner in place. This right here is why a small-sized upholsterer kicks booty. I fit where no one else does.

I aim the next comment at my cousin. "Do me a favor and stop reading the article, Jasmin. Check my email for me instead, will you? I haven't had time all morning. And I need to film again."

I steal a peek through the windshield to the open garage doors beyond. The oleanders are in full bloom, framing the entrance, and out beyond it I can see the busy street, and just past that the far-away ocean. The sky above is the burning blue of a truly hot day and it's definitely well past noon.

I haven't taken a break all day. Not that I need to. I can work steadily until dinner without needing to stop. But I *do* need to film the last stages of getting this headliner into place for tomorrow's upload.

There are a few moments of silence as Jasmin opens my computer and then I hear a choked gasp.

"You okay over there, baby cousin," I ask her, teasing. I leave the headliner mostly in place and hurry to adjust my camera. I've had it filming me all morning, and I plan to run that reel at high speed with voice-over while I discuss what I was doing, but at the end, I want to talk while I work.

"Umm ... Ada," she says in a choked voice. "You need to see this."

"If it's another bill, don't worry," Pops says with a grunt from under the roadster. "The guy's coming for this next month and I'll have cash to pay for my part."

He's not going to be done in a month. Even I know that. And he's not getting paid when "the guy" shows up in cash or otherwise. I've worked with my dad for years and his bill collecting skills leave a lot to be desired.

"No! It's an offer! It's from —" she's cut off by my phone ringing. I grunt as I try to stabilize the headliner and reach for the phone from my back pocket. Jasmin snorts a laugh and swipes it from my pocket, answering it for me.

"Ada Ford's phone," she chirps. "Jasmin speaking, can I help you?"

She batts her eyes at me and I narrow mine in a not-so-veiled threat but her eyes widen and she thrusts the phone at me before I'm ready for it.

I take it, still trying to balance the headliner on my shoulder. My voice is tight. "Ada here."

"Ada! This is Big Daddy Boom of BOOM Enterprises," the cheerful voice on the other end says and I freeze. *O. M. G.*

I should pause in my narrative to clue you in. New to the world of online vehicle channels? Well, then you won't have heard of Big Daddy Boom or BOOM Enterprises. Probably. You might have seen the online special 'BOOM Power,' or the Discovery Channel season of 'BOOM Off-Road Explosion!' But you won't know that he's basically a god in the online world and he has money to buuuurn. If I had even one joint video with him, it could make Pin Up Stitchin' take off enough to finally see some black on that ledger.

"Hi," I say. It's weak even to my ears.

"Who is that?" Pops asks, and Jasmin hisses at him to be quiet.

"I've been watching your channel, Ada," Big Daddy Boom says, "After my daughter, Gracie, brought it to my attention."

"He's been watching my channel," I mouth to Jasmin. She's bouncing up and down with a huge grin on her face.

"I'm flattered," I manage.

"It's great. Maybe I'll get you to do an interior for me sometime," he says, casually, like it's no big deal. "My helicopter is very blah. All grey inside. How great would it be with traffic cone orange seats and the BOOM logo?"

"Probably pretty amazing," I say. How did my throat get so dry? It's impossible to speak.

"But anyway, that's not what I'm calling for right now. I have this great little project that I'd love to get you in on."

I might faint.

I'm not the fainting type. I'm the slap your face with a gauntlet and duel you to the death type but I still might faint. This is ... this could solve all my problems. Immediately. This is the break I've been praying for every night and hoping for every moment.

"I'm in," I say in a rush, and he laughs easily.

"Well, don't say that until you've heard the details." He sounds like he's relaxing. I shift my weight so the headliner's on my back instead of my aching arm. "I'm bringing together four smaller channels of the best professionals, plus my own. Together, you'll go get Mikey Hunt's old '32 truck from his parents' mining claim. It's way out in the middle of nowhere. You'll film the whole thing. I'm pretty sure it was running when Mikey left it there, so it's probably just a matter of tuning her up, and then bringing her home. And then each of the shops gets a chance to work on her. We've got Bobby at Bobby Branson Body Shop doing the body and paint. Pin Up Stitchin' will do the interior — if you agree. Hollis Montieth has agreed to do the engine, and I have *Knockin' Rods* doing the overall work, tune-up, and assembly at the end."

My excitement is hit with a shot of dread and I have to fight back the panic clawing at my throat.

"*Knockin' Rods*?" I choke out.

"That's right! Nicola's known for putting together some excellent cars. You've heard of him?"

"Yes," I grit out, darting a glance to Jasmin who is watching me with her eyes bugging out. I think she can hear the conversation. My phone has this weird tendency to broadcast everything like it wishes it was always on speakerphone.

"Great! We'll schedule the whole thing out as a massive promotion. Make gear that goes with the build — it's called the Silver Bullet, by the way — and send traffic to your channel for your portion of it all. And then we'll all meet up at my place in Utah for a party at the end and the big reveal where we show it to Mikey. It's for his fiftieth birthday and he's gonna love it."

"Wow," I say and I really am stunned despite my reservations.

My online channel does okay. It makes enough to help cover the time and expense of filming and getting the right gear, and then just a little more. And I need that little more. I do great upholstery — the best — but it takes time and that means it's a while between paychecks. And I'm not just paying my own way. I'm floating Pops, too.

Pops has a passion for what he does and he's excellent at it. But can you guess what he's not excellent at? Turning a profit. He does free work for every person with an issue with their lawnmower, or boat motor, or weird tick in their car engine. He's forever stalling on the work that makes us money while he helps the kid down the road with his bike, or the old lady next door with her '80s Oldsmobile. I love my Pops to bits. Everyone does (right? How could they not?) but sometimes I wonder how we could afford to eat when I was a kid because time and money flow through his hands like the breeze on a sunny day. Thank goodness his dad left him the shop and the apartment above it or we'd never have been able to make rent.

"So what do you say?" Big Daddy Boom asks on the phone, his tone so bright and excited that it's contagious.

"Yes," I breathe. "Thank you for thinking of me."

He laughs. "No, thank *you*. I'll be excited to give Mikey a genuine Pin Up Stitchin' interior. I'll have Tanner send you the details and the contract and once we're all signed up it's a go. Do you have weekend plans?"

"I don't think so?" It comes out like a question and he laughs again.

"You do now. The details will be with the stuff Tanner sends. Feel free to let your channel in on some teasers, but keep a lid on things until we're ready to roll, okay? If we schedule this properly, we'll all be winners."

"Absolutely," I agree, both because I desperately need this, and because I understand how online marketing works, and I'm relieved that he has a plan.

We say our goodbyes and I turn to Jasmin just as she squeals and launches herself into the car with me to hug me.

"Adaaaa!" She says, turning my name into a whine of excitement. "It's really happening! You're going to be famous!"

"I don't think you should sign those contracts," Pops grumps from under the hotrod he's working on. I guess he heard the whole thing, too. "No amount of fame is worth working with a man who can't see the value in women."

"Big Daddy works with his daughter," Jasmin protests. "He's a great partner for this! And his channel has three million subscribers. Three million! If Ada could scoop up just ten percent of that she could clean up!"

"Not the internet-rich man," Pops says. "He seems fine, if a little lacking in judgment. I'm talking about the blowhard who writes those articles about you. Nicola."

"It will be fine," I assure him, trying to act breezy and confident.

He catches my eye from a gap between the roadster and the edge of the pit and lifts an eyebrow.

"Is there more going on here than I realize?"

"Just fine," I say with rolling eyes. He can't single-eyebrow me out of this.

But when I finish the headliner and open up the BOOM email, my heart is racing. Will it really be fine, trying to work with someone who treats me like a child? Or worse ... a barbie doll who is only there as some kind of decoration?

It will just have to be. I'm not losing this chance over Nicola Petrovic. In fact, I'm going to make him eat every word he ever said or wrote about me. And I'm going to enjoy doing it.

Chapter Two

NICOLA

I'M STILL STARING at the text on my phone when she pulls up. This is not what I expected. I thought there would be a buffer. There should be about a dozen other people here to help us remove this old truck from the mining claim and serve as an insulator between me and this woman who has seen me make a total fool of myself. Maybe if she wasn't so smoking hot I could have blown it off. But who am I fooling? She's a total smoke show. And I have no idea what to do around her.

I flinch at a stab of pain in my belly and take another bite of my powdered sugar donut. It's from the last gas station I passed and it's going to have to be lunch because I forgot to grab anything else on the way here. That's fine. There's supposed to be food that the guys from BOOM Enterprises are bringing. BBQ, apparently, and it's only for one day.

My phone flashes and I take a look. It's a text from Big Daddy Boom.

I hope you brought that trailer to get the Silver Bullet, buddy.

Uh oh. This text is time-stamped two hours ago. My cell has been bouncing between towers and somehow it didn't pull these from the cloud until I stopped.

But it's fine because I did bring my trailer. It's my twenty-four-footer and it will haul anything up to a full-size truck and a quad, both at once.

I watch *Pin Up Stitchin'* park her car in the gravel and shake my head. A '32 Ford Tudor Sedan? Is she kidding? This is not the place for a car like that. Not even when it's painted flat black. I can see chips in the gold metal flake wheels and I guaran-fuck-ing-tee you she got those on the way up that gravel road. If I didn't already know this was her rig, I'd go tell her how stupid it was to bring it here. Well, I would if I wasn't tongue-tied at the sight of her.

Again.

I swallow as she slides out of the car, aviators already on, a multi-color handkerchief wrapped around the front of her hair and the rest of it piled up into the world's largest braid updo. She's chewing on a toothpick and already scowling with those pretty pouty lips of hers. I'm pretty sure there are statues carved with those exact perfect cheeks and flawless skin in places far away from the wilderness of Northern California. Far from where we find ourselves now at the end of a dirt road that becomes a trail.

I swallow, grateful when my phone buzzes again, distracting me.

We've run into a little issue. It's time-stamped an hour and a half ago.

Still, I'm feeling pretty confident. I'm not a person bothered by issues.

Hollis has the flu. Or maybe something worse. Couldn't get on the plane. His whole crew is down with it.

Same with Bobby and his crew.

Okay, now I'm feeling a few butterflies in my belly with that stabbing pain. That's two of the five channels and more than half the manpower. I don't count Ada Ford in her cherry-red Doc Martins, black skinny jeans, and canary-yellow leather jacket. I'm sure she's great with a sewing needle — well, most of the time. At least half the time. And she seems to film reasonably professionally for her channel, even if her tone is a bit too chipper for my liking — trust me, it surprised me too after my first meeting with her sharp tongue. But I don't think she's dressed to get dirty, and someone's about to get very dirty hauling this truck out of the woods.

My phone buzzes a third time.

Tanner was on his way to you, but he blew his transmission on the road. Sending map. Hoping you can handle pulling the truck out with Ada. She can handle most of the B reel if you can get the truck running and haul her out.

I stare at my phone. This one's from an hour ago. He's kidding, right?

I swallow hard and look up at Ada who has her arms crossed over her chest and one leg crossed over the other as she leans against a tree studying the sky like I'm too boring for words.

City, city, city, is practically tattooed on that lovely forehead.

And she's my only backup here. That, or we both drive eight and a half hours back to our home city and call it a day. But I can't afford to waste two days driving here and back with nothing to show for it. And I need this build. I need it so badly that I can taste it.

The *Knockin' Rods* online channel has two thousand subscribers and gets about four thousand views when I post a video. It's small time. *I'm* small time. And I'm desperate to be more than that.

This right here — this is my big break and I absolutely refuse to lose out on it, no matter who I have to beg and cajole to help me go drag an old rust bucket out of the woods. Even if it's a smoke show with only two marketable skills — neither of which is off-roading *or* getting vehicles running — and the most sexy little curvy body I've ever seen.

No distractions, Nicola. Do the job. Work the plan. Get the money. Live the life.

It's my mantra and I'm sticking with it.

She spits her toothpick and it lands an inch from my boot.

Heat seeps up from under my collar and I grind my teeth. Even the mantra might not be enough.

"No distractions, Nicola," she says, wrapping her tongue around my name like it's a hard candy.

And it's not until she repeats it in a mocking voice that I realize I said it out loud. I shove the rest of the donut in my face to hide my embarrassment and chew it up fast to vent my frustrations. It isn't working.

"That car you brought is a waste of time," I tell her. "You shouldn't have come in that."

She lifts an eyebrow. "Excuse me?"

"Did you get the texts or what?" I ask her as I type "10-4" into my phone and hit send.

She looks away like she's embarrassed. "My phone has no service here."

I grunt and shove mine at her so she can read the conversation. My belly hurts worse than ever and it's making me start to sweat. I'd kill to lie down right now, but I have a job to do and the day isn't getting any younger.

"It's just us?" she says, like I've just told her we're scheduled to be eaten by wolves. "Well, then we need to come back another time."

She pushes off from the tree and starts to saunter to her vehicle.

Maybe she doesn't need this like I do.

"There isn't another time. I'm going now," I say, moving to

the trailer. I'd better unhitch the trailer and take the truck in. I'd hoped that someone else would be coming with an off-road vehicle and I could leave this truck here with the trailer but that car of hers has about four inches of clearance. It's barely capable of going off the pavement. I meet her eyes for a bare second. "It's probably better if you don't come."

I'm just finishing with the trailer when I see her storm past with her purse and a camera bag.

"Whoa," I say. "What are you doing?"

"Let me guess," she says flicking her chin like she's brushing me away with it. "You're wondering if my husband is here to help you. No luck. It's only me."

She opens my passenger door and flings her things into it, but she can't get in. Which makes sense. She's a tiny thing and the truck is lifted. I come up from behind her, grasp her hip bones firmly, and toss her into the cab, shutting the door behind her.

If she wants to come, we'd better get going.

When I hop in the driver's side, her aviators are on the top of her head and her nostrils are flared, her big brown eyes wide with fury.

"Never do that without my permission," she says tightly, biting off the end of each word.

"Help you?" I ask, nonplussed.

"Touch. Me." She sounds like she might kill me and bury me out here somewhere, but her full attention is on me, and I find I like the way it makes my neck feel hot.

When I look back at her, I drink her in, every last inch of her hostile, gorgeous, angry self.

"I'll never touch you again without your permission," I agree. "Not even when you're about to fall on your pretty little —"

I start the truck and rev the motor at that juncture on purpose and the 7.3 in this truck is loud and smoky and it drowns out the rest, including whatever her retort was going to be.

And yeah, this is a terrible start, but that doesn't mean it won't be a breathtaking adventure. Especially not with the enemy at the other end of the bench seat along for the ride.

Chapter Three

ADA

HE HAS GOT to be kidding.

I give him a long look as he turns the truck into the narrow dirt road. It's there, but it's grown over and I can only just make out that there's a trail here at all. It's going to do a real number on his truck body. And I don't care.

When he doesn't look at me, I start speaking anyway, "I don't care if you don't want me along. You still have to treat me with respect."

"Who says I don't want you along?" he asks gruffly and I just roll my eyes.

"That means no touching without permission. That means treating me as an equal partner. That means no making decisions without talking to me. I had more stuff back in my car, you know. I wanted to get it."

He leans over the steering wheel scowling at the road. Why the hell did God make him so pretty just to put the sourest soul inside that honey-dipped body anyway? What a waste.

He's seriously pretty. I think he's eastern European or something. His accent sounds Russian and that straight nose and chiseled jaw are working for me. But the scowl isn't. And neither is the way he is glaring at the trail like he plans to murder it and bury its body where no one will ever find it.

My phone rings and I take the call while I can. In the background I hear a series of pings as all my texts flood in so I put it on speaker.

"Oh my gosh, Ada!" Jasmin says through the speaker.

I catch Nicola's eye as he turns his scowl on me, his eyebrows pushing together as he turns that baleful blue eye my way, and I wonder if anyone has ever told him that he's adorable when he's mad. I want to see if he gets into outrageously-hot territory if I push him further. I turn the volume up.

"I'm bouncing in and out of service, so I might lose you," I tell her as the truck *literally* bounces, jarring my voice. He took that bump that fast on purpose, I just know it. I make sure to wink flirtatiously when he looks at me to tell him that I *do not care* what crap he pulls.

"I've had like a thousand calls from Big Daddy Boom!" she says. "On the landline. He says no one is coming to help you."

"*Knockin' Rods* is here," I say grimly and note Nicola's smirk at my use of his channel name. He likes that? Fine, I'm never saying it again.

"The asshole who wrote all those mean articles about you?"

"The very same," I agree, smiling sweetly at Nicola.

"I am *not* an asshole," he mouths and he looks appalled, like he honestly didn't expect us to think so.

"Like in the vehicle with you?" she asks.

"Yeah. He literally picked me up by the hips and threw me in his front seat."

"That's assault. You could sue him for that."

"I know that, but I don't think he does," I say pointedly. His cheeks are flushed red now, and they look great with his scowl. I should see how long I can keep them like that.

"Is he hot?"

"It's not that warm up here, actually. I probably should have brought a coat."

"Adaaa," she whines, but she composes herself. "So you're saying he's not your type."

I pause, waiting for him to look at me. Called it. He totally does. It's a furtive sidelong glance like he's wondering if he's my type and physically, yes, though if we're going by attitude then it's a hell-to-the-no.

"What is your type again?" Jasmin asks, fishing.

I answer long and slow like I'm considering it for the first time, but really I'm trying to see if his white-boy cheeks can get any redder.

"Hmmm ... maybe a hot dentist who talks about his feelings ..."

He's definitely redder and his eyes are wide as he focuses forward like he can't hear this conversation.

"So a unicorn," she says.

"As in there's only one of them?"

"As in they don't exist, and if they did then they wouldn't go for girls who smell like brake cleaner and think a good time is helping Pops figure out what's making that ticking noise in the engine."

"Easy," Nicola says, his pale eyes still on the trail as it jostles us side to side so hard that I'm nearly knocked across the bench seat and into his hip. "It's an exhaust leak."

"Do you have me on speakerphone?" Jasmin gasps, horrified. "He heard all that?"

"Sure," I say easily.

"But I called him an asshole!"

"I'm pretty sure he knows he's an asshole. We don't have to pretend we haven't figured it out, too."

"I am not," he says and his accent is thicker than normal. "Not. That."

"How's Pops?" I ask, changing the subject.

"Fine," Jamin says.

"And the shop?"

"O. M. G. Ada, it's fine. You've only been gone since early this morning. Just focus on your job and we'll take care of things here. Oh, and *Fab Fabrics* called. They say you're in arrears by six thousand dollars and they want payment on Monday."

"Okay," I say tightly, risking a glance at Nicola. Thank goodness he doesn't seem to be paying attention anymore. He's totally concentrating on the road as we come up to a rough washed-out area and a pink corner of tongue is peeking through his full lips as he concentrates, and it looks so soft beside his rough unshaven cheeks that I have the most terrible urge to catch it with my own lips and give it a new home.

"I've got to go," I say a little more hoarsely than maybe I'd like.

"Okay, love you," Jasmin says.

"Same to you," I say and terminate the call before scrolling through my messages. They're duplicates of Jasper's except two from Pops asking where I put the scrap angle iron and then claiming to have found it and one extra from Big Daddy BOOM.

The transmission is frigged. Tanner's stuck. We're sending a team. ETA tomorrow.

"Looks like the BOOM Enterprises team won't get here until tomorrow," I tell Nicola.

He grunts.

"A little communication would be nice," I say, putting my aviators back on. "You know — communication? The primary tool for working with others? Or is that not something you do in Russia?"

"I'm not Russian," he spits.

"Yeah, okay."

"Are you African?"

"No!" I'm offended. It's so racist to ask that. "My ancestors have been in this country since before it was a country, thank you very much."

"See?" he says, shooting a smug glance at me. "It's offensive when people make assumptions."

"I think we should stick to the point," I say, extremely grateful for my aviators to hide half my face. "Do you think it will be a problem that the Boom team won't be here until tomorrow?"

"I have a hotel booked for tonight in Sacramento," he says.

I do, too, but that did not answer my question. "So that's a no?"

"It's two o'clock," he says. "Assuming four hours in, we get there for six, an hour to hook up the truck or get it running, then four hours back out and two more to Sacramento. It's going to be a late night, but there's no reason to be worried."

"See?" I say. "Communication. It doesn't have to be like pulling teeth."

"You would know," he says, deadpanning. "You're the one who's marrying a dentist."

I don't dignify that with a response. I mean, I totally would have, but the next bump jars me way too hard, and my teeth rattle bad enough that I'm probably going to have to go see a dentist whether he's hot husband-material or not. Besides, I'm stuck with this guy for the next nine hours. I might as well try to keep things friendly. Lord knows he won't.

Chapter Four

NICOLA

SHE IS RUTHLESSLY INDEPENDENT, and as much as I want to be annoyed that I have to go on this job with a woman who thinks shiny red boots are a good choice for a ride into the forest, I have to admit that she hasn't complained at all. Not when she has to get out again and again to film the B roll of my truck going past corners or tougher patches of the trail. Yes, she has figured out how to get in and out without help. Not when she has to jog to catch up again. Not even when she has to fight her way up into the lifted vehicle.

"You shouldn't hang off the door handle," I tell her when she gets in this time. "You're going to break it."

It's the only helpful thing I can find to say. She's getting everything else right. It almost makes me feel kind of useless. Like, why am I even here if she can film it all herself?

Oh yeah. Because she brought a hotrod to do a truck's job.

It's been almost two hours and we should already be there. I'm not going to lie, I'm worried I've gotten us lost. Here's the thing, this trail isn't the clearest. But even if it were a six-lane highway I'd be distracted by the woman with me. Distracted enough to miss a turn? Maybe. To pass a landmark? Mmmhmm. To get lost? Look, I'm not perfect. I know that. Now you know it, too, ya?

She takes off her jacket and when I see the shirt below I swallow hard and I'm immediately annoyed. Yeah, that's what it is. Annoyed. Definitely not attracted.

"What is that?"

"It's a T-shirt. Most Americans wear them," she says loftily.

"What's *on* the T-shirt?"

"My logo. For *Pin Up Stitchin'*." She angles herself toward me and sticks her chest out to show me the logo as if the logo itself wasn't scandalous enough on its own, now I have the roundness of her chest emblazoned on my memory.

I scowl at her. And at the logo. It's of a woman in what could perhaps politely be called "burlesque" holding a huge needle between two fingers like a cigarette. A long tail of thread wraps suggestively around her.

"Is she gonna smoke that thing or make love to it?" I ask, deadpanning.

"It's a needle," she says bitingly. "It's for stitching upholstery. But I'm not surprised you don't know that. It fits with what I know about you."

"Which is?" I ask, squinting at the trail. It's probably right. It has to be right.

"That you know nothing about upholstery."

"And how would you know that?" I ask, but I'm distracted. I have a terrible feeling that this isn't right.

"Because I've read your articles and it's clear you're lost when it comes to upholstery. Not qualified to offer an opinion."

"I offer opinions on all kinds of things," I say, but I'm running this conversation with only half my brain. The rest of my brain is trying to determine exactly which of these options is the actual trail.

"And I'm sure they're equally valid," she says, smirking.

"Meaning?"

"Wait." Her tone shifts to urgency. "You're not scowling at me. You've been scowling for the last two hours."

She leans to look at my gauges like she can't trust me to tell her if something's wrong with the truck. I don't really mind her pressed up against me to look, but it's distracting. Maybe too distracting.

"The truck is fine," she says and then takes off her aviators to look at me more closely before saying, "Oh no. It's the route. You've gotten us lost."

"I?" I push back. I mean, she's here, too. She could have said, "Hey, that's not the trail."

"Yes, you. The one driving," she says, reaching for her phone. "No service. Shit."

She reaches for my glove box.

"No! Don —."

She has it open before I can finish speaking. A fountain of paperwork shoots out of the dash like cards from one of those shufflers in Vegas. Yeah. I keep a lot in there. But not maps.

"Oh." Her hands fly over her mouth and she's adorable in her panic. "Oh, I'm so sorry. What is this? Oh no!"

I feel my face flushing red as I try to grab for a photo that fell between us, but my grab pulls the truck into the weeds and I have to fight it to get it back onto the maybe-trail. When I have it under control, I stop and make a second grab for the photo.

It's me. Dressed in a white shirt and slacks with a bride in my arms. Amber. We were married for two weeks. Tied the knot in Mexico. I thought she was the love of my life until it turned out I wasn't the love of hers, and she took off with a bartender she met during ladies' night. He wasn't even the one she was with when she came back six months later to serve me with divorce papers. Turned out I was waaay down on her list.

But when I grab for the shameful picture of me grinning like a fool over a woman who obviously only married me for the free vacation, I realize that's not what Ada is staring at. My mouth opens. She's staring at a picture of me as a kid with my parents in Kosovo.

I swallow. Yeah. As private as the Amber picture is, this is worse.

We look upset. Understandable. We were fleeing our home and everything we loved. I was six. My parents were older when they had me. Both in their forties. They stare grimly at the camera.

I snatch the picture from her.

"My parents," I say gruffly.

"And the pleasant boy who won Mr. Popularity?" she asks with a smirk.

I don't answer. She knows it's me. The problem is that I see her side-eyeing the picture of me and Amber.

"Didn't know you were married," she says. "You don't wear a ring. What does she think about you being here?"

"She doesn't care," I say gruffly, tucking both photos above the sun visor on my side but I'm not fast enough. I swear Ada is a human squirrel.

"Wow, why buy a filing cabinet when you have a glove box," she chirps. She's flipping through my old canceled passport. You can see the hole punch marks from when they invalidated it when I became a US citizen. "Canada, eh?"

She says it like she doesn't know it's the most annoying thing to say to a Canadian. I'd care, only I'm not Canadian. Anymore.

"That picture of you and your folks was so dreary. I didn't know that everyone was so miserable in ... Alberta?"

"No."

"Quebec?"

"No."

"Manitoba?"

"Wow, you know a lot of provinces," I say as I pick up the

receipts on the floor. Have I really bought this many truck batteries? "Too bad you can't recognize Kosovo when you see it."

"Kosovo ..." her voice trails off and I look up, expecting her to say something like, "Oh my god, you were a refugee," but no, she's looking at a stack of handwritten papers and I'm not fast enough to snatch them from her.

"I know these," she says, and it's not awe in her voice, it's disgust. "These are your articles."

"You've read them, then?" I feign casual disinterest. She's really read my work? That gives me a funny feeling inside like the bubbles from champagne.

"You wrote them by hand?" she presses, turning over the first page and then lifting it up between a finger and thumb like it's a dead rat.

"They aren't infectious," I say, snatching up the last of the papers from the floor and stuffing them into the glove box. "You won't catch writing ability from them."

"No, but I might catch bad mojo," she says, flipping through them. "These are all the ones about me."

My neck and cheeks are suddenly on fire. I don't know where to look so I grab the entire handful out of her lap, not realizing that this means my fingers skim her thighs in really intimate places until it's way too late and the brief brush is burning through the backs of my fingers as I jam them with everything else into the glove box.

I slam the glove box shut, nearly pinching her fingers. Her nails are painted cherry red.

"You took the time to write that crap about me *by hand?*" she asks as if penmanship makes it somehow less worthy.

"I write all my articles by hand. It soothes me. Makes me more mellow."

"If that's the result of you mellow, I'd hate to see you wound up, buddy boy," she says.

I'm staring at her pouty lips. The way she said "wound up," all slow and drawling, is doing bad things to my imagination. You're not supposed to imagine kissing your collaborator, are you? And yet here I am, doing just that.

"Let's just drive," I say, feeling suddenly uncomfortable. The sooner we can be done, the better.

"How lost are we?" she asks as I start driving again.

"We're not lost," I growl, even though I have no idea if we are. I just don't like being second-guessed.

"I knew I should have been paying attention to navigating instead of filming," she says, leaning forward and peering out the windshield like getting her face five inches closer to it is going to make everything clearer.

"We're not lost."

"Let me see that map." She grabs my phone off the dash and unlocks it to look at my text from Big Daddy BOOM.

Having someone digging through my phone feels a lot like having someone digging through my pants. I don't like it. Not just because I don't know what she's going to get her pretty little fingers into, but because it feels incredibly intimate, and intimate is not something I do. Ever. Not anymore. Amber cured me of that for a lifetime.

"You have to treat me with respect," I say, echoing her words. "That means no touching my phone without permission."

The trail clears enough to see a gully ahead. It's washed out by the rain from weeks ago, dry and empty, but full of boulders and big rocks. My heartbeat kicks up into overdrive. I'm ninety percent sure we can clear it. Okay, maybe eighty-five. Eighty, if you twist my arm.

"So wait, you're comparing me touching your phone to you touching my actual body?"

I can tell she's incensed but honestly, everything seems to offend her, so what's one more thing?

"I just think you should ask permission," I say, stopping to hop out of the truck and lock the hubs. This is going to get rough.

By the time I'm back in, she's looking at me over the top of her aviators like a sexy diva. A tendril of hair has escaped her pretty updo and the contrast to her general put-togetherness makes my mouth a bit dry.

Focus, Nicola. You're here to do a job, not a pretty fox with molasses eyes.

I ignore her thousand-yard stare and lock in the four-by-four and start driving. This is about the limit of what my truck can handle even with the lift. I wonder if Big Daddy had any idea how rough this so-called road was going to be. I'm not entirely sure we can get the old hot rod over this.

I'm wheeling carefully over one rock and then another, trying not to hit my diff on anything, when she starts talking, and honestly, my hand to God, I don't mean to ignore her. I'm just focused on the thing that really matters — driving without doing permanent damage — and she's as much part of the background noise as the engine and the squeak of my tires when they slip on a rock.

"... which is why it was irresponsible to leave without a proper map," she says and then pauses for a breath. "Do you understand?"

Almost there.

So close.

"Nicola? Do you understand?"

I risk a glance at her. "Sure."

"Because if something happens to you, you know I'm screwed, right? I have no idea how to get out of here."

"I'm not going to let anything happen to you," I say firmly because that part I do know. Whatever else happens here, I'm the committed one. I'm here to get the job done, do it right, and get out of here, and part of that is keeping her safe. Why does she think I lifted her into the truck in the first place? "You're safe with me."

But I might have spoken too soon. The second the words are out of my mouth there's a clunk and a hiss and I know without having to look. I've popped a tire.

Chapter Five

ADA

I HEAR the tire pop the same moment he does. I see his cheeks flush hot, eyes still straight ahead like if he doesn't look at me he won't have to admit that I'm here.

I hop out the second he stops the vehicle. It's the back tire. With a sigh, I climb up his wheel and into the box. He has a spare tire back here — thank goodness — and some random tools including a battery-powered impact gun. I grab the gun, hop back out, and start to loosen the lugs while there's still weight on the tire.

It's the quiet that makes me look up and that's when I see him leaning against the side of the truck smirking at me. I wonder if he smirked at that wife in the wedding pictures that way. I wonder if that's why she married him or why she doesn't seem to be around anymore. Could go either way.

He's adorable when he's smirking — he has these deep smile lines that bracket his mouth that are utterly kissable, but that smugness is insufferable. It makes me want to open his phone again and slowly peruse through it until he can't breathe evenly.

"Planning to change the flat on your own?" he asks and the smirk deepens. Do men realize they look great when they lean against things? It makes them almost *have* to put one leg on an angle and that really ... um ... defines things they usually keep appropriately hidden. In this case, it's telling me very clearly and at eye level, that there's something there that I might like to see more of.

I give him a long look over my aviators. Adorable or not. Nice package or not. I don't go out with men who don't respect me and I don't sleep with men who don't think I'm something awfully special. I have this crazy thing called self-respect.

"I generally find that things get done right when I do them and done wrong when I trust someone else to do them," I tell him flatly. I hope he catches who I mean by "someone."

"Like what?" he asks defensively. Oh good. He's not an idiot. He caught the implication.

It's only when he smirks over his shoulder that I see he's set the camera up to film us changing the tire. Great. Just great. I'm going to look like a jerk on his channel when this is done. I'd better set the record straight. Yeah, I'm annoyed at him but it's for a reason.

"Like getting us lost?" I suggest. "Or getting a flat tire?"

"Look around, sweetheart, if you don't get a flat in here, are you even driving?"

"Should I assume you brought two spare tires then?" I ask, standing and cocking a hip to remind him he can't set the stage here. "And don't call me sweetheart. I'm Ada or ma'am to you."

"Ma'am?" He snorts at that. "What are you, eighty?"

"I need to be eighty to get respect from you? Did your mama teach you nothing?"

The look of pain that shoots through his eyes is enough to immediately make me regret saying that. I open my mouth to apologize, but he turns, grabs the selfie stick, and hurries to the front of the truck to open the hood.

"Impact gun," he says from under the hood, holding his hand out without looking at me.

Ouch. I really did hurt his feelings. But I'm not sure why. I put the tool in his hand. It's a nice hand. Large. It has a light sprinkling of hair on the back, thick knuckles, and callouses on the fingers and palms. Working man's hands. Just the way I like them.

Some girls are butt girls or eye girls. I'm a hands girl. Give me your soft tiny white-collar hand to shake and I'm out. It's the main reason that I'll never really marry a dentist.

"Please don't tell me there are more problems than a flat," I say lightly, trying to ease the mood. "Did your killer glare accidentally miss me and go straight through the engine block?"

"No. The jack's under here," he says, still not looking up. I think he might be mad. Like, actually mad. About nothing.

I hear the *zip zip* as he takes out the bolts holding his jack in place and then hands it to me while he gets the crank.

Okay. That's how we're rolling. With the silent treatment. Honestly, I have enough of a headache that maybe it will be a welcome break.

I go to the rear of the truck and set the jack under the frame but when he comes over, he grunts, takes it from my hand, and puts it under the axle.

"What's wrong with where I had it?" I grouse, but I don't wait for a reply before I'm in the back of the truck loosening the ratchet strap to get the spare. I'm not just decoration. Even though I look *ah-mazing* on camera. I can do stuff, too.

"Would you get out of there?" he complains.

"I'm getting the spare," I call out, shuffling backward to drag it to the open tailgate.

Something shifts — maybe the side he's jacking? — and I lose my balance just in time to also lose my grip on the tire and fall backward off the tailgate.

Right into his arms.

Like it's a freaking rom-com.

He catches me in both arms like he's going to bridal carry me over a threshold and my breath is still caught tight in my lungs — can you blame me? That all kind of happened at once! — so I can't find a word to say when he takes a long look into my eyes.

It's deep and intense and shockingly vulnerable and I have *no idea* what he's thinking. Which is weird for me because I can always call what people are thinking. But there's no smirk. No mockery. Instead, his cheeks stain pink — again! "Make Nicola Blush" would be the best drinking game! — and then he sets me gently on my feet like I'm made of glass, and puts a single finger in front of my face.

"Don't. Touch. Anything," he says with his dreamy accent before he grabs the tire and slings it to the ground like it weighs nothing and finishes cranking the jack up until it's fully extended. "Look."

He points at the jack and then carefully removes the lug nuts the rest of the way and eases the tire off. It takes a heartbeat before I see what he's pointing out. The jack is fully extended and he barely got the tire out. If I'd tried it on the frame, it never would have worked. This time it's my turn to blush but honestly, he just manhandled me again. And yes, it saved me from pain and maybe even a broken neck, but my dignity is smarting and I'd like his to sting a little, too.

"If this is a demonstration of your mechanical skills, you're going to have to do better than tire extraction," I say. "That's really not a great indicator. Or did you write a dozen articles critiquing that, too?"

"You're just sorry it's not tooth extraction," he says as he slides the fresh wheel on and tightens the lugs. "I've heard that gets your cylinders firing."

I grab the flat tire and manhandle it onto the back of the tail-gate. I think something might tweak in my back but there's no way I'm letting up until it's in the back of the truck. To my frustration, those big hands take it again and lift it the last inch to get it over the tailgate. I'm huffing and puffing as I release the tire.

In my defense, the truck is lifted. It's ten inches too high. Whose great idea was that, anyway?

"I told you. No touching," he says and there's a flicker of something in his eye. I want to know that flicker. I want to know — suddenly — what ignites it like that.

"And I told you no touching, but you touched when you saw you had to help. I'm just doing my part," I say, hand on my hip.

He crosses his arms over his chest and lifts one eyebrow and now I'm just annoyed because hours in front of a mirror have never gifted me with that ability. "If your part involves injuring yourself so we have to abort this whole thing and go home, then yes, I'd say you're doing it admirably."

"Nicola Petrovic," I say. "I think you might be falling in love with me. You should be careful. It would clash terribly with the I-hate-Ada-Ford vibe you've been projecting all this time."

And I know when I've said a killer line. I just did. And there's no way I'm letting him get a comeback in. I stride over to the camera, grab it, turn it off, and get into the passenger seat again before he can even close his dropped jaw.

Game. Set. Match. Or whatever those tennis-y people say.

Chapter Six

NICOLA

I CLENCH my hands on the steering wheel until my knuckles turn white, loosen them, clench them again. This girl is making me crazy. I haven't felt like this since Amber. Like I'm in the middle of a hurricane and at any moment I'm going to be swept away by the next wave or watch everything I've worked for tossed up in the air and dashed to the rocks.

I can still feel the weight of her in my arms when I caught her. Still feel how all her curves lined up in just the right ways, and I feel hot and like I need a moment to myself. Physical attraction is a wild thing with a mind of its own, and right now I wish mine would slink off into the woods and leave me alone. It doesn't help that she got on in there without complaint. There's something about a work ethic that does me in every time. Just thinking of her fighting with that spare tire makes my mouth a little dry. Enough, Nicola. Cool your jets.

It would be entirely foolish to make a move on Ada Ford. Not just because she's a known factor in our mutual business world which would make things messy, but because the pair of us are alone out here. Which means she trusted me enough to go to an unknown location with me, and that kind of trust from a woman should never be abused. I'll touch her to help her — to catch her when she falls — but I'd never, not in a million years, try to put a move on her when she's vulnerable and alone with me. Never.

Which brings us back to how my intense physical attraction can just go hang itself from a tree somewhere because I am not. Not. Not. Going to pay it any attention from here on in.

It's humiliating that she can tell I'm drawn to her. She wouldn't have made that clever remark about me falling in love with her if she hadn't sensed it. Which means I'll have to be better at hiding this … attraction? Crush? Ugh, that sounds very teenaged … from her. I'll have to limit my remarks to only the most important. Better yet, I should let her do all the talking.

I reach over to the seat and grab a donut to jam in my mouth. A full mouth doesn't talk.

"I think we should turn around and go back. Wait for more support before we drive the rest of the way," Ada says precisely.

I look at the clock. I look at her. I raise an eyebrow.

"You aren't even sure we're on the right trail and we're running on your only spare tire with no cell coverage here. Blow another tire, and it's you and me walking back for the next week with nothing to eat but one thousand sugary donuts," she says, picking one of them up and examining it like it might turn into celery if she watches it for long enough.

That's when I clock the camera set on the dash and the red light blinking on it. She's recording this. I'm pretty sure she's been recording most of it. And she'll have as much right to the footage as I will, so she can publish what she wants. Even more reason to keep my yap shut.

"Where did you get this many mini donuts?" she asks. "This package claims there are three dozen in here."

"Gas station," I say. I feel unaccountably cranky at the

thought of her judging my gas station diet. I bet she drinks Agua Fresca and eats only fresh-made local food like vegetarian burritos or salad or shit.

"Okay, let's find a place where you can do a fifteen-point turn and we'll drive right back to your gas station and await back up," she says. "We're three hours into this two-hour ride and it's getting dark."

It shouldn't be getting dark. It's only five in the afternoon. But she's right. I lean forward so I can try to peer up at the sky, but between the trees and the hills, I can't see anything worth noting.

I catch her watching me with a secretive look on her face. I must look like a fool.

"There weren't any storms on my weather app," I say, worried now.

"How would you know? We haven't been anywhere that a weather app works in hours," she says, but now she's looking worried, too. "I think we should go back."

"We must be almost there," I say. I am not going back and doing this a second time. Leaving my parents on their own once was bad enough. I can't handle twice. We're going to get to the cabin. We're going to find the truck. We're going to haul it out of here and we're going to do it tonight, rain or no rain.

And just as I think the word "rain" a drop splashes on the windshield.

"Oh no," she says like we just drove into a blizzard instead of a light sprinkle. She has her phone out in a blink, holding it up, trying to get a signal. And the screen looks way too bright in the sudden midnight blue of the surrounding world. This isn't going to just be a sprinkle.

A second drop hits the windshield. I swear it had an inch-wide diameter.

The third and fourth hit both at once, and now it's almost

blinding. My windshield wipers are on the highest setting and I can barely see the trail.

"You have to stop," Ada says, her voice about as high in register as I've ever heard it. "We can't drive in this. We'll get hopelessly lost. Just stop the truck and we'll wait it out right here."

I flick the headlights on and it doesn't help. The rain is slashing down so hard that it's all that lights up in the beams, so it looks like we're driving through 80's acid wash jeans rather than through the forest.

"Please," she says tightly. "This is crazy. At least let me drive."

I snort. One thing I won't be doing — letting her drive. No one drives my old 7.3 diesel but me. No one. No matter how lovely they are when they're panicked.

"I don't give up," I say grimly, eyes ahead.

"It's not giving up to admit you could get lost in a rain-storm!" she said. "They're not going to take your guy card away. It can be our little secret. Just please, please, please stop and let us wait it out right here. Think about it. Even if we get there, what are we going to do? Camp out in the rain? We can't work on a truck in weather like this."

But the headlights catch the edge of something and relief flows through me.

"Nope," I say, feeling hopeful as they light it up a little more.

"You are the most stubborn, foolish man. We can't even haul that Silver Bullet back in this. We can't see. We don't know where we are," she says, crossing her delicate arms over her chest. "Give me one good reason why you're still driving in this?"

I can barely hear her over the pounding of the rain on the cab roof. It will be easier just to show her. I ease up and park in front of the cabin. Or the wreck that was once a cabin. It still has a front door but that's hanging at quite the crazy angle.

"You stopped," she says and when I glance over her eyes are

closed in relief. "You can be reasoned with. It's a breakthrough. I'll alert the media."

When I say nothing, she opens one eye a crack and peers at me. "It was the question, right? When you had to explain yourself, it all became clear?"

It's hard to hold back a laugh.

"No," I say.

"Then what was it?" Her eyes snap open and meet mine, narrowing again. "Are you toying with me?"

"No," I say again, and this time I smirk. I can't help it. She's adorable when she's furious. Makes me think of a cat I had once.

"Prove it," she says, pulling back the same way that I'm sure Mr. Oolong would have.

I point out the window through the river of water streaming over the windshield. I forgot that it leaks in the passenger side corner. A drop falls down and hits Ada's cherry boot.

"We've reached our destination," I say calmly. "Look. There she is."

"Oh no," Ada says, and this time I agree because there's no way we're going to get the Silver Bullet going in this rain. It's going to be a challenge even when the rain ends. A tree has fallen right on it, one branch caving in the cab, one branch wedged between the motor and the grill shell, and the main bulk of the cabin flattened by the trunk. If Ada had been hoping to escape my leaky windshield any time soon, she might need to rethink that hope. There's nowhere to find shelter at all.

Chapter Seven

ADA

OKAY, let's recap. I'm stuck in a truck in the middle of a rainstorm with the world's most cranky man ever and my side of the truck is leaking. I'm cold, I'm already wet, it's dark outside, and there's no one coming to save us now or ever. There's a cabin out there in the rain somewhere, but from what I can tell, it's basically a heap of broken wood and squirrel nests, and there's certainly no warm bed or fire or anything else. And I have to pee. I've had to go for hours. And it's making everything else seem considerably less urgent at this point.

I'm not the damsel in distress type. It's not my style to look to Nicola to save me or make all this better for me — but could he have had a truck that didn't steadily drip on me? Was that really asking for too much?

"Your truck leaks," I say, and I put my aviators over my eyes. I know. It isn't sunny, but seriously, I'm worried that my eyes are giving away how incredibly *not cool* I am with this right now and I don't like that vulnerability.

He kills the engine and the lights go out.

"Ummm. Did you just turn out the lights?" I ask.

"It took longer to get here than I thought. It will take longer to get out again after. I need to conserve fuel," he says.

It's already getting colder in here. I snatch my aviators off my face again and peer outside. I can't see the moon. I can't see anything but darkness out there and a faint glow from the plug in on his dashboard for his phone cord. Fat lot of good that will do us.

"So we ... what ... sit in the dark together?" I ask, and I didn't mean to make it sound like I'd rather be murdered, but it definitely came out like that.

He doesn't answer. I'm starting to think he doesn't say much. Which is ironic since the reason I hate him springs from him saying much, much too much.

I hear the donut container open and the sound of chewing. Apparently, we're conserving fuel for the truck but not his donut-fueled belly. Which begs another question — I saw him reach for that spare tire. I saw his shirt ride up. His torso is toned. Not toned like a body-builder, but car-guy toned where most of the work he does is heavy lifting, but he's always moving and it makes for a lean build. That's not the look of a man who eats donuts for every meal.

He grunts when he finishes it like he's in pain or something.

"Surely, you eat something more than donuts as part of your daily diet," I say. "Or does your wife not feed you?"

"Amber," he says, clarifying.

"Amber doesn't feed you?"

"No."

"Huh," I say, and okay, maybe there's some judgment there because Nicola might drive me crazy but maybe he deserves someone who takes care of him a bit. Or maybe this is a cultural thing and his people think that's sexist. How would I know? I just know that in my world, a good woman makes sure her man doesn't get type two diabetes before he's forty from donut eating.

But hey, who's judging? Okay, it's me. I'm judging.

"You seem crankier when you eat them is all."

I hear the donut container open again. I guess my words have had the opposite effect on him.

"Look, I have to use the bathroom, so I'm going to have to duck out for a moment."

Like magic, this draws words out of him. Apparently, he can talk — but only if it involves criticizing me.

"You'll get soaking wet and have to sit like that all night."

"It's not letting up. Trust me, I've been waiting for it to rain less hard, but instead, it keeps raining harder."

I wish I could see his face in the dark, but I really can't. "You should have gone before."

"Before what? Before the flat tire, before you wouldn't turn around or stop for a minute, or before the rain started?"

He still doesn't answer.

"Look, if I wait here it won't just be me who gets soaking wet."

Still nothing.

I huff and open my door. His cry of dismay is lost in the howl of wind and rain. Fine. It's all fine. I'll just pee by the back tire. In this downpour, everything will wash away before I can get back in the truck.

I take care of business. In the dark. With a wad of quickly-disintegrating tissue from my pocket and the light of my cell phone — which is at 5% battery charge, if you were wondering. I was. And now I wish I hadn't looked.

By the time I get back in, I've solved one problem only to create another. I'm soaked right through to the skin. And I'm shivering.

"Don't —" Nicola starts to say but I cut him off.

"I am not in the mood," I say, trying to strip out of my

soaked leather jacket in the front seat of a crew cab truck. It's a bench seat. That should mean there's room. It does not. I feel like I'm ripping my own arm off. "I am cold, I am wet, I am hungry, and I have no room."

I don't mind stripping right down. It's too dark for him to see a thing. I don't even know where my clothes are going, only that my jacket and shirt are off, leaving me in my little lacy bra — it's pineapple yellow, for the record, and it makes me feel like I'm on vacation when I'm not soaked like a drowned cat. I'm an A cup and I need all the "vacation" I can find in a bra.

My boots are impossible. I hurt my hand when I'm trying to take one off.

"When I was a kid," Nicola says and I try to ignore him as I fight the world's most ornery boots.

They're basically the government and my feet are the taxes they want me to pay. They ain't ever letting go.

"I lived in Canada," he says.

He's a slow storyteller. I'd complain, but I literally have nothing else to do. A drop of freezing water falls from his windshield and hits me on the back of the neck and I bite my own lip to keep from cursing at the top of my lungs.

"And it got cold in the winters. I lived just north of Winnipeg. The locals call it 'Winterpeg' because it gets so cold."

"Charming," I say with a grunt as my boot finally concedes territory and flies off my foot.

"I hate being cold," he says. "I hate it so much that I usually bring a sleeping bag and dry clothes with me everywhere I go."

"If this is your smug way of telling me that I was unprepared for this Amazon-style downpour and camping with you in the cab of an F-350, then yes, I know. In fairness, I had other things with me, but you took off without giving me the chance to get the rest of them."

"You were already in the truck."

"Because you put me there."

There's silence, but I don't mind because I'm at a tricky part. I'm trying to stand-ish, because you really can't stand in the cab of a truck, to peel the wet pants from my backside and where my A cups are lacking, my butt has taken up the slack. It's not easy to wiggle all that lovely behind out of skin-tight jeans when they're dry and I'm able to fully straighten, never mind right now. I might need his winch for this. For real.

"My mother was always cold. I hated that. I wanted to warm her up, but we couldn't run the heat too high and so there was always a chill in the air."

I pause, still with my pants only down an inch.

"Are you close to your parents?"

"Yes," he says and this time his yes isn't a cut-off from the conversation. It's heavy with lots of thoughts. "I'm an only child. They need me. Especially as they age."

"I am, too," I say, the words coming out like a confession. "I have a father. He ... he's brilliant but scattered. He needs a lot from me and I feel all the time like I can't keep up with what he needs."

"Oh," he says, and it sounds like he's speaking inward, like he's correcting something inside. It's an odd thing confessing to him here in the darkness. I struggle the rest of the way out of my pants and have them almost to my ankles when he says, "You can borrow one of my hoodies. Here, I'll get it for you."

And without warning, he flicks on the interior light.

I scream and fall backward, my ankles bound by my wet jeans, and the look on his face — his flaming red face — as he takes in my bright yellow lace underwear and bra and all the rest of me as naked as you please — would have been priceless. It would have been. But I was too horrified to do more than let my jaw drop and try to scramble back into the seat.

The polite thing to do would have been to turn the light back off. I know this. You probably know this. He, for reasons unknown, does not know this. Instead, he reaches behind his seat, grabs his duffle bag, opens it, and proceeds to find his hoodie and offer it to me — all in the stark light of the interior lamp.

I take it from him numbly, still too stunned to say a word and it is only then that he flicks the light back off.

"Well," he says after a moment when I haven't moved a muscle. "I guess I know how to make you stop talking now. I just need to see you in your tiny lace underthings."

And if I was a little embarrassed before, I'm so mortified now that I can't speak.

Chapter Eight

NICOLA

I SHOULD PROBABLY GO OUTSIDE, too. A cold shower is just about exactly what I need right now. I can't erase the sight of her from my eyes. It's dark in here and somehow the sensory deprivation means that all I see is *her* all curvy and wonderful in those tiny lace underthings and my mouth is dry and my palms are sweaty.

Keep it together, Nicola, I tell myself as I ease my hat over my eyes. I think I'll just stay here behind the steering wheel with my arms crossed over my chest where they can't cause trouble and my eyes very shut where ... well, where they're causing me a whole lot of trouble because they're still just showing me one thing. Maybe a few things. And all of them very, very good. But not if I'm trapped in a truck with her.

People talk about cars like they're "she" all the time and part of that is because most car people are guys, and most guys consider something curvy and desirable to be a she. If Ada over there were a car, she'd be a Corvette Stingray, so freaking curvy and slender that a guy can barely keep a hold of himself. And she'd be painted pineapple yellow. With metal flake in the paint — just enough to make it pearly in the sun. And I guess she'd do her own interior. Something in leather, I think.

I hear the dripping from the windshield and it brings me back to right now.

"It drips on your side," I say.

Her response is slightly muffled by the hoodie I gave her. That means she's tugging it on while she talks to me. My stomach does a flip and I almost miss her response. "Yes, it really does."

"So, maybe you'd like to ride this out in the back? Other than the camera equipment, there's nothing too breakable back there and that stuff is all in hard cases."

I hear her hesitate but then after another minute, something slides against my arm and my breath catches. It's just some part of her brushing me as she crawls over the seat into the back. But telling myself that is not helping.

Some part? What part? Is it something soft and a bit intimate? Or hard and determined? Or risky and full of trouble? None of these alternatives seem like good ones when I'm barely holding on to good sense already.

I hear her breathing. It's ragged and is that a slight chattering sound?

"Are your teeth chattering?" I ask and it's almost a bark because now I'm envisioning those full lips slightly blue. Not on my watch. I freaking told her I would take care of her.

Also, now I'm thinking about catching those lips in mine. I'm thinking about working hard to warm her up. I'm really good at hard work. I can work hard for so, so long. And I would for her. I'd start with a little friction over her upper arms, and then lean in to wrap her in a hug, but everyone knows what really warms a girl up — skin-to-skin contact. The kind with sliding and friction and tangled limbs.

I would like that.

It turns out that I really, really like Ada. I didn't expect that. I expected snappy, grumpy, unfriendly Ada with her aviator shades and her frown. I did not expect to enjoy those snappy comebacks or find myself looking for those frowns. Since when did I become addicted to frowns? In one afternoon?

I can almost imagine her little hands roaming over me curiously as she fires off little zingers like, "What's this for? Oh, look! It did something to you!"

Nnngh.

"Yes," she grates out through chattering teeth and my mind has drifted so far that I almost forgot the question.

"There's a sleeping bag back there," I tell her. I have to clear my throat because the words don't come out properly. "It's on the passenger side, I think."

"Are you sure this is okay?" she asks in a small voice and she sounds vulnerable. I don't like that. She's a fireball. A land speed racer. She shouldn't feel unsafe. She should *be* unsafe for other people.

"Yep," I say shortly. I lean my forehead onto the steering wheel. It's not very late, but the wind is howling outside the truck, and I've been on the road since first thing this morning and I'm tired. I'm gonna sleep right here.

A drop of cold water hits the back of my neck and I hiss without meaning to. Great. Now, this side is leaking.

"Is your side leaking, too?" she asks and her teeth are still chattering.

"No," I lie, as a second drop hits me. I slide backward and rest my head on the door jam instead. A double drip hits my jeans and soaks right through. I shift my leg.

"It is leaking, I can hear it," she insists. "You can't hide from me, Nicola Petrovic."

That's the problem, though, isn't it? If I go back there, I won't be able to hide from her. Our already cramped space will reduce by half.

"I can do whatever I want," I say, putting as much surliness as I can into the words just as a gust of wind shakes the truck and a heavy shower of rain leaks through the upper edge of the windshield and spatters me.

"Come back here," she orders. I like her ordering tone. It sounds like it refuses to be disobeyed. "It's ridiculous for you to sit up there and get wet for no reason."

I feel a growl of approval start in my belly at how she worded that. Down, boy.

"If you don't come back here, I'll talk all night and keep you awake and miserable."

Look, I'm trying here, okay? It's not easy to be a good man.

I keep my damn mouth shut. It's the best I can do.

She must sense that I'm fighting her on this because she shuts up for a few minutes — long enough for my jeans to see a few more drops of freezing cold rain. There's seriously nowhere here that is immune to the leaking seal around my windshield.

Just when I think she's given up, she changes her strategy. "If you come back here I think I can tell you why you're so grumpy."

"Why am I so grumpy."

"Come back here and I'll tell you."

I could probably keep trying, but I don't want to. I've fought against comfort, desire, and now I have to fight curiosity, too? Not likely.

I make my way to the back, and I feel her shift to the passenger side, so I huddle against the driver's side door.

"Why am I cranky?" I ask.

"Do you have a belly ache?" She sounds so superior.

"Maybe," I admit.

"Because I noticed that you get worse after you eat those donuts."

"Maybe I just don't like donuts."

"Or maybe you're gluten intolerant."

"No," I say, but inside it's more like a question echoing through my head. Do the donuts make my belly hurt? But practically everything I eat has gluten in it. Sausages in buns. Pizza. Subs. Everything. Would I know? My belly seems to hurt all the time.

I'm quiet for a long time as I hear her shift back and forth trying to get comfortable while sitting up.

"You're not going to be able to sleep like that," I say eventually. "You'd better lean on me."

I expected some hesitation, but no, her head is on my shoulder almost immediately, and my nose is full of the scent of coconut — one of my favorites — and I should be professional and distant, but I'm not. Oh, I'm really not. I'm just sitting here with my fists clenched as hard as I can, trying to keep them to myself as I sink deeper and deeper into this scent, this warmth, this glorious feeling of someone so ... spectacular ... deciding to be this close to me.

She's here because there's no other option, I tell myself. Except that she invited me back here, too, instead of letting me suffer in the cold and wet, so I guess there were other options. And she picked this.

I'm congratulating myself on being someone who someone else willingly chooses to spend time with, when she asks me something out of the blue. It's a question that blows all that confidence away like the storm outside blowing around the truck.

"Won't your wife be upset that you're practically cuddling a strange woman?"

"No," I say shortly.

"That's ummm ... generous of her. Unless you plan to lie about it."

"I don't lie about things," I say, which is a lie since I lied to her about the drips a few minutes ago. But that was for a good cause, right?"

The silence ticks on. Neither of us can sleep. I don't know why she can't, but for me, it's pretty much that I can't stop my mind from racing around in circles over pineapple bras and coconut-scented hair.

"If you're not going to lie to her, then why will she be okay with it?" she says out of nowhere.

"Probably because she left me for another man two weeks into the marriage," I say dryly. I'm not sure why I told her that. I don't tell people that. My parents ask me if I don't go on dates because of them — because I spend too much time worried about them — and yeah, some of that is true, but mostly I don't go out because of Amber. Because I don't like having to tell people about her. I don't like them knowing how much she fucked me up.

"Wow," she says, and I realize I'm not going to have to deal with pity after all and it feels like relief in my chest. "She met a superhero? I always dreamed of doing that."

"A superhero?" I ask, confused. I can feel her warm breath on my arm when she talks. It's nice.

"Or was it a movie star? I'm not really into movie stars, although some of those Bollywood guys are cute."

"I'm so lost right now that I might need GPS," I admit. But I'm not annoyed. I'm actually feeling kind of relaxed.

"Well, I assumed she met someone pretty spectacular since she blew you off," she says. "Especially after that epic beach wedding. Was that a beer shirt you were wearing under your jacket?"

I bark a laugh. I didn't expect this at all.

"No, it was a car shirt. Obviously," I say and now she's giggling.

"You wore a car shirt to your shotgun beach wedding and your wife *still* left you for an Olympic athlete?"

She's still on that schtick, is she?

"I think you should go to sleep," I say repressively.

"I can't," she says and she sounds mournful.

"Let me guess, you're too busy imagining how pathetic my wedding was and it's keeping you up."

"No," she says and I can't tell if she's trying to keep from laughing or embarrassed about something.

There's a flash of lightning and for just a moment I see her cuddled in my too-big hoodie with my sleeping bag pooled around her waist and my breath freezes in my chest with a possessive feeling. I want her in all my clothes. And that's ridiculous. I barely know her. I don't know what she wants or if she has a secret ex-husband she married in a beer shirt who ran off with an Olympian, or anything really. And I still want her. Not just in a physical way but in an all-the-ways way. I swallow hard.

"Okay, so you can't sleep unless you get told a bedtime story?" I push.

"Yes," I hear her laugh all mixed up in the word. "And ..."

"And what?"

In a small voice she admits, "I've never been able to sleep sitting up."

"I'll go to the front seat," I say, already moving. I only stop when her little hand grabs my bicep. It does something stupid to me that sends all my blood rushing to all the wrong places.

"No, wait," she says. "You're not married, right?"

"No," I say. "No," says something that's waking up inside my pants.

"No girlfriend or someone else who might get upset about us both in this truck?"

"No," I repeat.

"Okay," she sucks in a long breath like she's going to do something brave and my imagination is all tumbling over itself to guess what that might be. "So we could like ... spoon on this bench seat and no one would care?"

I swallow and I don't answer because first, I'm not sure I can without betraying waaay too much, and second because if I so much as twitch right now, it's going to set things in motion that have real trouble stopping when they get started. I freeze like someone caught standing on cracking ice. Ice. Yes, focus on ice. So cold. So uninviting. So not a soft curvy woman who looks dead stunning in lace underwear who is currently wearing my clothes and suggesting we spoon.

"It's just, I'm really cold, and it's wet up there. It ... well, obviously it's not a sexual invitation, just a friendly one. I've spooned in the backseat of a Ford truck before. It can totally be done if we don't mind getting close."

Who, exactly, has she done this with before? And should I make sure to inform them that they are no longer allowed to do that with her anymore?

No. I should not. I swore I wouldn't touch her. Swore it.

I'm in real trouble now.

The minutes spool out silently. I don't know why she's silent, but I know that for me, I'm trying really hard to get this stiffness in my pants to calm down before I answer. It's not getting the message.

"Gosh, I'm sorry," she says eventually in a tiny voice. "You're offended. You think I'm putting the moves on you. You're going to like ... file some kind of charge against me for sexual harassment."

I hurry to say, "No. You're just offering a friendly place to sleep." My words come out gruff. I don't mean them gruff, but that's how they're coming out or not at all. "We can spoon. We might as well try to sleep. Just one condition."

"Okay," she sounds nervous now.

"You keep the sleeping bag for yourself," I say. That inch of padding in the bag is my only hope of hiding my growing — and I do mean growing, despite all my efforts to the contrary — interest.

"Great." She sounds relieved.

I have no idea why. I'm anything but relieved. As we arrange ourselves on the bench seat and the luggage, finding a way to fit a six-foot-two man and a five-foot-something woman into a pair of spoons with that sleeping bag wrapped up properly around her, means there's a lot of touching and a lot of coconut smell and the fact that I settle in with her without her rightfully complaining that something is pressing against her back, is the best I can hope for.

It turns out that she doesn't lie. Almost as soon as she gets settled in front of me (and yes, I keep my hands to myself) she falls asleep, her breath growing instantly heavy and deep. I do not sleep. I can't. I'm utterly overwhelmed by the sensation of her here in front of me, by the scent and warmth of her. Can a woman steal your soul with just her scent? I'm going with yes because it's happening to me right now. From this moment on, I think maybe she's going to own me. That's never happened before. Amber sure as hell didn't master my whole self with a no-touching cuddle. Even sex has never done this to me. It would be the kind of life-changing revolution people write about if it wasn't so damned inconvenient.

Because it doesn't matter that now I'm her creature. I can't ever act on it. Ever. And she can't ever know.

Chapter Nine

ADA

I WAKE up warm and for one glorious second I think I'm in bed at home — and then I try to move, and it all washes back over me. The drive into the woods. The storm. The uncomfortable spooning on the back seat of a truck. Behind me, someone is breathing heavily and his arm has slipped to fall over the crook of my waist.

Look, just because I feel bad that his wife left him, and I think it's kind of sweet that he lent me his hoodie, doesn't mean that I've suddenly warmed up to the man who either tried to trash my career — which I need to pay the bills, thank you so much — or did it without trying because he's an old crank. This overnighter is a one-time thing. My career is an all-the-time-only-way-to-pay-the-freaking-bills thing.

Which means I should not be charmed by his masculine woodsy scent or the weight of that lightly furred arm hanging over my waist. I shouldn't be intoxicated by the warmth sealing my body to his or the way his breath gusts out softly against my hair or how he moves very slightly in his sleep, nestling into me. Yeesh.

He has car-guy hands. Which I guess means he's not a total fraud. The knuckles are big, there are callouses, and the cracks of his fingers are dark with grease and ancient dirt. I like car-guy hands. I know where I stand with them. Even if I don't know what to do with their owner.

I slowly — so slowly that I could be percolating coffee, and wouldn't that be like heaven right now? — ease his arm off of me and sit up. I do not want a repeat of the embarrassment of last night.

He hasn't woken up yet and he's definitely adorable when he's asleep. And gorgeous. When he isn't grunting or giving one-word answers, it's hard to believe he's single. That chiseled jaw is darkened with the shadow of his beard coming in and his eyelashes are ridiculously long. His lips are parted in sleep, giving him a vulnerable, swoony look that makes me want to curl up against that gorgeous masculine body and run my hands all over it. Seriously. He looks like a whole snack. And that makes him and the donuts the only edible things in this truck.

A thought that reminds my stomach that it's empty. It rumbles unhappily. Wow. Loud much?

I steal a glance at Nicola, but he doesn't seem to have woken up yet. Maybe I can sneak forward and slip back into the world's wettest clothes.

I ease over the seat and just as I am almost there I see him shift and I freeze. He opens an eye and catches me like that, half slung over his seat wearing only his hoodie that goes midway down my thigh like it thinks it's a fashion-not-so-forward dress. I feel like a kid in it. A kid who fell into a pond, and got wet and their parent put their own shirt on them to keep them warm. And I realize a little too late that it got caught on the upholstery of the truck seat and has ridden up nearly to my breasts, showing my whole entire ass to him in nothing but my tiny lace under-wear. Awesome.

"Morning," he says muzzily, and his voice is all low and raspy and sleep-worn. It sends a little frizzle of heat into my chest. I mean, if you could get over the personality thing, this guy is all sexiness.

And if I could get over the fact that he's woken up to a very revealing look at me. Oops.

He wrote mean articles about your work, I remind myself. He thought your car was built by a guy because he doesn't respect women.

Usually, these reminders make me want to see red, but they aren't working today, for some reason. Maybe I'm just too tired to think. Yeah, that has to be it.

"Good morning," I say brightly with my best smile as I scramble the rest of the way over the seat. We'll keep it profes-sional. That's the best thing to do here. No nighttime confes-sions. No wearing other people's clothes. "I'm just going to get dressed."

"There's a T-shirt in the bag," he murmurs, adjusting his position in that kind of slow grace people sometimes have when they're sleepy. Okay, that *he* has when he's sleepy. He's the only one I've noticed being all lion-like. He adjusts his position so that his hip is suddenly tilted up and over the ball of sleeping bag I left behind me, and his shoulder muscles flex under his light T-shirt. It gives me mental images of him cuddled like that over me instead of over a rumpled sleeping bag and no, Ada, no. That's a really bad idea.

"It's okay, thanks," I say brightly, grabbing my wet clothes and leaping out of the passenger door before he can say more.

Here's a thing about me — I don't accept gifts. I mean, I borrowed his hoodie and sleeping bag last night, but it was a one-time thing so I didn't freeze to death. And I'm pretty sure he only offered me exclusive use of the sleeping bag to try to hide his raging boner. Yeah, Nicola, it did nothing to disguise that.

But I can forgive him for that because seriously I'm a sexy little thing — there's no point pretending I'm not because I know I am, and it would just be a silly attention-getting thing to pretend otherwise, right? You're only in your twenties once. Might as well admit it's the best you'll ever look.

He can't help but like what he saw, and for guys, that means there's consequences. I felt the consequences pressed against my back but I'm not going to hold that against him — even if he held it against me. Ha ha.

Here's another thing about me — I laugh at my own jokes.

But back to what's relevant. No, I won't borrow his T-shirt. I don't take gifts, mostly because my Pops is always giving them. To everyone. All the time. And it's sweet, and generous, and totally comes from the heart. But also his credit cards are maxed out, and the debtors call almost daily, and as hard as I work, and as much as I pay down, he still seems to find ways to spend, so that it's always two steps forward, one step back. And that's how I know that just because someone offers you something, doesn't mean that they can afford to give it to you. I don't take gifts on principle. I look after myself, and I hope that they look after themselves. I won't ever put someone in a position where they're giving me things they can't afford.

Which is why I'm huddled in a clump of wet trees getting slapped by soggy leaves as I change out of a warm, dry, cozy hoodie into damp pants and a damp shirt. I slide my soaked leather jacket over it all and I'm cold and miserable. I wish I'd taken his T-shirt and kept the hoodie.

I wish it even when I bring it back to the truck where I find him standing outside the cab changing the battery in the camera I had set up on the dash.

"Must have forgotten to shut it off," he says when I approach. "Ran the batteries right out."

He doesn't mention that I look ridiculous in my damp clothing. Or that we spent a night side by side. Or that both of us have morning breath.

"Thank you for lending me your sweatshirt," I say, handing back his hoodie.

He grunts and places it on the front seat of the truck, hands me the camera, and then, to my surprise, he offers me a bottle of water and a protein bar. And there's a look in his eyes that doesn't fit with the man who wrote scathing articles about my upholstery. It's … is it kindness?

"I found these in the bottom of my bag," he says — and yes, I see now that he's in fresh jeans and a House of Kolor T-shirt, which shows that he knows a good paint when he sprays one, and that automatically gives him points in my book. "They're for you."

I want to grab them. I'm both hungry and thirsty, but I don't take gifts.

"I'm good, thanks."

"It's going to be a lot of work to get the truck free," he says curtly, nodding to where the tree is down over the cabin and the truck. "You'll get hungry."

He blows so hot and cold. Wait. Is that powdered sugar in his whiskers? Did he eat another one of those donuts even after I warned him?

I cross my arms over my chest. "I'm fine. You didn't eat one of those donuts, did you?"

He shakes his head, annoyed, and then shoves the water and protein bar both at my chest so I have to grab them or risk having them pushed against my body. And then he reaches into the truck, grabs one of his mini donuts, and bites it at me.

Yeah, *at me.* Like it's a challenge.

"I'm not the one who is going to get a gut ache and get cranky from that," I warn. He's already moving past me, grabbing a hand saw from the truck. But just like that — with our sharp exchange — I feel like myself again.

I retrieve my aviators, fix my headscarf, and then I steal a swig of water — because okay, I do want some.

I hurry to set up our cameras, and by the time I'm done, he's hard at work and most of the branches are sawed off.

"I'll get the tree off. You get that thing running," I say, grabbing a hold of the first branch and pulling it out from the engine compartment.

"Running?" he scoffs. "In this shape, we'll be lucky if we can get it rolling."

His skepticism doesn't prevent him from pouring gas in the tank and hooking up the spare battery he brought while I pull the rest of the branches off the truck. It's in good shape for a truck left to rot on a claim. Other than a few dings from these branches and sun-faded paint (light blue, if you were wondering), it's pretty much perfect. I must say that out loud because Nicola scoffs at that, too.

"It's not perfect," he says. "It's a good start, but definitely not perfect."

I'm pretty sure he'd say that about a mathematically perfect circle. Nothing is good enough for Nicola.

He tries to start the truck and it turns over but doesn't fire.

"Old gas," he says.

"Or the ground is bad," I argue.

"The ground won't be bad because this used to run before. Why would it suddenly not be grounded?" he says, crankier, meaner — exactly as I predicted.

I move so I can lean in and look at him through the windshield and raise an eyebrow. Does he hear that tone in his voice? Does he not realize how he sounds?

He ignores me. Intentionally. I can tell because he gets out of the driver's seat, rounds the vehicle, pulls the hood side up, and starts fiddling with the engine.

"Spark plug?" I call from where I'm pulling a few more branches off the truck in the back. It's in pretty good shape, all things considered. There's air in the tires. The floors and box are solid. Roof is dented but fine. Creatures have been living in the cab and it smells of their nests, but otherwise, it seems okay.

"Yes," he says and then he curses. "It won't be running on its own power."

I never thought it would be, so I'm not too concerned.

"Okay, so we'll run the rope you brought and you can steer while I pull you out," I say casually.

He turns to look at me and he crosses his arms over his chest to smirk at me.

What?

He looks from me to the broken hotrod truck and back again.

Oh no.

He smiles.

No, no, no.

"Why do you hate me?" I ask dismally.

"No one drives my F-350 but me," he says, nodding to the truck we came here in — as if there are other F-350 diesels with 7.3 motors in them lined up in front of the cabin.

"I think you mean no one *wants* to drive your truck. Newsflash. It's because it leaks in the rain," I say. "But I'd still rather drive it than the rat motel."

"This needs a steady hand doing the pulling."

"And what, you don't want me to do it because I'm a girl?" I challenge.

"It's my truck. I drive it," he says, but there's a moment of uncertainty in his eyes as he says it, like he's not sure he can go through with forcing me into the mouse mobile and if I push back again, he'll probably cave and let me drive his diesel truck instead.

But here's another thing about me — I have issues letting

people sacrifice things for me. All my life I've had to give things up for people.

"Oh sorry, honey, I gave the cash to Jerry. He needed smokes. You don't need a school lunch this week, right?" Pops would say. Or, "We just bought you socks. You can go a few more months without new ones, right? Martha's kid needed a new bike and I gave her what I had."

It's tough to give things up. Especially when you're forced into it. Which is why I try to never put anyone in that position. And also why when I see that uncertain look in Nicola's eyes I hop in the driver's seat of the old Ford truck. The Silver Bullet, we're calling her. Maybe Nicola is a werewolf and this project will kill him dead.

Thank goodness my pants are already soaked, or I'd be mad now that I have a wet butt from this upholstery. Plus, I was already gross from putting on old clothes, right? So it's not a big deal that I now smell like vermin? I hope it's not.

"Just make it good for the cameras," I warn. "Make it worth our while."

And he looks appropriately guilty as he hands me a dash cam and gathers up the other camera and tripod so we can get going. That's okay. I would never have really made him do this. Besides, if there's one thing I've learned, it's that if you want something done right, you have to do it yourself.

He finishes with the cameras, snugs the tow rope tight on my axle and on his, and then he swaggers back to peer in my window at me.

"Just like old times," he says with a half-smile.

"Yes, all those old times that I rode around in a rat mobile while you practiced knots like a trust-fund kid with a sailboat," I shoot back.

He laughs but then he pauses and his face screws up and he looks like he wants to confess something. I hope it's not that he really found something dead back here. That might be too much even for me.

"Ada?" he says and I swallow at his concerned tone, especially when his blue eyes flick up to meet mine and the look in his eyes stops my heart for a second. It's sincere, and concerned, and sexy as hell, and the combination makes my mouth water and my knees weak. It's like I want to kiss him. Maybe I do. What the hell do I know?

"Yes?" I say, trying for cool instead of close-to-heart-attack, which is how I actually feel right now.

"I don't hate you," he says and there's something about the way he says it that makes it sound like he's saying "I really like you" and I can't take it. It's too much.

I hide in flippancy.

"Sure," I say. "And donuts don't make you cranky."

Because I don't believe him. Even after he lent me his hoodie and gave me water and kept me warm all night, I still don't believe it, because I've read all five of his freelance articles that feature my work, and I feel safe in saying that if there's one thing that Nicola Petrovic feels about me, it's definitely hatred.

He opens his mouth and then shuts it, like he's out of words and they won't flow anymore, like someone shut off his water because he didn't pay the bills.

"Let's just do this thing and go back home to real life," I say and he nods in agreement — maybe a little too fast. His eyes shutter and whatever emotion he almost let me see is gone.

And for just a moment, I miss it.

Chapter Ten

NICOLA

I'M NOT sure what it was that turned my head around so bad. Maybe it was waking up and realizing that the cold spot beside me was warm all night and that I missed it. Maybe it was how she looked wearing my hoodie this morning — like she belonged to me somehow. Or maybe it was how she refused both my dry clothes and my help. But here's the thing. I'm supposed to have my head in the game and tow this hot rod truck out of the woods. That's what I'm meant to be focused on, but what I'm actually thinking about is her.

I'm thinking about what it would be like to take her for a real meal, not just an energy bar and water. Would she snipe at me from across the table? Would she have something snappy to say about what I chose to order? I think I'd like that.

I've been alone for a long time and that's never been a problem for me. And now, out of nowhere, I want acid and sugar in equal parts. I want a new kind of adventure.

I'm wondering what it would be like to show her my shop, to explain my hopes for the future and why I'm busting my butt

so hard to make my channel work. I feel like she'd understand —
maybe even approve.

Could I let her in? Show her my secrets? Even the dangerous
ones?

She's guaranteed to mock them. To tell me how badly I'm
managing everything. To say something cutting. I think I might
like that. It might suddenly be my favorite idea.

The distraction is enough that I don't see the stream until I
have to jam on the brakes. I throw my truck in park to see what
we're dealing with and I hear her cursing out my open window.
Oh. Yeah. She didn't have much warning to brake there. Well,
best not to acknowledge it, or she'll know I messed up.

"Look," she says, blowing out an angry breath as she comes
up from behind me. I stare out across the rippling water. "I'm
not going one more foot until you stop and listen to me."

"I'm listening," I growl. This is bad. Really bad. This was
not here yesterday, but all that rain must have run down into this
exact gully. The one where I popped a tire yesterday. Dammit.

"When I call you from the truck and tell you I need help,
you have to stop," she says and there's something about the tone
of her voice that gets my attention.

I turn away from the disaster in front of me to see her
standing there with one hand on her hip and the other holding
the camera on a selfie stick. Her chest is heaving, she's breathing
so hard, and her eyes are flashing. Which might be because there
are leaves and sticks in her hair and she's soaking wet.

"Why are you all wet?" I ask.

"Why am *I* all wet?" she repeats, like she thinks I'm an idiot.

"You weren't wet when we started," I say, confused.

"I got wet when I screamed at you to stop because every
branch in sight was hitting the doorpost and slapping me in the
face with wet leaves and spiders and who even knows what, and I
couldn't see a thing."

Did her voice raise to an even higher pitch? Maybe.

I might be in trouble with more than the full gully. I don't like having two problems at once. I prefer to tackle my issues one at a time.

"Why didn't you shut the window?" I ask.

"Because," she says and it sounds like she's trying to hold her temper and failing. "It. Doesn't. Roll. Up."

"Oh," I say. "Well, that would have been useful to know sooner."

"That's why I've been screaming to you for the last half hour! But you didn't stop and you didn't listen."

"I couldn't hear you," I say. This can't possibly be my fault. Except it is. But I don't know how to deal with that so I push on. "Is that why you steered into all those rocks? To get my attention? You know that every time you do that it increases the bodywork that needs to be done, right? Every single one of those dents will need to be pulled."

"I'm aware!" she snaps back, crossing her arms under those pretty breasts and scowling that delicious scowl I love so much. "And I'm done. I'm not driving in that thing anymore. I am covered — covered! — in gross old-car smell. I am soaked, and I'm cold, and my bones have been jarred and rattled until I'm going to wish I'd found that dentist to marry because all my teeth are loose from this ride. I'm not going even one more foot."

I look her up and down. This is not the time to quit. The road we already passed was fairly easy. The real task is right in front of us now.

But also I totally admire this woman. She managed that ride as well as anyone I've ever met.

I'd never say that. Obviously. When you tell people stuff like that it goes to their heads and then they immediately stop being admirable. Or, worse, neither of you can speak to each other again because it's so unbearably awkward that you said such a personal thing out loud. I've experienced both.

But I do admire her. I don't know many people who would drive in an old wreck just because it's the job at hand, or who would do it in such terrible conditions with so little drama. And she did a great job of it. I couldn't have done it better. Not that that makes it perfect. There's always room to improve everything and telling people how to improve is a way to show them that you think they have potential. But she's right. She can't drive the Silver Bullet for this next part and she shouldn't be the one to take this next risk.

"That's fine," I say absently as I finish making a plan for this part in my head.

"Oh," she seems to deflate like she was running on the fires of her great hatred for me, and now that I've agreed with her she's lost power and is bogging hard. She needs to downshift. She does. Her deflation turns into squinted eyes and a turned head so she can give me literal side-eye. "Why? What are you planning?"

Clever girl. What am I supposed to do with a girl who is capable, pretty, *and* clever? Normally, I'd avoid her because I know better than to shoot for what I can't ever hit, but we're stuck together which means I'll have to live in the orbit of all this total feminine power with no defense except growling inaccessibility. And I'm not sure how long I can maintain growls right now — well, not defensive growls. I could work up a very real growl of desire if the occasion presents itself.

"The gully where I popped a tire yesterday isn't there anymore," I say, stepping to one side to give her a view of what we're dealing with. "It's a full-on pond. A pond with a current because the rainwater is flowing through it. But I'm sure you remember what it was like. There are rocks all through it and the water is well above my truck's running boards."

She looks from the stream to me and back and she looks a bit grey, like she just realized what I realized a few minutes ago. We ford this pond, with or without our trophy, or we're stuck here another night. Or we have to hoof it on foot. None of those options is very palatable.

She swallows. "I'm pretty sure that the Silver Bullet will sink to the windshield in that water. I'll drown."

"Exactly." There's always something thrilling about working with someone who can keep up. "Which is why you'll drive the 7.3 through and tow the truck as far as you can, but we'll swap out the tow rope for the winch cable and when the truck gets stuck — which it will — we'll let out cable until the 7.3 gets across. Once you're on the other side you can use the winch to bring the Silver Bullet in to shore."

"And what will you be doing?" she looks skeptical. "Are you half fish? I don't see any gills. You won't be able to survive an underwater journey any better than I will."

"Once it gets too deep, I plan to stand in the box and watch for obstacles and yell at you if I see an issue," I say calmly.

She lifts an eyebrow. "Note to Nicola, it's already been established that yelling can't be heard in the big truck. Hence my wet face and leaf-decorated hair."

"We'll work out hand signals."

"And if you get stranded out there? If the winch cable gets hung up on something or the truck gets wedged?"

"Then," I say with absolute confidence that I do not feel, "I will swim and untangle the cable. I'll be able to see it all from the box."

"But you're dry and I'm the one who is wet. If you do this, you'll be wet, too."

I pause, eyes widening. Is that concern for me that she's showing?

She freezes, too, like she just realized she's revealed she has a beating heart. That's okay. I knew it all along. I rip my hoodie and T-shirt over my head in one motion and throw them in the cab of the truck. I'm shrugging off my boots and socks when I realize she's still frozen there, shocked, her pouty lips parted.

I look up long enough to smirk. That's right. I get stuff done. I'm not one of those guys who's all talk.

I throw my socks into the cab and start to shuck off my jeans. It's only then that I hear her tiny squeak and I pause with my jeans unzipped and my thumbs in the waistband.

"What?"

Her eyes are too bright. She snaps her mouth shut and then her eyes run up and down my body and she spins around to look at the problem ahead of us. Good idea. It's going to be a doozy. I shuck my jeans off, grab my phone from my pocket and throw the jeans on the seat, pull my boots back on, not bothering with the laces, and then I slam the truck door and tap her on the shoulder.

"Yep?" she says, and her voice sounds tight. She doesn't turn around.

"Can you hold onto my phone while I'm in the water?" I ask, and she finally turns, eyes fixed on mine like we're in a staring contest. I carefully put my phone in her hand.

"I'm not your secretary," she snips, but it seems to bring her back to herself because her expression transforms from stunned to focused. She snatches the phone from my hand and hops into the driver's seat of my truck with a lot of help from the steering wheel. She practically hangs off of it like a spider from a web. It's only once she's seated and has pulled the seat as far forward as is physically possible that she pulls her aviators down from on top of her head and squares her shoulders like she's going into battle.

"I thought no one drives the 7.3 but you," she says, glancing down at me only to turn right back to face forward again. Her jaw is tight like she's clenching her teeth and her knuckles are tense on the steering wheel. At least I don't have to tell her to take this seriously.

"No one drives it but me *and you,*" I growl, and then I quickly run her through the hand signals and make sure that she isn't going to take off while I unhook the tow rope and swap it out for the winch cable. She still isn't looking at me when I knock on her window. Not even when she unrolls it. I straighten, tightening every muscle in my body as I get ready for this.

We can do it. It's no big deal. Besides, she's proven she's competent, so I can put my safety in her hands. Right?

"Just take it easy when you go through the water," I tell her. "Not too fast. We don't want to kick up waves that swamp up into the engine compartment. Slow, steady, let her crawl over the rocks in four low."

"I know how to drive," she says, shooting a chastening glance at me over the tops of her sunglasses, but her eyes immediately widen and she's back to looking forward again before I can snarl back. Do those wide eyes mean she's worried? She doesn't need to be.

"Don't be anxious," I say, trying to reassure her.

Nothing.

I reach through the window and put my hand on hers on the steering wheel and she jumps, her foot hitting the gas pedal. I jump, too. Fuck. Maybe this is going to go to hell. Maybe she's not as steady as I thought she was. Fortunately, it's in park so all it does is rev my poor engine up.

I swallow. Too late to back out now. Better to pretend everything is fine so she has the assurance to make the pass.

I leave my hand on hers. "You're going to be fine. Just make sure it's out of park when you go to drive it."

Another angry look over the shades. Good. We're getting somewhere.

"I'm not going to let anything happen to you." I'm speaking as calmly as I can.

"No," she corrects me. "I'm the one driving. *I'm* not going to let anything happen to *you.*"

I nod curtly, my mind already back on the job. Confident as I try to appear, it's going to be a tough ride. I'm most of the way back to the Silver Bullet when I shoot a worried glance over my shoulder, but there she is in the side mirror watching me. Okay, good. At least she's alert.

And then all of a sudden her door is open and she leaps out of the truck and is running over the rough ground toward me and for a moment I get the strangest feeling that she's going to wrap me in her arms and something in my heart splits in two and I'm already opening my arms to welcome her when she stops and reaches up to put my hat on my head with the go pro on it. It's already blinking to record.

Oh.

Yeah.

Filming.

I'd completely forgotten.

"Film it or it didn't happen," she says, and then she spins on her pretty red boots and sprints back the way she came and my open arms fall empty to my sides and disappointment rushes through me like an ill wind.

You didn't come here for hugs, I remind myself. You came here to get a job done.

But as I watch her pretty little behind sway as she runs and then curve sweetly as she pops back up into the big truck, the reminders fall pretty flat.

Chapter Eleven

ADA

So, apparently, I'm driving his diesel truck now with him in the other truck and he's wearing a pair of the world's most form-fitting boxer briefs. They're multi-colored if you were wondering, which maybe you weren't. I wasn't until I saw them, and now I think maybe I should have been because if my pineapple bra screams "Hawaiian beach" then these scream "Fireworks!" and they make my cheeks too hot for words. I keep thinking of things exploding.

Focus, Ada. Now that he's given me the job of driving his truck through the pond, I'd better not screw it up. Especially since he popped a tire in here before, and even if we had spares there's no way we could change a flat in three and a half feet of water.

I concentrate, try to forget he's back there, and just drive. It's not easy and I'm sweating before I've gone more than a few feet. I have to keep my eyes on the mirrors and watch for his hand signals, and he's trying to backseat drive — of course — which is as annoying as it sounds. What does he think, that I can follow his minutia of "left, right, left" in hand signals while watching where my tires are going and where his are going? I only have two eyes. I use my best judgment with them.

We're halfway through when the Silver Bullet gets hung up and now I'm letting out winch cable as I drive. No big deal. I've never done it before, but I've let it out from a stationary truck and I've driven a truck so it's just a matter of combining the two. By the time I make it to shore, I'm shaking with effort.

It's done, Ada. You can calm down, I try to tell myself, but nothing about this feels done. It feels like it's just begun. I look out the rear and see him in the box of the Silver Bullet gesturing to me to tighten up the winch line. I missed him moving from cab to box. I bet that was a sight.

I follow his instructions and wait. The Silver Bullet moves, dragged along the gully floor like the hulk it is, but then it falls forward and the cable slides over a rock and gets stuck on the wrong side. Nicola gestures to me to let out some slack and then he leaps into the water. I don't envy him this part. A bunch of rainwater run-off is bound to be cold and it's so murky that it's hard to see through, though maybe it's not as disgusting as what I've been sitting in all this time.

Bring Bring.

That's not my phone. I look around and find his on the dash. One bar. We must have slipped into service somehow. His texts come pouring in, but this call comes up on his ID as "Emergency." I shouldn't answer it, right? There's probably some rule about answering other people's phones. It stops ringing. Okay. It will go to voicemail.

Nicola is over the rock now and trying to tug the cable back the way it should be. He signals for more slack and I give it to him as his phone begins to ring a second time. It's "Emergency" again. And now I'm not sure. Should I pick up? Will that make me a nosy person or a helpful one?

It stops and starts again while I'm still deciding. If it were me, I'd want it picked up. After all, it might really be an emergency.

With a worried huff, I grab his phone and take the call.

"Hello?"

A string of words in a guttural language I don't know come pouring out before I've even started my greeting, never mind finished it. This is Serbian, right? Nicola must speak it, or this person wouldn't be pouring the words out like he gets charged for them by the second and is trying to get in as many as he can in a short time.

"Whoever this is," I break in, "I am not Nicola. And if this is an emergency, and you speak English, you'd better speak fast because the cell here is the pits."

"Where is Nicola?" a heavily accented deep male voice asks me. "Why is he not answering?"

"He's swimming through a pond right now," I say, distracted as Nicola waves a hand signal at me.

I start to reel the winch line back in — I could have sworn that was the signal he gave me but his sudden yell arrests me and he makes the stop sign urgently, a pair of slashed hands over his chest before making the same sign again. I let line out and he sags with what I can only assume is relief. Oops.

"A pond? Where is he? Why is he not answering his calls?" the man on the line asks.

"He's north of Sacramento rescuing a vehicle," I say as Nicola paddles to a rock and stands on it, distracting me with more hand signals.

"That was yesterday," the man says.

"Do you need something?" I ask as I try to interpret the signals. I can't tell what Nicola wants.

"Reel it in!" I hear him call and I give up on hand signals and bring the winch line in. It snags and I try to sign that we're hung up while the man on the phone rants to me about children who do not keep their commitments.

"Well, I can't get you another child," I snap, realizing this must be Nicola's parent, "but in lieu of that, could you tell me if there's something else that you need because I need to get off this line."

"Try again!" Nicola calls. "Slower."

The winch only has one speed. I try to reel it and I hear his loud curse as he scrambles back over the rock, his tight butt revealed in excruciating detail in his wet shorts as he hurries to untangle the line again.

"You're going to have to try a tug with the truck," he yells.

"You're too close to the line!" I yell back.

"I am not too close!" The man on the phone objects. "Put Nicola on the phone."

"He's busy right now."

"Would you focus?" Nicola barks from the pond. "Put down your phone and drive the damn truck!"

I make a frustrated sound in the back of my throat.

"That is no tone to take, young woman!" Nicola's possible parent says. "Tell Nicola I can't find the pills for this morning. I don't know where he put them."

I turn to call to Nicola, "Where did you put the pills?"

"The what?" He calls back. "Would you just put that thing down and drive?"

"The pills!" I call again.

He shakes his head, flushed in his fury and glorious like a god of war before he leaps into the pond and swims to me. He's a fast swimmer. Like, Olympics fast. And then he's finding his feet and emerging from the water with rivulets of dirty water pouring from his slick black hair and every plane of his beautiful body.

And can I really be blamed if my mouth falls open and the phone falls from my hand? I can't right? Because this is like some kind of alien mind ray that wipes your thoughts clean. He's all I can see and I'm pretty sure this memory is now imprinted on the hard drive of my mind in a way that you could sure try to write over, but you can never, ever, ever erase.

He snatches his phone from the ground where it fell and barks, "Hello?" Before falling into rapid Serbian, his bright blue eyes catching mine, locking on, and narrowing. When he puts the phone away he scowls.

"Why are you answering my calls?" he asks. And he's pretty rude about it to someone who voluntarily called back and forth between him and an equally annoying relative.

"Because the ID said 'Emergency,'" I say.

"I told you that you could drive my truck, not run my damn life." His eyes are stunning when he aims that wry look at me. I can't tell if he's serious or not.

"Oh, excuse me for hearing that your dad needs his pills. I can see why that's some classified shit," I say, peering over my aviators at him. "That *is* your dad, right? Deep voice? Cranky, just like you? Maybe consider telling him to lay off the donuts so his tummy doesn't hurt and make him intolerable to be around."

With me in the truck and him on the ground, our eyes are exactly level. He smirks at me and for a minute I think he might laugh, but instead, he reaches out, lifts my aviators back on top of my head, and looks in my eyes for what feels like a long time. I don't know what he's looking for or if he finds it, but eventually, he gives me his phone.

"Let's wrap this up, Pineapple," he says.

"Sure thing Mr. Fireworks," I shoot back.

He looks down. Looks up at me, blushes so pink and wide-eyed that he could be the sunrise to my Hawaiian beach, and then he smirks again — this time with extra dimple and my heart does some kind of double flip that would kill someone who ate like he does. I can't speak for a moment, which is probably for the best when he calls over his shoulder.

"And this time, make sure to follow my instructions so we actually make some progress!"

Chapter Twelve

NICOLA

MY HEART'S still racing as we get the truck the rest of the way out of the pond. She talked to my dad. She. Talked. To. My. Dad.

That's part of my life I don't share. Ever.

It's more intimate than all the rest of this — even with bench seat spooning and seeing each other in our underwear. This is already more than I've ever shared with a woman. And that includes Amber. I married her, sure. And lived with her for two weeks. But she didn't meet my parents, not even on the phone.

She also never helped me get a truck out of the mud, which, now that I think about it, probably would have been a great way to discover who she really was inside — a quitter.

But I can't really drum up my usual bitterness toward her. Not when my chest feels all strange.

I feel this weird kind of softness inside and I'm not sure what to do about that. I'm not a soft person. I'm the kind of person who is tough for everyone else. I'm strong and capable, and I keep things focused by watching for imperfections and ruthlessly destroying them. I don't think soft thoughts about girls who take my parents' calls because they look important.

I certainly don't get impressed that a girl managed to make my dad say, "Who is that warrior queen I was talking to? Bring her home and give us grandchildren."

What did she even say to him?

I'm still thinking about it when the Silver Bullet is finally free and I'm shucking my clothing back on hurriedly. I'm damp underneath and I smell like a ditch, but that's better than Ada, who smells like disintegrating truck seats.

She's practically hopping up and down while I get dressed and I'm pretty grateful for the smell right now because this softness is trying to convince me that I want to kiss her, sink into her arms and just breathe her in until everything inside me melts. That would be a terrible idea. The worst.

"Your phone got service but mine didn't," she says, leveling her intense look at me.

I want that look leveled every morning. It would be better than an alarm clock to get me out of bed — or keep me in it. What sort of orders would a girl like Ada issue in bed? I'm worried that I want to find out a little too much.

"You got all kinds of texts," she says, trying to thrust my phone at me.

"What do they say?" I ask.

She's silent until I look up and see her doing that one-eyebrow thing. "Wait, I'm allowed to read these? That isn't considered 'running your damn life?'"

I bite my lip.

Oh. Yeah. I said that.

I could say nothing about it ... but the softness makes me want to explain.

"My parents are ... vulnerable," I say eventually.

"So you worry about them." For once her voice holds no judgment.

But I can't tell what she's thinking. Her sunglasses are over her eyes again. I reach out and lift them onto her head and to my surprise she lets me.

"Yes."

"They can't remember to take their pills on their own." It's not a question. She knows that now. It should make me itch all over that someone knows that. Instead, I get this terrible warm feeling. I'm weakening. My defenses are lowering. This is horrifying.

"No." I feel like the confession has been torn from me. Like maybe she's a priest in a confessional, but with a gun in her hands for immediate added authority. I feel more exposed than if I'd taken off my boxers with all the rest.

We look at each other for a long time, and I can't help but think that this is just like our first meeting. Her, sitting in a vehicle. Me, outside, talking through the window as she judges me.

"My dad can't remember to stop charging things to his credit card," she says eventually and I feel like the breath has been knocked out of me. She knows what this is like. "I never stop worrying about him. I might get home to find he's racked up more debt than I can pay this month." She pauses to swallow. "More than I can pay this year."

I'm nodding along.

"He lives with me," she says, sticking out her chin like she's challenging me to contest this. I think it's funny that when she feels insecure she gets so aggressive.

I clear my throat. I'm not good at vulnerable. It's not my thing. And on top of that, I can't admit how close my parents live to me. Not just to her, but to anyone. Ever.

"I worry all the time, too," I say, finding something I *can* talk about.

I hold her gaze and her brown eyes are electrifying. I can feel their touch on mine as if it were a physical thing. And then, just when I think I might shiver from it all, she breaks the spell.

"And you speak Serbian. I heard you. It's a sexy language."

"You thought my father was sexy on the phone?" I give her a dry look.

She rolls her eyes at me. We both know she meant me. What is making me smile like that? It's undignified and I need to stop it right now.

But somehow knowing that she likes the curve and flow of my accent lights a fire deep in my belly. I don't know what to do with it. Is it going to burn me? Is it going to burn everything?

"Are you going to read those texts, or what?" I ask her as I go to unhook the winch and replace it with the tow rope again.

"Sure," she says, hopping out to follow me as she reads. "Oh. Oh wow."

"Try out loud," I growl as I work.

"So, these are — a few from your dad. His autocorrect has it in for him. A few random ones that have nothing to do with me, and then a ton from Big Daddy Boom."

"Read them out," I say as I reel the winch back in.

"So apparently, Big Daddy Boom says that a bunch of our footage is automated to upload direct to the satellites, and it has better signal than our phones do," she says and she sounds surprised. I mean, I am, too.

Does that mean that Big Daddy Boom has already seen some of our raw footage? He's going to kill us over this gully crossing.

"I meant verbatim," I snap, worried now. Umm ... weren't those cameras on all night? When we slept together? The blood is rushing to my cheeks so hard that they feel stinging hot.

Ada reads in a really deep voice like she's trying to be Big Daddy Boom.

Hey guys, great footage. Love it all. Get as many shots as you can. You're both champions! she reads.

"*Tanner is having continued issues with his transmission, but the guys are picking him up, and they're still on their way. Stay cool.*"

She laughs before she reads the next one. *"Big weather blowing in. You guys need a lift in the chopper?"*

"That's all last night," she says. "This one is from this morning."

"Showed the early footage to a buddy at a HUGE streaming service. They might be interested in a show."

Exactly *which* footage did he show this guy?

She doesn't look too worried. "I bet high rollers like Big Daddy talk like that all the time. It's probably nothing."

I'm not sure why she thinks that, but to me, it doesn't sound like nothing. It sounds like guaranteed income. It sounds like a way to set my parents up.

She goes back to reading. "This one is from while I was on the phone with your dad."

"The streaming service saw some of the river crossing. There's a potential deal with them, guys! You have no idea how huge that is! You'll be stars," she reads and she doesn't sound like she believes it.

She laughs kind of hollowly. "Well, that's nice. Maybe some of them will subscribe to our channels."

"Or," I prompt.

"Or what?"

"Or, they might give us the show." I shrug.

She stares at me before reading the next part, *"But they only have the budget for one show. Which of you wants it the most?"*

"Me, obviously," I say immediately. When she says nothing, I feel like I need to explain. "Maybe it's no big deal for you, but I have aging immigrant parents to support. They worked their whole lives for minimum wages. Do you think it's easy to pay for what they need now? I want this kind of thing more than you ever could."

"Woah," she says, putting a hand on one hip and popping it. She's turned from playful to stern in a heartbeat. "You *want* this more? Really? Are you kidding me? Did you not hear what I said about *my* dad? How could you want it more than me? We both want this."

"Sure," I say, trying to mollify her, but she throws her hands in the air.

"You know what? Just drive. Let's get this over with."

She turns like she's going to walk to the Silver Bullet but I reach out and grab her by the hips to spin her around. Her mouth falls open in maybe surprise or maybe horror.

"You said you wouldn't touch me except to keep me safe," she objects, arms folded over her chest. Her eyes are a bit pink. She's not upset, is she?

"I am keeping you safe," I say in my quiet voice. The one I use on children and dogs. "From yourself. It's not smart to drive angry."

"Then I guess whole race tracks shut down the minute you show up."

I smirk at that. Nice dig.

"Listen," I say, "don't be mad. Come on. We make a great team. Maybe they'll decide they want both of us."

I can tell by the look on her face that she's listening to my argument.

"Besides," I say "If they really are considering offering us a tv deal, don't you think they'll judge us by the footage? We can't stop now. This is our best shot at getting a crack at this — even if only one of us makes it in the end."

She doesn't answer, but she doesn't roll her eyes at me either. Instead, she snatches up a Go Pro from in the truck and beelines it back to the Silver Bullet. Not my first choice to end this argument, but I'll take it. At least she's making money out there for us, and we certainly both need it.

"And Ada?" I call, almost surprised when she stops and looks back at me. "Be more careful driving. I've seen enough of your pretty skin to know I wouldn't want it bruised."

"What about you?" she quips. "Maybe you're the one who will end up bruised."

I shrug.

"I look good in anything," I say and then I hop into the truck and end the conversation.

Chapter Thirteen

ADA

So, it turns out I'm attracted to the man who has made my life
and career so difficult — still no apology from him on that, by
the way.

I steer the Silver Bullet the rest of the way out while he tows
me. There aren't any incidents. I'd say it all went smoothly, but I
don't know. I'm distracted by a swooping feeling in my belly
every time he looks in his rearview mirror and our gazes
intermingle.

I try to turn my mind to what I need to do when I get home
to prepare for the next part of this build — how I'll pitch it to
my subscribers, how I'll fit it into my regular content schedule,
but the ideas aren't flowing. All that's flowing is the feeling of
him behind me when I woke up this morning, warm and safe.
The way he lifts my aviators so he can look at my eyes. That
accent. The shape of his body when it's dripping wet.

My mouth is very dry, by the way. Just thought you should
know.

I don't know what to do with any of it. Except I do know I can't let him know about it. If he had the power to ruin me before, he'll have it doubly now. All he has to do is wink and murmur something in Serbian.

My phone buzzes in my pocket. Service! This is amazing! But I can't look at it until we get to the road and the Silver Bullet finally comes to a stop.

When we finally pull out to the gravel road, the first thing I see is my car. I could almost cry, it looks so good.

I can drive home.

I can shower at a hotel.

I can be ... not covered in grossness and how great would that be?

The first drop of rain hits when I open the door of the Silver Bullet. And then the second. And then the sky opens up and pours down on me.

Well, I guess I don't have to wait to have that shower.

I jog up to Nicola's truck and knock on the window. He rolls it down and looks at me with a blank expression.

"Yes?"

"It's raining!" I gasp.

No change in expression. "Really? Shocker."

"Do you think we can load up in this?"

"Is there a reason you're standing in the rain and not hopping into my dry truck?" He's really getting that eyebrow lift down.

"I thought I'd take a shower," I say. "Wash that disgusting truck off myself."

"Is your phone waterproof?"

"Oh, crap!" I'm sprinting around the truck and leaping into the passenger side before he can rescind the offer. I do feel cleaner. And very, very drenched.

He has donut dust on his chin.

Uh oh.

His dark eyes meet mine and I'm braced for whatever is coming next.

"How does your hotrod do in the pouring rain?" he asks.

"Fine," I say and maybe I sound a little belligerent, but people are always knocking my car because it's old, even though I've rebuilt practically everything on it. It gets annoying. It's like they don't trust my work. "How's your truck in the pouring rain?"

He smirks. "The windshield leaks."

"I've noticed." A cold drip hits the back of my neck just on cue.

"But we could trailer your car, too," he says, looking at me hopefully. "The trailer is easily long enough for both vehicles. And it would be cheaper than driving your car and my truck both. Less fuel."

Am I hearing him correctly? Does he *want* to spend more time with me here in his vehicle?

He clears his throat. "That journey took longer than I thought. By the time we load up, I doubt we'll make it further than Sacramento before we have to stop for the night. I don't know about you, but I'm starving and I didn't get much sleep last night."

His phone rings then and he answers it, immediately switching to Serbian. I check my own phone. It's back in range now. I have a bunch of texts from Jasmin.

Are you okay up there?

The Weather Network says the storm is going to last all night.

How hot is your rival when he's soaking wet?

Can you snap a pic for me?

Also, have you killed him yet? And if so, maybe don't say, just send me a random emoji and I'll help you bury the body.

That was all last night. The ones from today tie a different kind of knot in my belly.

OMG. Boom Enterprises is already airing teasers for your trip and just mentioning that you're on it got you three thousand new followers. Three thousand, Ada!

Umm, also I think your dad did a thing. Don't call. You'll want to hear about it in person.

When you're sitting down.

He's fine. He's fine. He just ... bought some stuff.

Crap.

Seriously, don't worry. Just ... maybe get back as soon as you can.

The rain stops as fast as it started and I hurry out again while Nicola is arguing on the phone. My bag is in the back of the car. I rush with it into the woods far enough to get changed into something dry. The relief of clean dry clothing makes the blow from Jasmin's texts a little less hard.

Okay, so my dad did a thing. I knew he might. It's why I begged the family to keep an eye on him. As long as he didn't hurt someone it should be okay, right? And Jasmin always exaggerates. Just because she is freaked out doesn't mean I need to be.

By the time I get out of the woods, I'm hastily jamming my wet clothes back into my bag. There's nothing I can do about the boots and I'll just go without a jacket for now.

I pull up short.

Nicola has already winched the Silver Bullet onto his trailer and is finishing tightening the ratchet straps. He nods to the spot behind it with an easy smile.

"See?" He says, grinning so that his dimples show even under his dark scruff. "There's room for you." His brows pull down. "Where's your jacket?"

"It was wet." Whatever else might be true about Nicola, he's a hard worker. He loaded that fast.

I hop into my car and fire it up. He already has the ramps down. I ease up onto his long trailer. If I had a place to park one of these I'd be crazy jealous. It's amazing.

I'm gathering ratchet straps from his truck bed and carefully strapping my hotrod down when he comes back out with his GoPro in one hand and his House of Kolor hoodie in the other.

"Here," he says as I finish up. "It's getting colder."

"I don't take gifts," I remind him, but it feels like a silly policy right now.

"Ada," he says slowly and his blue eyes are so intense I have to look away. "You're cold. And I think you should be warm. Either take the hoodie and wear it, or I'll have to warm you another way."

He's looking at me with naked hunger in his eyes and I forget he's holding a camera. I forget he wrote all those things about my work. I forget everything except how powerful he looked when he was tightening those straps and his triceps were flexing, and how bright those eyes are, and how incredibly sweet it is that he's trying to force me to take his only warm sweater, and I melt.

I take a step forward without meaning to. A drop of rainwater is sliding down his unshaven jaw. I want to trace it with my fingertips. There's rain clinging to his eyelashes. Something inside is screaming at me to kiss him. I can already feel that kiss on my lips.

"How would you do that?" I ask a little breathlessly and yeah, my heart seems to stutter at the end of that, too.

"I was thinking," he says, stepping a bit closer so I can see his Adam's apple bob. "That I could hold you close against me and rub you with my hands to warm you up."

I clear my throat. "So it's a worn hoodie or your hands all over me? Those are my options?"

That something inside is moaning now. She wants this bad.

"Sure," he says. "Unless you can think of a better way."

And I can think of a better way. I can think of so many better ways. I can think of his naked skin all over mine and seeing what might be inside those boxer briefs he was wearing earlier. I swallow, but I am a smart girl and I know better. We're too tangled up in business for me to risk everything on a fling with him, no matter how dry he makes my mouth. And how wet he makes other things.

Time to murder that voice in my head. Or at least lock her away in a closet with a very strong door.

I snatch the hoodie and pull it over my head. "Thank you."

"Mmm," he says noncommittally, "I'd say 'You're welcome,' but you're kind of not. I was hoping for the second option."

And the bold look he gives me makes me feel tingles all up and down my legs and low in my belly and I want so badly to feel those hands all over me, inspecting me like he inspected that truck before he tried to make it run. I want him guessing at what drives me like he was guessing about it. I want him tinkering with everything and getting up in my undercarriage.

"Get used to being surprised," I say but it's too breathless to be as badass as I was hoping for.

I'm thrilled when he takes one more step forward so that we're chest to chest, leans in, and says in a low voice. "I don't think I will. I think I'll let your surprises keep me on my toes until one day, I give you the biggest surprise of your life."

I look down and then up again. Slowly.

"If that's supposed to be a euphemism, you have forgotten that I've already seen you pretty close to nude, Fireworks. And it was not the biggest I've seen."

He chuckles, low in his throat, and gives me a dangerous look before leaning down and whispering in my ear, "Keep telling yourself that, Pineapple."

And then he's gone, loading up the ramps, and back to business like nothing happened while I'm still trying to bring down my increased heart rate and the very agitated buzz in the less-used areas of my body.

Wow. He's good at that.

Does he toy with everyone he hates like that, or just me?

I'm still wondering about that as I get back into the front seat of his truck.

Wrapped in his hoodie.

Toasty warm.

Chapter Fourteen

NICOLA

I LOVE DRIVING WITH HER. This is a surprise. I usually prefer my alone time. I'm a happy tenant in my own head. It can take hours for my thoughts to calm enough for boredom to even be a possibility. When people are with me they buzz with chaos and intensity and I need time afterward to find that stillness that can only come from running all my thoughts out until there are no more thoughts left.

Not today. Today, I'm charmed by her sharp chatter.

"Tell me about yourself," she'd started, but mostly she's telling me about herself.

About growing up in San Diego. About her doting father who was so obsessed with cars that, of course, she would be, too. How he'd take her to the drag races when she was tiny, put a pair of headphones on her head, and then have to carry her to the car when she fell asleep in his lap. How every Saturday was a swap meet somewhere. Every Sunday, a day spent building in his father's old shop. How her aunt — a restless soul much like her father — would drop her younger cousin Jasmin off for the day while she went to a folk festival with a new boyfriend and then maybe not come back for three weeks, or how when they got older she'd take both Ada and Jasmin with her.

"I smoked my first pot at age eleven at one of those festivals," she tells me with a scowl from under her aviators.

"I don't doubt it," I say, trying to wind her up further.

"I never did it again. I don't like being out of control. I feel like my whole life is out of control sometimes."

"You seem to be the most in-control person I've ever met," I say, and I try not to look at her too long because when I do, it brings back that softness that's killing me. "Self-reliance is hard to find."

"Self-reliance comes when you know no one has your back — that you have to make it happen or just live with the consequences." Her tone is sharp.

I nod.

"You look like maybe you know about that," she says, and when I don't answer she digs in. "You came to Canada from Serbia."

"Yes," I say.

"As a refugee. Did you speak English?"

"Not at first," I say tightly.

"Sounds like maybe you know about being out of control," she says and I nod.

I do know. I know all about it.

We're both quiet for a long time. It's getting dark outside and I'm deep into memories of my childhood when she speaks again.

"When I was a kid, I never knew what we were going to do, or where we were going to go, or whether I would be dropped off with Auntie Mary at two in the morning because Pops needed to help a friend who was stuck somewhere."

I match her confession with my own confession. "When I was a kid, I lost all my friends and my home to come to a country

I didn't want to even visit. I watched my parents have to take jobs for which they were overqualified. I watched them go from vibrant people to ... hollow. They're still hollow."

She's gentle when she speaks again. "When I got older, I never knew what bills might come in that needed to be paid yesterday with no way to pay them."

I can match that, too. "When I got older, they needed me. Just when I thought I'd finally escaped. Would finally get a chance to live my own dreams."

I glance at her expression, lit by dash lights and oncoming traffic. She's biting her lip before her eyes meet mine and for a flash, I'm too vulnerable. Too exposed. She must see it on my face.

"You know, then. You know what it means to be out of control. We don't get to pick these things. We just have to roll with them."

"We could leave," I say quietly.

She scoffs. "I never would. If it was in me to abandon someone who gave me what little he had, I would have done it already."

Her words are like a knife slicing into me, cutting right to my heart because she *gets* it. That's exactly how I feel. Exactly.

"I think it's the same for you," she says quietly and my breath grows ragged.

She knows me. I'm choking on the idea. She understands that part of me I keep hidden. I don't dare acknowledge it. If I do, won't that mean she owns some part of me? The part she has seen that no one else ever has?

"That doesn't explain Amber, though," she says. "She wasn't part of your controlled life."

That pulls a snort from me. "Sometimes you just don't want to think. You want to do."

"So you did her?" She snickers and I roll my eyes.

"So, I tried." I leave it there. I've been open enough. I don't want to confess that I made such a mess out of things with Amber that I haven't bothered to try to see anyone since. I've given up with women. I can't make them happy and take care of my parents, too. And like she said, what kind of person doesn't repay the ones who gave up everything for them? I throw it back on her instead. "What about you? Any Ambers?"

"If you mean, have I been married for two weeks and then dumped? No. Shockingly, I'm better with people than you are."

"Who says I'm bad with people?" I can't help the complaint in my tone. She could probably help that laugh, though. It doesn't need to be so obvious.

"*I* say you're bad with people," she says. "Me. The one you've been bad with."

She has a point. But eventually, she actually answers my question.

"I have this thing."

Her voice is hard like she's steeling herself to tell me something crazy about her. Suddenly, all my senses are on the alert.

"What thing?" I ask and I'm thinking about leather and whips and blindfolds, and feet in stilettos, and after that, I'm out. I'm not one of those guys who spend their time on internet porn. I build cars and that takes all my time and creativity. So, my list of possible fetishes is very short.

She hesitates. "I shouldn't have said that."

"Well, now you have to say," I growl. "Because I'm imagining all kinds of 'things.'"

"Stop it! Stop it right now! You don't get to imagine me and *things*."

I keep my tone dry, but it's hard to keep my eyes on the road. I want to see that gleam in her eye. My imagination is full to the brim with Ada.

"I'm imagining so many things. Things you've maybe never heard of. And the longer this takes, the crazier they get."

In actual fact, I got as far as imagining her naked, and then I hit the rumble strip on the side of the highway and had to pull my mind back on target again so we didn't crash. Awesome, Nicola. Really well done.

"Don't try to rattle me to get a confession!" she snaps but then she sighs. "Fine. I'll tell you."

But she doesn't tell me. The minutes draw out.

"Yes, that's quite the story," I say eventually and she laughs before hitting my arm.

I don't think I've grinned this hard in a long time.

"Fine. I have this thing about respect. I won't have sex with a man I can't respect. I just can't ... get into it, ... okay? Like, it doesn't work for me."

"You've tried?"

I wish I could see her flush but it's dark. And despite it being dark, she's slipped her aviators over her eyes to hide from me.

"Of course I tried," she snaps. "It doesn't work for me."

She's so adorable when she's mad that I want to laugh and kiss her all at once. I'm smart enough to do neither.

"Doesn't seem to be an issue. Just limit yourself to people you respect."

She snorts. "Yeah, because that's so easy."

I almost laugh at that, too, but then it hits me. This girl doesn't hold many people in high regard. Maybe she doesn't hold anyone in high regard. Has she ... is she ... my mind derails again and I hit the rumble strip *again* and she lets out a little startled cry.

"You have to stop doing that. It's not the effective interrogation tool you think it is."

I say nothing. I don't want to confess that every time I think of her naked I almost kill us both.

"How about I just tell you, and you promise to stop doing that," she says and her voice is tight with annoyance.

"I promise," I say grimly because seriously, Nicola, get it together.

"I ... don't think most people are all that respectable."

"Mmmhmm."

"What I mean to say is that I've respected one or two, but I find they are unavailable."

"Meaning?"

"Meaning I've never *dated* someone I respected, okay?"

"Meaning?"

She makes an annoyed sound in the back of her throat and I have to grip the steering wheel doubly hard to keep on the road because my mind wants to go there sooo badly.

"Ada Ford," I say eventually and can I help it if my voice sounds all growly? No, I cannot. "Are you confessing to me that you've never been with a man you respected and so you don't ... how shall I put this ... *light up* for anyone?"

Her whimper tells me I've guessed correctly.

"Hmmm."

"You sound far too happy for a priest who just heard my confession," she snaps.

"Oh, so I'm a priest now?" I laugh. "Celibate and doomed to never love a woman? I don't think so." Not with these thoughts in my head, at any rate, though I won't tell her that. Instead, I say. "I'm just thinking about how it would be fun to earn your respect and then see what you do with that. What might you do, Ada Ford, if you suddenly found you respected a man you claim to hate?"

"Not going to happen," she snaps.

My laugh is low. "I guess we'll see."

"I think I know my own mind."

"Do you, though?"

We're quiet again until civilization arrives and I see the sign for a truck stop restaurant lit up in the darkness.

"Hungry?" I ask and she laughs.

"Have you seen me eat anything in the last twenty-four hours?"

I guess we're past the awkward — and extremely beguiling — sex talk and back to normal friend talk. Are we friends now?

"An energy bar," I say because I like to be accurate.

She laughs again. "Just pull into the stop here."

It's pretty empty since it's past supper time but they serve all-day breakfast and I order eggs and bacon while she orders some kind of fruit thing and eggs. I don't even care what they taste like. I inhale them. I'm surprised to see she's done the same.

It's only when we go to pay that things change. Her credit card is denied. She tries to hide it from me but I see her face go pale and I wonder who was spending all her money while she was with me.

"I've got this," I say. "Least I can do when you've kept me awake on the road."

She isn't wearing her aviators and I can see the turmoil on her face. She doesn't take gifts. But it's too late to say no.

"Okay," she says. "Thanks. But maybe no hotel tonight, okay? Can we just keep going until we get to San Diego?"

"Fine," I say because I'm a moron and I swear I'll agree to anything if it just means more time with her. But I'm going to need coffee and ... I don't know, maybe a bag of ice to sit on so that I don't keep thinking of her and her *thing* and drifting right off the road.

Chapter Fifteen

ADA

I DON'T REALIZE I'm asleep until I wake up and he's right there. It's dark all around except for a neon sign above his head that reads "Beach Inn," and below it in blinking neon, "Vacancy."

"Can't go to a motel," I mutter, fighting eyelids that I swear weigh a thousand pounds, and then just like that, I've been swept up into arms and I'm being carried. "I said no touching."

"No touching except to help you," he murmurs in my ear. "Don't fight me on this one, Ada Ford. It's midnight. I barely slept last night. I can't drive anymore, and you fell asleep while regaling me with your best high school stories. We're both done."

I try to muster an argument and leap from his arms. The best I can do is a muttered, "Can't pay" and a spasm that puts my lips somehow in contact with his neck. It's seriously everything I was dreaming about just now. Strong and firm, rough from stubble, smelling of man, and rust, and gear lube. I want to die. It's so good. Can I sleep right here? Please?

I've barely registered that we're indoors before I find myself gently put onto a bed. I think it's a bed. That's definitely a pillow. I moan, so tired I can't muster the effort to kick my own boots off. Someone else pulls them off for me, pulls the covers up and over me, and then I could almost swear I feel someone kiss my hair before he whispers to me.

"Sleep well, Pineapple."

When I wake the next morning, it's to an unfamiliar motel room.

I blink in the morning sun as it all comes crashing back. I'm in a motel. With Nicola.

I sit up, panicked, only to realize that there's just one bed in this motel room and no one else is sleeping in it but me. No one did earlier, either. The other side of the bed is made up motel-style with the hideous coverlet tucked around the pillow.

I'm still in Nicola's hoodie. The House of Kolor one.

I rub my eyes muzzily. The things I had with me are on the little table beside the window. So is a pair of yoga pants and a hoodie with the logo of "Beach Inn" on them and a tiny note placed on top with the key to my hotrod.

The note is scrawled on motel letterhead and when I read the cramped doctor's handwriting — or maybe, *ha ha* dentist's handwriting — I feel a little stab of something hot and intense and melty like bubbling caramel.

It reads.

I never said I hated you.

Nicola

555-307-2219

And suddenly I'm panicked all over again. This is a goodbye note. I can tell.

I open the motel door and I see it right away. My hotrod. Parked neatly in front of the motel. And no sign of his truck or trailer anywhere.

I'm so disappointed that I just close the door and sit down

on the bed and put my head in my hands. This is crazy. I don't let people disappoint me. And besides, why would I be disappointed because Nicola's gone? Nicola, who I didn't want to work with in the first place. Nicola, who trashed me in those articles. Nicola, who paid for dinner last night and carried me into my own motel room and maybe kissed my hair.

I'm not one to linger in sadness. There's always too much to do. I hop up and get in the shower and when I'm thoroughly clean, I dress in the motel clothes he clearly bought for me — what kind of jerk ignores you when you say no presents? And I march to the front desk.

"Room 13?" The white girl behind the counter asks, lifting an eyebrow. She has those watercolor tattoos of lilies and roses that are so popular climbing her arms, but apparently, no one told her that having them tinted pink makes it look like she has a bad rash.

"Yes. I'm checking out," I say.

"Cool, just leave the key in the room." She seems bored and way too into her book to deal with me. The title is *A Court of Something Something* — I can't really read the part her fingers are sprawled across — and she's nearly at the end. Her eyes have yet to leave the page.

"Don't I need to pay?" I ask.

"It's already paid. He said to text him if there's a problem."

"He?" I press, though I'm pretty sure I know who *he* is. There are only two *he's* in the world who would pay for a motel room for me, and one of them has already maxed out my credit card.

"Some hot older guy with an accent." She looks up then. "He's not trafficking you, is he? We have a hotline if he is."

Oh. God.

"No," I say and it comes out in a rush.

She shrugs and goes back to her book. "The pamphlets are

by the door if you need one. Oh, and he said to give you this. It's for the place across the road."

I take the paper in her hand. It's handwritten on the back of a receipt for Stella's Muffins and it says, "*Gift Certificate: One muffin and a Coffee.* And is signed, *Stella.*

I stare at it and look up again and then back down at the pamphlets. I'm not sure if I should be horrified that the desk girl thinks I'm being trafficked or grateful that she offers this to other women who come through. Beside the pamphlets are the hoodies, yoga pants, and ball caps with the motel branding. Nicola paid way too much for what I'm wearing, but it's pretty comfortable if you can get past the ugly neon logo. The thing is, there's only one hoodie I want to wear, and it's in my hotel room right now and is roughly five thousand sizes too big because it was made for a huge Serbian dude. And I'm mad as hell that he didn't let me give it back. Or say goodbye. Or anything.

I go back to the room, grab my phone, ignore all other messages, and type in his number.

Goodbye to you, too, I text him, furious.

His answer comes back lightning fast. *Is this Stella?*

How many girls have you failed to say goodbye to this morning? I type as I gather my things. My clothes reek. I'm suddenly more grateful than I can say for the ones he bought me.

I loved the banana chocolate chip. I could almost marry you just for that.

I look down at the slip of paper the front desk girl gave me and back at my phone. Did he really give his digits to the woman who runs a muffin shop, or is he pulling my leg? I can't tell. And I should probably leave it at that, hop in my car, and head the rest of the way home. But instead, I find myself bundling everything into the hot rod and driving next door.

The muffin place is darling. I hate it on principle.

The woman behind the counter is a fresh-faced forty and I hate her, too. How old did Nicola say he was last night? Thirty-six? Thirty-seven? I think it was thirty-six. Which means he's closer to this woman's age than my twenty-five.

The shop is painted in a turquoise so soft it's barely discernable as "not white" except that it's paired with vanilla that looks like ice cream, and the combination is just so pretty when combined with the stainless chairs and tables that I'm a little wistful when I show my handwritten gift certificate to Stella — who is way too pretty to bake muffins, by the way, like model-pretty with her blonde hair untouched by grey and her make-up clearly tutorial-worthy. She takes it and gives me a black coffee.

"There are fixings for the coffee on the end. The honey is locally sourced," she says with a smile. "Which muffin would you like?"

"Cranberry lemon," I say, choosing from the case and her smile lights up the room. I can't help but ask, "Is that your favorite, too?"

But she laughs, "No. Mine is the apple cinnamon, but that sweetheart who came in and had me write this for you told me that he bet me one smile and a dollar that you'd pick the cranberry lemon. That's his dollar on the bulletin board."

I follow her finger to see a dollar bill pinned there on its own. When I look back at Stella her smile is all warm and soft and she tilts her head to one side in an "awww" expression.

"You're so cute!" She says. "I wish I could find love like that."

I have literally no idea what to say to that, so I snatch up my muffin and coffee and manage a, "You have a lovely place here, Stella," before bolting to the door.

It is lovely.

And I am not in a couple with Nicola. Am I?

Am I? I ask, as I hop into the car and follow the signs onto the highway.

I can't be, I think as I downshift while simultaneously

tearing into the muffin. It's an amazing muffin, if you were wondering. No wonder he loves her.

My phone buzzes and I look down.

I'm kidding, Ada. I know this is you, his text reads. *If you picked the cranberry lemon, then you owe me a coffee sometime. I bet on that one.*

Why that one? I text back.

There were no pineapple muffins.

That's the last thing he texts and I know I should pull over and send him a long thank you for all these gifts and something professional about how we'll see each other later when he drops the Silver Bullet off to me or something. I should. But I can't bring myself to do that, because then it really will feel like goodbye, and it turns out that I don't want to say goodbye.

I've never felt lonely when I was alone before. I do now.

I want to have to fight every bit of information out of Nicola like I did last night — I learned that he doesn't talk unless you guess the right answer about him. I want to fill all his silences and solve him like a puzzle. I want to kiss his neck again.

And even if I can't do any of that, I'm not quite ready yet to say goodbye to the possibility, so I let the text hang there, and I just drive, and drive, and try to tell myself that it's only been two days and I still don't really know him, that I'm just tricked by spending all that time forced together, that I'm just desperate because it's been so long since anyone made me curious about them.

But none of it is working.

I left San Diego a self-made woman with a great opportunity ahead of her. I was certain about who I was and what I wanted.

I'm coming back someone who has no idea what she wants and is just a little bit scared to find out.

Chapter Sixteen

I GUTTED the Silver Bullet on my first day back, amped up with bright energy from the drive and the way I felt purged from all those confessions. I was spurred on by the need to do something — anything — to keep me at home rather than chasing off through the city to find her. I'd searched her online, obviously, and found her shop and her dad's shop. Pin Up Stitchin' shared a building with her dad's garage and the street view showed a charming shop with such a classic feel that it could easily have been the same in 1950 as it was now.

So, I worked, and I waited. I waited for her to answer my text. But there was nothing. No response to that last one at all. Was she angry? Of course she was angry. She was always mad at me. I just wanted her to be mad nearby instead of far away. Was that so much to ask?

That same day, Big Daddy Boom called me via video chat and let me know how sorry he was to have left us hanging. I showed him the Silver Bullet with my phone camera and he hooted like a little kid.

"Listen," he said. "We're sending over disclaimers and legal stuff for you to sign. Don't post more than teasers about the Bullet yet, okay? I'm still talking to the guys at the streaming service about a deal."

I'd nodded along.

"I'll be in San Diego in three weeks. I want to meet with both you and Ada then for dinner. I'll have Tanner send you details. Can you get this truck stripped down before then and send the motor off to Hollis Montieth? We'll send you shipping details. It's all covered."

"Sure," I'd agreed, feeling deflated. I wouldn't see her for three weeks. That felt like an eternity.

No distractions, Nicola. Do the job. Work the plan. Get the money. Live the life.

I sank into my work. I had to upload my teasers and send all the videos to both Big Daddy and to Ada to sort through for their channels. I had to show progress on the giveaway vehicle I'm working up for the channel — an old Ford Falcon — and install the speaker system my sponsor sent for the build.

I had to deal with everything that went wrong for my parents while I was gone. Get them groceries and prescriptions. Clean the place. Do laundry. All that super glamorous stuff that comes with having your aging parents live in the second bedroom of your two-bedroom home.

And ... okay, this is going to sound crazy but I cut back on the donuts, too. And the other things made with flour. Look, she's not wrong. They give me gut aches. And that makes me cranky. She's right about that, too. It's actually kind of nice to know *why* it hurts.

By the time I have a handle on things it's been a week and there's still no text from Ada. It's midnight after a long day and I'm eating a burrito that I made for myself — my parents won't eat "foreign food" which is practically *everything* in their view and just a bit hypocritical if you ask me.

I don't know why I'm so weak, but I open my phone and reread my texts with Ada, and wonder what I did wrong. Is it the nickname? Or is it just that she was stuck with me before and now that she's home again she'd rather do anything but spend time with me?

I shake my head at myself and dig out the articles I wrote about her. I write articles freelance for all kinds of car magazines. I'm not sure I'm much of a writer, but the editors seem to enjoy the sharp eye I have for inconsistencies.

The first time I submitted, I was trying to pull together some money for rent and I figured it couldn't hurt to try. My article was picked up that same day with a request for more and an e-transfer of fifty dollars. After that, I just kept going. I don't do it full-time, but if I'm at a car event anyway, why not type up a report on what I saw? Maybe highlight a few of the better cars or some of the more interesting work? Point out how to make it just a touch better next time, right? It can mean seeing my time compensated, on top of whatever else I get out of the event. I've always thought that was a good deal.

I'm not sure right now as I reread everything I've written about Ada's work. Obviously, the sheer class of it caught my eye immediately. She has an eye for fitting the perfect style with every vehicle but leaving it just enough "her" that you can imme-diately pick out her work from the rest. I loved it before I knew who was doing it.

But do these articles express that, exactly? I'm not sure. That I wrote them at all is almost embarrassing in how much it shows that I'm obsessed with her work. I mean, who writes eleven arti-cles for seven different publications on just one woman's work? Did anyone else notice that I'm hung up on it? I hope not. I tried to be extra objective to make up for it — to point out all the flaws along with the genius. I think they're fair. They defi-nitely highlight both.

But somehow, out of all this, she got the idea that I hate her.

And I just don't see it. No matter how many times I reread them, all I see is my poorly disguised attraction.

I sigh, put them back, and I don't think anything of them until the next day when my dad tries to throw them out.

"What did I tell you about messing with my papers?" I ask him in Serbian as I snatch them from his hands. I'm not sure why my heart has kicked up a gear but it has.

"You need to get it out of your mind that you are a writer. Focus on the cars. Stop with these videos and articles and things. They only distract you." He means well. But his head can't wrap around what the modern work world is like.

"I need those things for my work to sell, Dad," I say, shoving the articles into the top drawer of my desk. "And I need you to stop trying to interfere with it."

"Who is interfering?" He asks, shaking his head. "Why don't you bring that nice girl over. The one I spoke to on the phone. She was snappy. You need snappy. Someone to draw you out of these funks you get into."

"I don't understand why you can't just forget her," I grumble. I wonder if I'll look like him when I'm old. He's worn and stooped and six inches shorter than me, even though he was easily my height when he was young.

My dad slowly makes his way back to the living room, grunting in pain as he goes — or maybe in judgment of my choices, sometimes it's hard to tell.

"You're thirty-six Nicola," he says as he goes. "You should be out there meeting a nice girl and giving us grandchildren. When was the last time you were with a nice girl, hmm? I haven't seen one around here. Unless you keep her at your shop. But there's no bed over there, so it can't be a very hot love affair."

"I need to be here, working to fund our lavish lifestyle," I say wryly, ignoring his cringy reference to me, a girl, and a bed. The last image I ever want in my head when I'm with a girl is my dad talking about my 'hot love affairs.'"

I help him find his seat in the chair he likes. My mother is asleep on the couch, her COPD machine whooshing as she breathes. She'll probably sleep the morning away restlessly. She's slipping away from us a little at a time. We both know it. We both don't want to say it.

"You need to move us out so you can have a life," my dad says. "Meet someone. Take adventures. Have children."

Every time he says something like that a surge of panic claws up my throat. I remember all over again that I'm trapped. I can't get out. I can't ever leave them. I can't have a life. It's good Ada hasn't texted because what could I offer her anyway? I'm stuck here in this house forever nursing my elderly sick parents.

"You know that's not an option," I remind him. "You need help. I can't ship you back to Canada without me to help you. You need family. And because I immigrated and became a citizen of the USA, I can't go live with you there."

"You can put us in one of those facilities where nurses do it all."

I give him a long look. "You know I can't afford that. And where would that leave you? Would you be happy alone in a facility with nurses doing everything?"

"You could put us in one here where there's a little help and you can come by now and then."

"And what? Admit I'm hiding you here illegally? They'll ship you straight back to Canada and we'll be back to where I can't help you."

"You shouldn't have come here, Nicola. You should have stayed in Manitoba. Was it really so bad?"

It was.

Sometimes I still have dreams that I'm living in that little town just north of Winnipeg and when I wake up I feel like I can't breathe. The cold is crawling down my throat and my eyes are iced over. I shiver now with the memory of it. People might laugh if they knew that what scares me most is small-town, friendly prairie life with a side of minus thirty degrees Celcius weather. They can keep laughing and I'll keep living as far away from that part of the world as possible.

"What's done is done, Dad."

He's quiet for a while. It's hard for him to admit that we're all trapped here. Him, me, Mom — all of us. It's quite the impossible situation we got ourselves in. And now our only option is to wait it out.

"At least call the girl. Go out. Do something other than stare at cars, or at us."

"Mmm," I say noncommittally, but his words are sticking with me. I pull my phone out again and tap in a new text.

If you want to see what the Silver Bullet looks like when it isn't in a pond, swing by my shop.

I include the address, which — thankfully — is not the same as the home where I live and keep my parents. It's not a good idea to mix business with your personal life. I learned that a long time ago.

It's not until the next day that I get a text back. I'm under a vehicle when my phone buzzes and I nearly bang my head on the muffler in my scramble to get my phone.

You want me to see your shop, Fireworks? That's awfully personal, don't you think?

I blink and run my hand through my hair. There are so many reasons why I shouldn't bring Ada into my broken mess of a life. There are so many reasons why it would be better to leave her alone. But right now, they aren't actually coming to me. And yes, I want her here. I want to hear her tell me everything that's wrong with the place just so I can hear her voice.

The offer was for the Silver Bullet, not to see the shop. If you want a tour, that's extra. Come prepared for up-charges.

I'll pay in coffee, she texts me. *No donuts, though. We talked about those.*

I glance guiltily at the half-eaten box on my workbench —

look, it's harder to quit those things than it might seem. But they aren't making me cranky right now, even if my belly does feel like someone broke a bottle and left it in there.

Deal, I text back. And I hope she doesn't get here too soon because I need time to wipe this goofy grin off my face.

Chapter Seventeen

ADA

"Can you hold things down until I get back?" I ask Pops nervously.

I've been working like a hamster in a wheel all week and I'm exhausted. I need to get jobs finished yesterday. I need to collect on invoices. I need new business. I posted a teaser about our trip, but I haven't sorted through the footage yet to do anything more, and besides, the contract that Big Daddy Boom sent puts limits on me until after we talk with him in two weeks.

My head is buzzing and it's hard not to take it out on Pops. He maxed everything out while I was gone — my credit card. His credit card. Everything.

"I'm fine," he says. "I have Marvin, here, don't I, Marvin?"

Marvin gives me an apologetic smile. He doesn't know about the debt.

Marvin's an old family friend. An immigration officer who just retired, he wants to relive his glory days while he's still young enough to enjoy them with a perfectly restored Shelby Mustang.

He asked my dad to get him one. Which explains the credit situation.

Marvin found the "perfect thing" and bought it. And brought it here. And Pops bought all the parts he needed to fix it up. Which will be great. When it's done in a year and we can give Marvin the bill, but not so much right now when I'm going to be pretty hard-pressed to fill my tank with gas this week.

"It will all work out," is what Pops said when I told him how stressed his choices made me.

"Couldn't we have bought the parts in waves?" I pled with him. "Then I could afford more than noodles for food this week."

"You worry too much," he shrugged, drinking the home-made kombucha that Auntie Mary brought by this week. At least we have that. "Everything always works out in the end."

I wanted to scream.

Everything works out. Yes. Because I make it work.

Getting Nicola's text was a welcome relief. Sure, I might have to dig through my dryer vent for change for coffee, but I need a break from Pops and Nicola's the perfect thing. A few snappy remarks and a man who can keep up is just what I need to forget that it's up to me to make everything work out.

"Just stay out of trouble, okay?" I beg Marvin and my dad.

Jasmin rolls her eyes at them from where I can see her behind her laptop. She's been camped out here all week and I can't be more grateful. Her sunshiny attitude and her whispered teasing about my weekend away have made the week bearable.

"You, too, Ada," she chimes in, eyes wide with feigned innocence. "Stay out of trouble."

My phone buzzes and it's Jasmin.

Or rather, please get into trouble. For me. I want to hear all about it. And try to get me a selfie with him.

Not happening, I text back.

Or … I could take your dad shopping… she teases.

No, I text back. *Please, no.*

SELFIE. I can hear the capitals in her text.

"Go, don't worry about me, pumpkin," Pops says as he takes another pull on the kombucha. "Marvin and I will be jawing all day."

I wave goodbye and hurry to my car and I'm checking my updo and my aviators and making sure that my fitted jeans and sandals are clean and don't have grease stains on them before I realize what I'm doing. This isn't a date. It's a work thing, right? But I can't help it. I run upstairs, change into my favorite handkerchief shirt and freshen my makeup before I run down to my hotrod and peel out. It's about a twenty-five-minute drive to Nicola's shop and every minute of it is spent with me second-guessing myself.

I want to see him so badly. And yet. He gave me gifts. Things I can't repay right now. Shouldn't I be embarrassed to see him again? I actually feel a little warm. A little feverish, like I am doing the exact thing he said he did with Amber — throwing caution and control to the wind and just going for it. Does that mean it will end as badly as it did for him with her?

I'm so jittery that when I grab coffee from a fast-food place, I don't even take a sip. Yeah, no Starbucks here, this girl needs to pay in linty change. I find his shop eventually, set in the hills on the outskirts of San Diego where the mountains roll down toward the sea. It's pretty and wreathed in sunrise colors and I can tell it's his place immediately.

The door of the shop is open. It's a rented space on the side of a dairy distributor's warehouse, but he's put his *Knockin' Rods* sign up on the front and it's huge and lit in neon so there's no mistaking it. Palms wave on either side of the door. I see the Silver Bullet through the open door just waiting to be inspected.

When I park and get out, Nicola is cursing from under the hood of our project. The sound makes my heart stutter for a moment — which is crazy, right? I came for a distraction, not for flutters.

"That bad?" I ask, pulling my aviators up onto the crown of my head. "And here I thought you were picked because you're good at this stuff."

"I just wanted to try to start it before I have to pull the engine and ship it to Hollis Montieth to be rebuilt," he says without looking up.

His voice is exasperated. And I love it. I wonder if he'd sound that annoyed if he lived with me. Annoyed that the tomatoes are too soft when he wants them in a salad, annoyed that socks get lost in the dryer never to be seen again, annoyed when I roll over in my sleep and end up on top of him.

My cheeks blush hot at that last one and I'm glad he's not watching me.

"What's happening?" I ask, doctoring up my coffee with sugar and cream from little fast food packets. I leave him both.

"It's not starting."

"Spark plugs?" I ask, sipping my coffee. I don't know what this fast food place puts in their coffee — cocaine? — but I feel bouncy and happy like the whole world is sunshine and rainbows.

"I already checked and they're fine," he snaps. But I know him now. His snapping doesn't scare me.

"Did you just eat a donut," I ask with a dry tone and a nod to the open box on his workbench.

"I can eat what I want," he says. "And before you ask, yes I checked that it's not a ground, I even added this ground strap."

Oh, that's what he's wrenching on. I suppress a smirk.

"Does your belly hurt?"

"It would hurt less if this motor would start and it *should*. It's surprisingly clean and I flushed out the bad gas and old oil. You'd think it would be fine."

"You know you'll keep getting belly aches for as long as you refuse to admit that you're gluten intolerant," I say blithely and when he finally looks up I offer him my most angelic grin.

I can barely hold it.

He's gorgeous. I forgot how gorgeous. It makes my stomach swoop and my face feels hot and flushed. I want to lean him back against this car and ... hold up, Ada. You came here to get distracted, not to get some action. But my imagination won't listen. It's already stripped him half-naked and is working on the other half. It's already accessed memories of him in dripping wet boxer briefs that clung to every dip and rise. It's already telling me that the trail of light hair I saw arrowing up from those shorts would be fun to follow back to its origin.

I cough in an attempt to get a hold of myself.

"Solenoid?" I offer.

"It has one," he confirms.

"Then it's the solenoid," I say firmly.

"Why?" His blue eyes narrow with suspicion and I love it.

"It's always the solenoid," I say with a shrug as I hand him his coffee. "I didn't know how you took it, so I brought all the things."

I hand him a fistful of sugar and cream.

"I like it black," he says. "And it can't be the solenoid."

"It's always the solenoid." I round the car. It looks great now that he's gutted it and cleaned it. The dash is out and sand-blasted. The seats gone and stripped to the springs. I point at one. "That's for me, I take it."

He nods. "Once we've met with Big Daddy Boom and he tells us his vision for the truck."

"Classic tuck and roll in white with baby blue piping," I say. "This old girl needs to look like a classic nineteen-fifties hot rod. Like from the Beach Boy's *Little Deuce Coupe* album cover."

"Well, that car wasn't period correct." He's trying to pick holes in a very sound theory, thank you very much, as he scowls into his coffee.

"I'm just saying it's that kind of surfy hotrod vibe," I say shrugging.

"What's a surfy hotrod vibe?"

Fuck, I love his frowns. I want to collect them and pin them up on the wall of my shop the way some guys pin up mostly-naked women — no, boys, that narrow ribbon you call a thong does not count and I'm not looking at the car with her ass in the air like that, and neither are you or you wouldn't have put the poster up.

"I'm a surfy hotrod vibe," I say, pointing at my handkerchief shirt and aviators.

He laughs and it's throaty and lovely and it matches his angry smile.

"What's it going to take to get you to drop the gluten?" I ask, putting my aviators down. "I can see you hunching over stomach cramps."

He slinks back to the front of the car and starts removing the solenoid and he doesn't talk again until it's off. "One solenoid, removed to perfection."

"Sure," I agree sipping more coffee. "How about, if it's the solenoid, you give it up for one week?"

"Just one?" He quirks a scowling eyebrow at me. "I thought you had to give up that stuff forever."

"Well, if you're smart you give it up forever, seeing as you clearly have celiac disease, or something similar, but for the purposes of this bet, one week."

"Okay," he agrees, and to my surprise, he walks into the back and comes out with a new solenoid. He had one sitting here? "What do I get if you're wrong?"

And how is he suddenly so close to me. I have to lick my lips because they've gone dry and he's leaning over me like he wants to make me his shadow. I can see his throat bob and hear his breath hitch.

"How about I pay you back for all your gifts?" I ask in a

strangled voice that's meant to be playful and I wish I wasn't betting this because I really can't deliver right now.

"Those are gifts. You don't pay people back for gifts unless you're an asshole." He's giving me a top-tier scowl. It would go right near the window when I mount it on my wall.

"Who says I'm not an asshole," I say, pouting prettily.

"I have a better idea." His whisper is husky. "Bet me a kiss."

"How do we know that solenoid even works?" I ask, but what do I even care? I want to be wrong. I'm dying to taste that scowl. I bet it tastes like goddamn lemons. I could bake it into a fucking pie. Oh — did I mention that my language gets R-rated when I'm turned on?

"It's brand new out of the box," he whispers, and how the hell does he make that sound seductive? It sounds like he's saying, "I could fuck you until you're a new person" instead of something about an auto part. I should film this and sell him as ad material to the manufacturer. There'd be lonely women everywhere lining up to buy solenoids for cars they don't even have and I'd be at the front of the line.

"If you say so." It's a weak reply, but the best I can do under the extreme duress of his ridiculous hotness.

I don't know if I'm relieved or furious when he moves away to install the solenoid. And, I mean, I should want him to lose this bet so that he stops getting bellyaches. That would be the neighborly thing to want. Apparently, I'm no fucking neighbor. I want to lose so hard that people who owe mafia bosses feel bad for me. I want to be the loser of losers. I want that kiss like I want to pay off my credit cards. I'm so crazy for it that none of my metaphors are working and I don't care.

I'm practically gasping when he slips into the cab to fire up the engine. It flares to life and I want to curse. And then it sputters and dies and when he turns the key again he gets nothing.

He slips out of the cab. "Well, I guess I'll just stop messing with it and send it to Hollis."

He's not looking at me.

"So who won?" I ask because I don't understand this sudden miserable mood of his. He kicks the tire of the car and doesn't look up. "Is it me because it started, or both of us because it died."

And on the word "both" his eyes kick up to mine and I see a look in them that makes my belly backflip twice.

"Both," he says, like he doesn't believe it but really wants to.

I try on a fake stern expression. "That means no more gluten for you for a week, Petrovic."

"Petrovic?" he echoes. "Not Fireworks?"

I shrug one shoulder casually, teasing him. "I don't know, Nicola. I haven't seen any fireworks yet, have I?"

And when I look up at him, I swear he's flushed as pink as the sunrise.

He moves so suddenly that I gasp, swiping my aviators off my face as he sits on the front tire of the Silver Bullet and pulls me in close between his legs with a gentle tug.

I can't breathe.

He's right fucking there, all muscled and warm. I'm tracing the lines of his torso with my gaze, letting my eyes catch on the dimples in his cheeks that are popping when he gets this predatory look that's not quite a smile but is definitely reminiscent of a hungry wolf.

He sets my glasses on the hood of the car and his hands trace my waist lightly before climbing up my back, soooo slowly, as if by his very touch he's trying to coax me close.

"Just one?" he asks, raising an eyebrow.

I scowl, but it's so hard to do right now. I want to grin. I want to give him everything. But that's not how I roll.

"That was the bet, wasn't it?" I say, placing my hands very deliberately on his shoulders.

Our heights match with him sitting like this, and I'm conscious of exactly how close I am to where his legs are spread to make room for me. I'm wondering if it helps to have them spread — if it keeps him from getting uncomfortable in those jeans because I'm sure as hell feeling uncomfortable right now. Parts of me are waking up and deciding it's growing season and they're going to focus on the watering part of that.

I lick my lips again and his part as he watches me — part and inhale in a crazy sexy way.

"I hope it's worth it for you," I whisper. "I hope it makes it easier to live without donuts, or pizza, or birthday cake, or muffins, or cinnamon rolls, or —"

He doesn't let me finish. His lips have caught mine and they're hot and fevered but so soft and gentle that it almost hurts. I want more than he's giving. I want the scowl as well as the smile. It's like he's caressing me with this kiss, like he's trying to lure in a wild thing, when all I want is to be devoured. I try to seize control and turn this into what I want — a feasting, consuming, demanding kiss. But he won't let me and his insistence brings me back to sweet and soft and so fucking much longing that I might come just from this. Can someone do that? Come from just a kiss. I'm about to, I think. I'm so close I'm practically buzzing with it.

Remember when he called it "lighting me up?" I sure do. I'm remembering it right now.

And then suddenly it stops and he laughs and pulls me into a hug. He's hard against my right leg and I'm practically crying, I'm so frustrated. I want to slap him for stopping. I want to insult him until he tries to prove me wrong. I want to kiss him forever.

"You even taste like fucking pineapple," he says and his voice is so husky it could pull a dog sled. Ha ha.

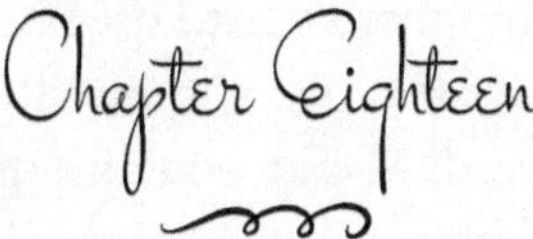

Chapter Eighteen

NICOLA

SHE TASTES EXACTLY as I expected. She's so sweet it almost hides the acid, just like with a pineapple. Any time I eat one of those things I forget they're acidic and end up with sores in my mouth. It's the sweetness that hides it, that tricks you into thinking that there's no sting.

Ada is the opposite. It's her sting that hides the sweetness underneath, and I'm addicted. She tries to take control of this from me, to force it into a tumultuous thing, but I keep her right where I want her, slow and sweet and gentle. She deserves to be honored. She deserves to be slowly savored.

We break apart and she smirks. "Okay, Fireworks, I guess you get your nickname back."

I smile, I think. I'm so buzzed on touching her, kissing her, that I can't quite think straight. I think I might bite my lower lip. I think I might reach a hand up to cup her cheek and run my thumb over her cheekbone, but when I lean in for another taste, she laughs and steps back.

"The bet was for *one* kiss, Fireworks. If you want more,

you'll need to bet again."

I should probably say something snappy back. Or even something smooth. But I've got nothing. I know it's going to make me look like a fool to just stare at her like the only glass of water in the desert, but that's what I do. I'm trying to memorize her. Trying to drink deep of her without drinking at all. I could try to express it in words — but wouldn't that break the magic? Wouldn't that wash away the sweet taste still lingering between my lips? My eyes fall to her lips and I think I might sigh, or at least exhale because they draw my breath away, like a fisherman hauling in his catch. I'm done. Who would have thought one kiss would slay me?

"Wasn't there going to be a tour?" Ada asks with a quirked eyebrow, scooping her aviators from off the hood and slipping them expertly back onto her nose. She's cool and collected like some kind of billionaire CEO and even though I know she's almost too broke to buy coffee, I still feel like she's too money for me.

"This is my shop," I say and my voice is so husky it's like it thinks we're going to bed together. Maybe my dad is right. Maybe I should set up a cot in the parts room. Or something. Anything. I start to point at things to try to convince my mind that we're in a garage, not a boudoir. "Workbench. Project. Lift. Other project. Forklift. Tools. Compressor. Welder. Plasma cutter. TV. Cameras. In the back are parts," I gesture to one door. "And a computer for editing."

"Comprehensive," Ada says breezily. "What do you usually charge for a tour like that, because I'm thinking the crumpled Washington I paid for this coffee with might be a bit much."

"Most women pay me in kisses."

She snort-laughs. "Sure they do, Nicola."

I love how she says my name, like it's still foreign to her even though she's said it before. Or like maybe she doesn't believe it's mine. It makes the competitive side of me want to prove something, although I'm not sure what. That I'm really Serbian, maybe?

I speak to her in Serbian, so I guess that's what I wanted to prove. And since it's safe to say anything I go ahead and say what I want to say. "You're like fire in my veins, you terrible hot vixen."

"If you're calling down curses on my family," she says, looking over the lenses of her aviators, "then you should know that there's only me and Pops and Jasmin and Aunt Mary and Aunt Mary is probably already cursed from messing with the occult, Pops' life might actually improve with a curse, and poor Jasmin doesn't deserve that shit, and you should be ashamed of yourself for cursing her."

"And you?" I ask, finally calming down enough to stand.

"I'm already cursed," she says breezily. "Obviously. I just kissed you and you didn't turn into a frog."

"It's frogs that turn into princes, not the other way around," I growl and my accent seems more pronounced than normal — it always does when I'm so turned on that I can't think.

She waves a hand as she circles the Silver Bullet, inspecting it. "I don't think so. What girl would want a prince when she could have a perfectly good amphibian as a friend. Princes aren't all they're cracked up to be. They have soft hands."

"Like dentists?" I ask and she startles, and I'm so pleased with myself that I grin. "You're the one who is marrying a dentist. Maybe you'll get lucky and when you kiss him, he'll turn into a frog."

She flips her hair and it's such a dramatic gesture that it makes me laugh. "This conversation has gone off the rails. I refuse to dignify it with a response."

And then she peeks into my storage room in the back and then into my office before sauntering back to where I am.

"No bed?" she asks, quirking one eyebrow and suddenly I'm feeling hot again, like I'm coming down with something.

I frown hard at her. "I don't always kiss hot women in this place. I usually work."

She frowns back as if she doesn't like being called 'hot.' "With you being dedicated to your *work* above everything, I'd expect you to have one here."

"I don't need a *bed* to work," I say, with a wink and she rolls her eyes.

"Stop working your moves on me, Fireworks, and let's go see if there's anything to eat around here."

But my phone buzzes before she's done talking and when I pull it out, it's a strange number.

"Hello?"

The voice on the phone is all I hear for a moment and everything else fades away at the urgent, quick explanation. I think I'm about to collapse, but to my surprise, I've been maneuvered onto a stool and Ada is propping me up as I take in a deep breath.

"I heard," she says, her tone suddenly quick and businesslike. "I'll drive you. You're in no state to drive yourself."

And she's right. I'm not, because my mom had a stroke and the nurse on the phone said to come quickly because they weren't sure if they could stop the brain bleed. I feel like I might throw up. I feel like I'm forgetting something.

She jams something in my hand and I look down to see it's my wallet and then she's guiding me out of the shop and into her car, locking up for me, and putting the keys and my House of Kolor sweatshirt on my lap as she fires up her car and drives like she's trying to win the Speed Demon of the Year award from the devil himself.

"It will be okay," she tells me. "People have strokes all the time."

I shouldn't have left Mom on the couch this morning. I should have checked on her more thoroughly.

"You don't need to do this," I say which is pretty weak since she's already doing it.

"And you didn't need to buy me a motel room or a muffin, but you didn't hear me complaining," she growls.

"Only because I didn't stick around to hear it." I'm coming back to myself from a long way away.

"Well, then maybe I'll do the same thing," she says, adjusting her sunglasses as she throttles down. There are no seatbelts in the hotrod. They didn't make them in cars this old. I've never worried about it before, but when she passes someone on the right, I start to think that maybe they were a great invention.

"I'm not the one who will do surgery on her, you know," I say sharply. "It's not a race to get me there."

"Maybe I just don't want you in my car for very long. Maybe you cramp my style," she says, but I hear the emotion in her voice.

"Is that pity I hear, Ada? Pity?" I'm aghast. But my mind is finally clear again and I can think. Talking to her is like having ice water dumped over your head in the best possible way.

"I don't pity you, Fireworks," she says as she turns into the hospital parking lot like she thinks she's drift racing. "*You* don't have soft dentist hands. It's those guys I pity."

"Checks out," I say as she slides into the idling area by the main doors and I hop out.

"Your phone," she reminds me and I grab the phone, keys, wallet, hoodie, and just for good measure, I lean in and steal a kiss, catching her surprised exclamation in my mouth.

"That's bad language, Pineapple," I say. "But I'll forgive you as thanks for the ride."

And her angry scowl makes everything okay as I dash into the hospital. It's what gets me through the anxiety as I find my mom and dad in the channels of hospital wards and floors, as I talk to nurses and doctors, as I beat myself up for not being a better son. That scowl could power a drag car and it's powering me when everything else feels adrift.

Chapter Nineteen

ADA

THE NEXT WEEK is a flurry of work, work, and more work. I manage to get a project complete and I'm stunned when the customer shows up with cash in hand. It's enough for groceries and a few other small essentials like insurance and electricity. You know, those crazy things that people buy like suckers.

I text Nicola, but he doesn't text back until five days later.

Sorry. Overwhelmed. Parents. If I say 'thank you' will that make you angry?

Is your mom okay? I text back and "okay" feels like a stupid word because what I mean is "alive" and I wish I had the guts to just say it but I don't, so I fall back on "okay."

He doesn't answer that text for two more days. Either he's arranging a funeral or things are even crazier there than they are here. If I didn't have the happy routine of working and keeping Pops out of trouble, I'd be going insane. Marvin is here almost every day, though, and that changes things up as he absorbs enough of Pops time that I don't have to constantly watch that he's not giving away our groceries or bits of our shop.

I'm covering a seat when the text from Nicola finally comes through.

She'll survive. It was uncertain for a while. But I have an issue.

There are so many jokes I could tell after that line, but seeing as it's part of a text where he says his mom didn't die, it feels wrong to exploit it, so I text something kind instead. It almost hurts to be kind to Nicola. I want to be not-kind to remind him that he stole a kiss he didn't ask for or earn.

What do you need? I text and I send a surreptitious glance at Pops as he laughs over the Shelby. I feel a little too much like him offering to do a favor without knowing what it is.

I didn't get the engine pulled for Hollis and the truck is coming to get it tomorrow at noon. I need someone who isn't me to pull the engine and crate it for shipping.

I don't reply right away. Not because I can't do it, I mean losing a morning of work is going to hurt, but I can film it for my channel and it won't be a loss in the end. I'm just shocked that he's asking.

I know it's a big ask, he texts at the same time I hit send on my message.

Is Nicola "I need this to be perfect" Petrovic asking me for help?

I'm not worried about your skills, he says and for a man like Nicola that's almost as huge a thing to say as "I love you." My eyes feel like they're going to fall right out of my head.

Jasmin appears then and reads over my shoulder. "He trusts you with his *truck?*"

"It's a group project," I say defensively. "It's as much my responsibility as his."

"Who trusts you with his truck?" Pops bellows, startling Marvin enough that he jumps.

"No one!" I shoot back. "Just a colleague."

"The man you went up into the woods with? You stay away from his truck!"

"His mom had a stroke," I say. "What do you want me to do? Force him not to take care of his parents?"

Pops' mouth closes with an audible click and I almost feel smug until he says to Marvin, "See? I told you she has a good heart under all that crankiness. Just like her old man."

And I'm both oddly touched and also want to shake him because hello, why does he think I'm cranky? Might it be because he spent all our money? Again? On helping Marvin, who doesn't need it?

But I brush it off with a shake of my head and start to gather the tools I need.

"Won't he have tools at his shop?" Jasmin asks, following me.

"You aren't going to his shop," Pops says from under the hood of the Shelby.

"He won't even be there."

"That's what you think!" Since when was he so protective? "I've seen how you jump when he texts. How you drop everything. You have a good life here. Don't go ruining it with a man."

I roll my eyes. Like that's a thing that's going to happen.

"I'll bring Jasmin!" I call, grabbing my purse and the last of my stuff and frantically signaling to her to follow.

She rolls her eyes at me in a really good impression of *my* eye roll — trademark, Ada Ford, two thousand and something — but I know she'll come with me. She's too curious to pass this up.

"Fine," she hisses as we jump in my hotrod. "But you owe me lunch."

Lunch is bought from the same fast food place as the coffee and paid for with actual crumpled dollar bills instead of change. Yeah, baby, I have made my way up this week. I skip the grease fest and go for a coffee instead. My stomach is already swooping enough at the thought of going to Nicola's place without him there. I can still hear that accent in my mind if I close my eyes. And if it was a curse he was putting on me, then it was the sexiest curse ever. Maybe he was cursing me with wanting him, and if so, he should hire out for curses rather than mechanical skills because he's deadly good at them.

My phone buzzes and Jasmin grabs it.

"It's your man!" she sings out and I roll my eyes.

"Nicola."

"Whatever. He says not to bring any dentists with you. What does that even mean?" she asks but she's already typing.

"What are you typing?"

She doesn't answer, screwing her face up in concentration. I make a swipe for the phone but she dodges it and I have to stop because I'm driving.

"Nothing that doesn't need to be said," she says, laughing.

When we pull into the shop, I grab my phone from her. I need to ask Nicola how to get in. I see the text stream.

"There's way more than one text here, Jasmin!" I say but she only laughs, jumping out and pressing a pin into the door lock until it releases.

Quickly, I read the texts while she pops open the bay door and explores Nicola's shop.

The code for the door is 77777

Don't laugh. I don't like forgetting things.

The time stamp on this one is later. *I bet you have the engine extracted in an hour.*

An hour? Jasmin had typed back. *You expect me to pull an engine in an hour? Sweeten the pot, precious. If I do it, what do I get?*

Precious? I put my hand over my face. How am I going to live that down?

Okay... how about this. Get the engine out and crated and you win, he texted her back.

And my prize?

I look up from my texts, feeling like I've been slapped. "Are you flirting with Nicola on my phone, Jasmin?"

"You said he wasn't your man, so fair is fair," she calls from inside the shop.

Something hot and jagged claws up my throat. I don't want other girls flirting with Nicola. Not even Jasmin. And he's been surrounded by nurses all week. You know, the kind of women who work a job that pays well and requires cleanliness. The type of women who fill out a pair of scrubs nicely. Is that my heart racing like that? Why would it race over the idea of a pretty nurse stealing Nicola's attention? That makes no sense at all. It must be the coffee. I swear they put something in it. Maybe I should call the authorities on them.

I go back to the texts, not feeling any better but definitely feeling worse.

Your prize? his text reads.

Wait.

And then five minutes later by the time stamp. *This isn't Ada.*

Who is it, then? Jasmin had texted back.

Jasmin.

Ooooh, look who knows so much, Jasmin had texted for me.

Stop messing around and help your cousin.

I storm over to the Silver Bullet and get to work, annoyed when I hear Jasmin chuckling from behind me. But I can't be too annoyed. He could tell it wasn't me. We barely know each other and he could hear it wasn't my voice. That shouldn't make me feel warm and fuzzy, but it does.

"Admit it, Ada, you love that I teased him," she says.

"I don't."

"Because you don't flirt with him but you wish you did."

"None of that is true," I say, but it's a little true. I don't flirt with him *enough* and I wish I did. Not just because life is too short, although it is, but because I have this sudden possessive feeling inside that's screaming "Mine, mine, mine" and really hates Jasmin right now.

"Look," Jasmin says, pushing a curl out of her face as I pull the engine lift into place. "You're overreacting."

This actually shouldn't be too bad. Nicola took most of the car apart already. Even the transmission is detached and off to one side. It's just the suspension and engine left in the frame. I bolt the chains from the engine lift arm to the block while Jasmin talks.

"Nicola is a good distraction for you," she says, studying her nails. "This crap with your dad is a lot. I know. Why do you think I've never let my mom anywhere near my finances."

She gives me a long look and I feel myself flush. She's right that this is partly my fault. I should have known not to lend my card to my dad.

I know she's about to make a big speech because she tilts her chin and stands as tall as she can before she starts.

"You deserve to be distracted with hate-loving your professional nemesis. But don't forget that he wrote all that crap about you and that you probably lost business because of it. So go ahead, mess with his head. Have some fun. But don't you dare get involved with him." She levels a finger at me. "He screwed you before. He'll screw you again. One hundred percent."

I shrug. Everything she's saying makes perfect sense. And yet. I might like getting screwed by Nicola — literally, not figuratively. That man bought me yoga pants. And he kisses like he knows me. He cuddled with me for a whole night in the back of a truck. And he curses in Serbian. And he loves his faulty parents.

There are a lot of "and yets." I'm not sure I'm ready to be logical about this. Not when I could be *illogical* and keep having the time of my life.

"I have something to tell you anyway," Jasmin says, leaning in so she can look at my eyes as I jack the lift arm up.

"Okay, but can you watch the engine to make sure I don't hit anything while you talk?"

"Mmhmm," she says, watching. "An online shop saw my designs on social media. *Threads That Shred.* They're about sustainable clothing and timeless polish. And they want to carry a few of my pieces."

She sounds almost giddy.

"Really?" I say, forgetting the engine and the question of Nicola. This is huge! This could set Jasmin up so she never has to rely on our shaky family for funds ever again. I hurry to hug her. "I'm so proud of you!"

We sway back and forth for a minute before she breaks the hug and points at the Silver Bullet. "I want the same thing for you. Don't lose track of this opportunity. Don't let some man take what you've earned."

Her eyes are hard as rock and even when we move to other topics, I see her shooting little looks my way like she's trying to make sure that I take her advice. I ignore them as I finish pulling the engine, crating it, and leaving it in the right place for the shipping company, being sure to film the whole thing in time lapse so it can be sped up for our channels. It comes out perfectly and Jasmin looks so happy in the shots that I should pay her for spreading her positivity to my viewers.

I'm just wrapping up when I get a text from Nicola.

You made it in under an hour.

He sends a pic of me on his security camera and what do you know, Jasmin was right. There's totally one here sending pictures to him and I look like a freak on them with my face all stern and my body exaggerated by movement.

And then a second text comes in.

That sounded creepy, didn't it? It was meant to be a thank you.

You can thank me later. I was thinking with printed retractions, I text, and I'm kidding, but also I'm kind of not kidding.

His texted reply is so long in coming that I don't get it until we're well away and Jasmin has gone home for the night. I'm just turning in myself when it pops on my phone screen.

I'm addicted to perfection, Pineapple. You should know that by now.

And I do. Which is why I can never fully soften around him. Even if I love his frowns. Even if I want them all to be mine. I can't be vulnerable with a man who is always looking for something to judge. Who could? Not Amber. And not me.

Chapter Twenty

NICOLA

THESE LAST FEW weeks have been trying. My mom still hovers on the edge of death. We aren't sure how much brain function she'll get back. She can communicate. Slowly. Barely. But she can't sit up or lift her hand on her right side, or even do much with the one on the left.

My dad is a basket case. Just trying to keep him fed and together is a fulltime job. The nurses keep hinting to me that I need long-term care for both of them. They tuck flyers into my bags and gently tell me that one man can't take care of all of this on his own and do I have any siblings?

By the time I manage to get back to my shop, the engine has been expertly pulled by Ada and the Silver Bullet is sitting there ready for me and I can't even get to it. Instead, I throw myself into the paid work beside it, blasting through a guy's midlife crisis car with all the frustration and sorrow that's welling up in my chest every time I stop long enough to breathe.

It's only the morning before we're supposed to meet up with Big Daddy Boom that I finish stripping down the Silver Bullet and making a list of parts to find and what needs work — everything, obviously.

I'm so harried and rushed that I don't notice the text on my phone until it's almost too late. It's from Big Daddy Boom.

Changing the venue from the restaurant to my beach place. My chef is here visiting family so I got him to come in for an evening and it will be so much better than in public. Come as you are.

There are directions and an address sent next and it's going to be tight to get there through traffic at this time of day and still swing by my house to shower and check on Dad.

I'm running basically from the second I get the text. I hit home at a full run, throw dinner on the counter for Dad, and take a literal sixty-second shower. I'm out and toweling off as he complains to me in Serbian.

"You can't go out. You need to take me to the hospital."

"We were there this morning." Clean jeans. I must have clean jeans somewhere. But where?

"And we need to go back tonight. What will your mother think? That we've abandoned her?"

"Dad, I have to take this meeting."

"A meeting? In jeans? Ha! You are lying to me."

I'm quick to button my cotton shirt up over my hot rod T-shirt. It's white. And the jeans are ... sort of mostly clean. It will do.

"I'm not lying, Dad."

"Give me a reason. One good reason why you can't take me to see your mother tonight." He holds up a warning finger as I slide my motorcycle boots on. "And don't say business. Don't you dare. You are my only son. Your mother's only son. We gave up everything for you. Everything. Our home. Our friends. Our lives."

I grit my teeth, wracking my brain for how to tell him that if I don't get this deal there's no way I can keep supporting him without having to remind him that his funds are not sufficient and he didn't save enough. Embarrassing your father is never the best option. The second another alternative comes to me, I take it.

"Did you want me to see that spicy girl? The one on the phone?"

He pauses and his answer comes out like a question, "Yes?"

"Well, if you want me to bring her here and convince her to bear Petrovic babies then I need to actually see her."

"You're seeing the firecracker?"

"Yes." It's not a lie. She'll be there.

His eyes narrow. "Tell her you're an idiot and not worthy of her but that she could do worse."

"I'm sure she'll take that well," I say wryly and then I flee. I'm already five minutes late by my best guess and I need to move.

I'm so amped by the time I get to the gates outside the beach house that I can barely sit still, my fingers tap on the steering wheel as I speak my name into the intercom. I need this to work. I need it so badly.

I'm buzzed in and I hurry to park. My only consolation is that Ada pulls in after me, three minutes late, just like I am.

We meet outside the front door and my jaw drops. I wore clothes that can best be described as "presentable." Ada, on the other hand, is stunning.

She's in yellow, of course. Pineapple yellow. My mouth waters at the sight of it and I can taste her kiss in my mouth all over again. The dress is a tiny strapless cocktail dress that flutters in the breeze. I don't know about women's fashions. But whatever this is, it looks amazing on her.

She quirks an eyebrow at me. "Did you come straight from the hospital?"

"What?" I ask, taken aback.

She just shakes her head and huffs like she's been given a job she didn't want, and then before I can stop her, she straightens my collar and brushes something off my jeans and I'm hot caramel under the stare of those brown eyes. I'm a marshmallow on a s'more. I'm wax in the sunshine.

It's been a tough week. And there's been no one — no one to confess all my fears to, no one to share the tears I've been holding back as I grapple with what to do with the two people who depend on me, no one to take care of *me*. And I don't like to admit it, but I want someone to take care of me just a little bit. Just to where they criticize my clothing with little huffs of annoyance. Just that much makes me feel like my heart is molten.

"I don't recall you complaining about my clothes when you borrowed my hoodie on our trip," I say huskily, trying to disguise how I feel.

It's not much of a comeback. Not only am I bowled over by her sudden attention, but I'm also distracted by how she looks in this little dress as she moves around me with her critical frown. She's a glitter bomb in human form. She's smart as a whip and enormously capable. How can she look this good on top of all that? It feels unfair to everyone else. Maybe leave something for the rest of us, Ada.

Fortunately, I don't have to say anything. The door opens and it's Big Daddy Boom himself. I thought that they edited those clips to bring out his big personality. I was wrong. He's tall, sure, and muscular, but he seems to fill not just the doorway but the entire entrance of his house as his exuberant voice booms out.

"Our guests of honor!" His smile is contagious. And I guess I didn't need to worry about formality — although, I still kind of am — since he's wearing his typical BOOM T-shirt complete with cut-off sleeves. "You've made it! Excellent! Eddie is getting ready to serve and we're all having drinks on the patio. Follow me."

And follow we do. Adam Boomhower — "Big Daddy Boom" — is a very rich man despite his welcoming, good-natured attitude and his beach house is basically a mansion on the beach. The patio he takes us to is natural rock cut from some land far away and reassembled to provide a picture-perfect hangout place ringed with palms on three sides that merges straight out onto white sand.

My eyes are probably huge. I'm suddenly grateful to Ada for tweaking my appearance. I feel like a rusty truck in a lot full of waxed sports cars. What must she think of me? *She* looks the part. Like she was born for this.

At the table, I recognize Tanner — Big Daddy Boom's right-hand man — and Pretty Boy — one of the video editors from his crew. They're sipping beers and fortunately are dressed in branded BOOM T-shirts and jeans so I don't look as much like a fool as I feared.

I take a seat beside them and Adam pulls out a chair for Ada. I feel my face growing hot. I should have done that. It's what gentlemen do, isn't it? But I didn't. I take the beer offered to me with a red face and I don't know where to look.

"I'm so glad to have you here in person," Big Daddy Boom says. "We're all excited about this surprise for my partner, Mikey Hunt, aren't we boys?"

"We really are," Pretty Boy says enthusiastically. He has a weedy little goatee and a backward baseball cap and somehow both those things make me feel less intimidated. "When Adam said that he was bringing on a few smaller vlogger channels we lit right up. This has great potential."

"Big Daddy Boom, not Adam," Tanner corrects him protectively.

I steal a glance at Ada who lifts a single eyebrow and I can tell she's missing her aviators. She's replaced them with about six gold rings on her fingers and delicate gold chains wrapped artfully around her updo, but it's not the same when it comes to expressing disdain.

"They can call me Adam," Big Daddy Boom says with a huge grin. "We're all family here." He clears his throat. "We were sorry that Tanner and the crew weren't able to help you pull the Silver Bullet out, but you two rose to the challenge like champs!"

I hate how the way he talks makes me want his approval — but it does. No one makes me feel like that. I try not to scowl, though. I need this. I can't afford to be my usual nonconformist self in the face of it.

"The way things worked out ended up being perfect," Adam says, leaning in over the table.

He's also in a BOOM T-shirt with the sleeves cut off, and I'd be tempted to think he hijacked this house except there's a professional chef in a white jacket and hat setting up beside our table and cooking as we speak together. The food smells ridiculously good. I think it's BBQ.

Adam lifts a hand and starts counting off on his fingers.

"First, with our guys unable to get to you, the secret has been even better protected from getting out to Mikey — and that's awesome!" He lifts another finger. "Second, the footage we got of you two working together is going to go over great with viewers. The tension is sizzling, but so is the skill you both display. I'm seriously stoked about it." His grin now is so wide he looks almost manic. "Third, having you both on camera and working like that gave us an in with the streaming service and they're going to consider giving you a show. Which is why we're here. We're going to change the plan."

"You said there was only room for one of us in the streaming deal," Ada says carefully. I know what she's thinking because I'm thinking it, too. We both need this. We both want it. If only one of us gets it, the other will resent them forever.

Adam smiles and his smile is predatory. "That was before. The deal is different now."

"Different how?" she presses, frowning. I love that I don't have to talk. I can rely on her to be annoyed enough for both of us.

"Different because they want you both," Adam says and, impossible as it might seem, his presence grows again until it's filling the whole patio. His eyes are little-boy bright and big as he drops his next comment. "They say both of you or neither."

I glance at Ada and find her gaze catching mine and for just a moment she looks as panicked as I feel. I can't work with her every day. I like her, but I can't do that. Not with it all filmed and broadcast. Because this — whatever this thing is between us — is real and a camera would steal that away. It would sink it before it could even swim. It would ruin that tiny thread we've been weaving together.

"How does that help you," I ask, trying to buy time.

"Well, the show would be the pair of you working together doing projects for my shop. I'd be on camera, too, giving you the jobs and inspecting them at the end of the builds. It's great for my brand, and for you it's even bigger than what I offered in the first place. But right now, in this minute, it means we have to pivot with the Silver Bullet build."

"You're delaying it?" Ada asks.

Adam laughs and so do his guys, like this is a joke and they all know the punchline. He leans forward.

"We're speeding it up. We get this one chance to pitch this thing both to our audience and to the streaming service. We need you to work double time to get this done — together. On every part of the build."

"The engine has already been shipped to Hollis," I protest.

"And he will ship it right back," Adam agrees. "These kinds of things have to be fluid when you're talking big-time online marketing. Plans have to change and move as the opportunities do. We both know you can handle an engine rebuild, Nicola. Especially with the help of the daughter of Pops Ford, so Hollis is out, you are in. He doesn't mind. I'll have other opportunities for him."

Ada and I share a look again and she looks ill.

"The paint?" I try again.

"Can happen in your shop. I'll get you a mobile paint booth," Adam says with a dismissive wave.

"I don't know about ..." Ada, begins but he interrupts her, too.

"You were perfect together. That zip and zing? Amazing. And guess what? I'll let you pick how to style the truck. You can do anything you want to it in terms of modifications, colors, upholstery — anything. And all paid for by me," Adam says confidently. That's outrageous. He must really want this. "But there's a catch."

"There always is," Ada mutters.

"I'm going to start streaming your video right away. We're going to pitch you as a couple. And you're going to have to make it believable to the audience. If it works, it will segue perfectly into a streaming video series. If it doesn't, then we all lose."

This time it's my turn to open my mouth.

"Don't answer yet," Adam says. "Right now, let's eat some BBQ and talk details. Then you can go home and sleep on it. I can't make you two do this—"

"Though he has in the past," Tanner whispers, snickering with Pretty Boy.

"— but I sure hope that you do!"

Adam's grin is so warm that it's hard to say no to anything he wants. I'm glad to have a day to think or I'd definitely feel pressured.

I glance at Ada as the BBQ is being served and her expression when she looks back is tight with determination. She wants this. She'll do whatever it takes to do it. Even work with me.

I see this as clearly as if it were written on her forehead. She's not worried about messing up the hint of a real thing we might have. It's not even a factor for her. So I can't let it be one for me, either.

I'm trying to relax, joking with the guys, eating the best BBQ, and reminding myself that even if this ruins things that might have been with Ada, at least it's great for the future of my career, when Big Daddy turns to us again.

"We have all the uploads of the footage of the extraction and the work so far. Great job! If you want, the guys can send you edited clips to save you time, right boys?" They give him thumbs up. "But you need to get me a comprehensive design by Monday. And I need more footage of you working together by Tuesday and then every day after. If we're going to sell this, then it needs to be your top priority."

And that's when I know I really can't do this. Even for Ada. Because I have a sick mother, and a scattered father, and I can't just drop them both for this opportunity. Not even with my dream on the line and Ada's future with it.

Chapter Twenty-One

ADA

I WAS PREPARED to be told that they could only choose one of us and that it was Nicola. I was almost certain it was going to go that way. After all, why would a popular video streaming service want a deal with a lone upholsterer even if Pin Up Stitchin' had the best logo around and the cutest owner? Nicola does the full deal at his shop — total rebuilds and restorations from start to finish. I just make them plush and pretty inside.

But when Big Daddy Boom announced that we could have it together, my heart began to race. Because I could do that. I wouldn't even mind the fake couple part.

I haven't dated in ages but back when I did, I dated some real winners. After those fools, I could basically pretend to date anyone, and I actually *like* Nicola. It won't be a hardship. After all, we worked well together on the trip to grab the truck. We even had some fun afterward before his mom's stroke. I'm still half-swooning over that kiss. Sure, it means keeping myself buttoned up enough that he doesn't suspect I'm more attracted to him than I should be, but I can do that. I'll just wear my aviators all the time and practice my level stare in the mirror.

I can totally do this.

Big Daddy Boom talks us through how our channels are going to work together. And — side note — the plan is fantastic and likely to launch me from small time to the big leagues. I can't be thankful enough to Adam Boomhower for this. He's making our careers, and yes, it gives him a bit of content, too, but we're the real winners here. I want to find a way to thank him, even if it's just by agreeing to all his asks — including this ask that I be in a fake relationship with Nicola.

The problem is, as the evening progresses, I'm starting to worry that Nicola is not on the same page. His quiet turns to brooding. He's catching my gaze less. Laughing less. If I hadn't spent all that time with him I wouldn't be noticing it now, but it's unmistakable. Something is wrong.

I try to nudge him under the table with my foot but after the third time he just leans down slightly — those long arms come with the tall frame — and catches my foot with its cute little heeled sandal in his broad hand and holds it there like we're teenagers holding hands at the movies, only the hand he's holding is a foot.

No one else seems to notice he's checked out so I wait until we leave —hours later — with full bellies and big hugs from the BOOM guys and a massive box of BOOM Merch that Pretty Boy hands me to use in the videos.

"Just wherever you can," he says and he seems so excited that I almost laugh and have to pretend to cough instead before I agree.

When the swag is loaded and a second round of hugs given, I head out to my car, and only then do I text him.

We need to talk.

He does not reply. Hardly unexpected for someone who

doesn't communicate well. His truck peels out of the driveway ahead of mine, his wheels screaming like his repressed soul.

I bite my lip as I briefly consider chasing after him, hunting him down wherever he's headed, and making him talk, but he might be headed to the hospital. He might be going to check on his mom. It feels selfish to make it about me if those are the circumstances. Even if I'm a bit sore that I had to hug sweaty Tanner twice, and didn't get to say goodbye to Nicola at all. And especially since his growly sneer was getting under my skin all night in the very best way.

Instead, I go home and when Jasmin hops up and down asking me what happened in the meeting, I tell her it's still undecided. And when Pops grunts and says that I don't need a rich man's channel to have a happy life, I just smile and don't point out that we desperately need this money, and if I don't get it we're at the point where we will have to start cutting essentials. Like phones. And electricity.

The next morning, I text Nicola again the second I wake up.

Seriously. Don't give me the cold shoulder, Fireworks. I need to know.

I give him an hour. Now, you might argue that I should give him more time. You might argue that I'm being pushy and men don't like pushy girls who scare them with all their neediness, and maybe you'd normally have a point, but it's Saturday. We need a design we both agree on by Monday. That's not much time, especially with our history of agreeing on things.

I've already drawn up what *I* think the little truck should look like. I've pulled swatches for the interior and picked paint chips. Yeah, I'm that good. But it will mean nothing if he isn't on the same page, so I go hunting for change again and find a fistful of coins in a bolt jar in the shop. Enough — I hope — for a pair of coffees.

I get on the road, noting that my fuel gauge is getting lower with no more income in sight, step on the gas, and bring myself, my bright beautiful ideas, and two cups of the hottest most mediocre fast food coffee I can find to the *Knockin' Rods* shop.

I walk in with extra hip sway in my cherry skinny jeans, and my aviators down low where they can disguise the mad desperation in my eyes.

"Mornin' Honey," I drawl and wait for Nicola to look up from his desk.

His eyes are red and puffy. He's still in the same clothes he was wearing last night — though now they're rumpled and dirty and the look on his face is fully defeated.

"Not today, Pineapple," he says and I've never heard him so low and sad. So dejected. I look around for a clue. His office has a few photographs — unframed and not even pinned in place, just jammed into the window frame. They're mostly of cars, but a few with an older couple that I assume are his parents. He has one of those photos in his hands. There's a kid with them — a young Nicola, I'd guess. It's the picture from his glove box.

"You're already caffeinated?" I ask, plopping his coffee onto his desk anyway. He might not think he needs coffee, but he certainly does.

He puts his head in his hands and now I'm really worried. His face is practically white. His throat bobs. His arms shake a little just from holding his head and none of that is right. I want my stormy Nicola back. I want back the angry eastern European devil who makes my life miserable. I have no idea what to do with this Nicola.

I swallow. This feels important, like I could easily get it wrong.

He speaks suddenly, "My dad went to visit my mom on his own while I was at Adam Boomhower's beach house eating fucking BBQ."

I feel cold suddenly. This isn't going to end well. I put my coffee on his desk, too.

"He made it there. And then he had an episode. Confusion, they called it. He admitted some things he shouldn't have."

"Is he okay?" I feel cold. Worried.

"For now."

"What did he admit?"

He grips the back of his neck with his hand really tightly. And it's a long time before he says.

"I shouldn't be telling you this. I shouldn't be burdening you with it."

"No," I say, calmly, precisely.

There's a cold feeling in my belly. I know this one. Disappointment. I'm used to it. And I'm going to do what I always do. Clamp it down. Refuse to be ruled by it. Become its master instead. I steer hard back into control.

"Nicola," I say, "you *should* be telling me that you're going to play my boyfriend for the cameras and make us both a ton of money and cement us forever as car-building legends because we scoop the best streaming show ever. You *should* be looking at the samples I've pulled and the design I worked up to bring to you for discussion. But I don't think you're going to do those things, are you?"

There's a tense moment but he finally lets go of his neck and looks up and his icy blue eyes meet mine and swallow me up. I've seen people low before. I've seen them broken. I haven't seen them like this, and now I'm really worried.

I clear the knot from my throat. "And since you're about to disappoint me on a deep level, I think that maybe you should at least tell me why."

His voice is husky when he answers.

"I don't invite people to my home. That's why I don't have any friends. I don't have time for things outside of work. Ever. I haven't had time since Amber. Not since my parents got ill."

"They're both ill?" I ask and he nods.

"I don't let people in," he says simply, like it answers everything. Not hardly, buddy.

"Is this you telling me to fuck off?" I ask brashly but he's already flinching, shaking his head.

"No." It comes out like an exasperated sigh. "It's me about to let you in."

I take a step forward. I don't even know why. I just feel like I should be touching him for this. Like, if he's going to open his whole truth up to me, maybe I should be there to catch it, right?

"We've seen each other in the most ridiculous underwear," I say softly. "I think you can show me this."

He huffs a bitter laugh. "The irony is that even if we were fake dating ... hell, even if we were real *married*, I wouldn't tell you this." I feel my eyebrows rise and he snorts. "Don't look so sanctimonious like you've never had a secret."

"If I had a husband, I would share all my secrets with him," I tell him firmly in my scary voice — the one that says, obey me or risk dismemberment. "And I would expect him to share his secrets with me. And if he wasn't man enough for that, I'd leave him faster than Amber left you."

Look, I know that's playing dirty. It's a straight-up kick to his balls. Dirty is how I play.

His nostrils flare and I step forward, hands on hips. I plan to be clear about this. I'm not sure why since we clearly aren't going to date, but it feels like the time to draw a line in the sand.

"And he'd deserve that, Nicola, because trust requires truth. I wouldn't respect a man who didn't give it to me."

That does something to him — something that makes his eyes darken and the line of his jaw stand out. He watches me for a beat, nostrils still flared, cheeks red and then he just deflates before rallying, and looking me defiantly in the eye.

"My parents are illegal," he says. "I've had them here for two years. Way past when they're supposed to be back in Canada." He closes his eyes as if in defeat and sinks his face back into his hands. "And we're going to be in so much trouble."

Chapter Twenty-Two

NICOLA

WELL, there it is. I've confessed to her that I've committed a crime — or at least that my parents have under my guidance. That we've been found out. That my sand castle is washing away with the waves. It's her chance to get out and, of course, she will now, but I'm still grateful to have had one more whiff of her coconut-scented hair before she is gone, one more conversation where she snapped at me and told me to be better.

I think that maybe this version of her will take up residence in my head and I'll get to hear her snap at me and tell me to be worthy of respect every time I feel like shading the truth. I hope this version of her fights dirty like she did with that Amber comment. I hope this version wears skin-tight red jeans like she is right now because it will make the upcoming legal situation slightly less torturous. In the end, the memories are the only things you ever get to keep. I'm going to remember her just like this.

"I ..." There's a lot I need to say but somehow I can't remember what any of it is. "I need to apologize."

"Yes," she snaps. "Quite frequently, and yet you never do."

I bark out a laugh. One of those grim laughs you can still find when the rest of the world has gone to shit.

"Well, then take this one," I say, still not looking up. I feel like shit. No. I am shit. I've ruined everything and I'm going to lose everything. Everything I've built. Everything I wanted. Even my parents who I was just trying to protect. I hate myself fully right now. "I apologize to you, Ada Ford. For ruining your dreams and your chance of seeing solvency and not having to worry all the time."

It's silent for so long that I almost look up but as much as I love her frowns and her judgment, I'm afraid to look because this moment is thick with something and it's not rage. I'm afraid of what it might be if it isn't anger.

"No," she says in that firm, woman-in-charge tone of hers that I love. "I don't accept."

I nod. That's totally understandable. I shall treasure her rejection the way some men might treasure a "yes" to their proposal of marriage. I'm proud to be thrown aside by her. Maybe I should get her a ring. With the last of what I have. What kind of ring do you give someone who hates you? Diamond, maybe, like their cold, cold heart? Though I think citrine would suit Ada better.

"Look at me." Her voice is audible fire.

I look up, despair and misery heavy in my heart and I swear that traitor mind of mine thinks she can burn away all that thick disgust I have for myself if I just let her. I want it so very badly.

"This is completely unacceptable," she says. Her lower lip is trembling. Fury looks amazing on her. Better, even, than that yellow dress. I try to memorize how it shades her cheeks and brightens her eyes. "As in, I refuse to accept it. This is our big chance, Nicola. My big chance. I'm not going to hear a no from you. I don't care if you've been hiding your parents in the country like a stash of weapons in a fallout shelter. I don't care if you hate me."

"I don't hate you," I say and a smile is playing at the edge of my mouth. In a moment, I'll have to go back to real life where I need to find a lawyer and hope none of us does actual jail time for this. In a moment, I'm going to have to go to the hospital and explain to my incapacitated parents why they'll be seeing immigration agents soon. And that it's my fault. And that I can't save them.

But right now, I get this lovely unreal moment to hold onto and I'm going to hold it tight.

"I don't care if you do hate me," she says, lifting her chin in challenge. "But I refuse to accept that this is over."

"Okay, Pineapple," I say and I hear the sadness and resignation in my voice, but I hope she doesn't. Because I want her to fight me every step. I want there to be one person who doesn't give up on me.

"Good," she says, taking a step nearer. She puts the papers in her hand on my desk. "These are the samples and drawings I made for the Silver Bullet. I kept another copy with me. You need to go over them and make comments or accept them before Monday when I'm going to turn them in."

That took a turn I didn't expect.

"I'm sure they're fine," I say. I just don't care. I won't be working on that project anymore. "You have good judgment. Do whatever you want."

"I should record you saying that," she says, smiling slightly. "For the future when you need to hear from your own lips that I have full permission to do as I please."

I smile wistfully at her. This could have been amazing.

"Now," she says in her take charge kind of way. "That's the first thing. Second thing."

"What's the second thing?" I start to ask, but my rolling desk chair is suddenly hitting the wall behind me as she leans down and pushes her weight against it and into me so she can steal a kiss.

It actually might be more than a kiss. It feels like she's taking me apart — disassembling me for a full rebuild. That's quite a trick with only a pair of lips and a few well-timed gentle moans. I reach up, tentatively, to cradle her face with just my fingertips, keeping my touch feather-light. I can't believe this is happening. I don't want it to stop.

My heart is racing like a car making a land-speed run at Bonneville. I don't even try to slow it. Don't even try to tame my imagination or the parts of my body that are suddenly standing at full attention.

I gasp for breath and my gasp opens me up more and she takes more of my lips, caressing them, filling them, and sinking her tongue into my gasping mouth. I'm not sure what her hands are doing. I'm lost to sensation. I think one hand is tangled in my hair and pulling it.

When she's done, she smirks at me. "That's to remind you we aren't done here."

"Of course it is," I say and I feel like she's stolen all my thoughts and feelings. Blown them away like hurricane winds. I reach for them but all I can find is stunned blank nothing.

She seems happy enough with that. Her smug smile deepens, the corners of her mouth sinking into her cheeks enough that I see dimples. And then she turns on her heel — her pretty heel — and leaves. I listen to her engine fire up and slowly grow fainter.

She's gone. And that's fine. She gave me a parting gift of numb nothing and it's priceless and precious. I wish I was better at thanking her for things because it was exactly what I needed.

I drink the coffee she left for me — both cups. Hers is way too sweet.

I lock up the shop.

I find the number for a lawyer.

And through it all, I don't have to hate myself or taste bitter despair because I'm still tasting sweet pineapple and the wonderful sensation of being completely unable to think.

Chapter Twenty-Three

ADA

I'm not really sure what came over me. I don't do things like that. Like kissing men and telling them what to do. Well, unless you count kissing Pops' cheek and begging him not to spend money today.

But it felt like he needed it somehow and maybe I have more of Pops in me than I thought because the instinct to yank him out of his despair with an unexpected gift was so overwhelming that I didn't question it. I just did it. And it turned out it was hard to stop once I'd started. I want to explore this man. I want to find all his dips and peaks. I want to map them and know them until I'm the acknowledged Nicola Petrovic expert and anyone who needs information on him comes to me first. They'll have to call me Dr. Ford because I'll have a Ph.D. in Nicola.

My heart's racing so hard that words fail me and I end up fleeing his shop like it's the scene of the crime. Maybe it is. What's wrong with both of us that neither of us can be mutual in our kissing? I always feel like a thief or the one who has been burgled. And I love it. I'm getting just a little addicted to it.

Maybe it's the way he gives and gives to me and won't take no for an answer in a world where everything feels scarce, he's plentiful. Or maybe it's how he gasps and clings to me like he needs me and knows it.

I'm afraid I'm getting in too deep. Like I've gone so far up Mount Nicola that I can't back up to get down again, I can only crest the hill and hope to make it down on the other side.

But here's another thing about me, in case you were wondering, I don't take difficulty sitting down. I don't put my head in my hands and give up — not that I blame him because that was a lot, but surely he has that end of things covered, and I don't need to demonstrate my mourning skills along with him. Besides, I am *not* losing this chance just because a hospital reported a pair of old people to immigration.

I speed home, irritated that Nicola doesn't live closer. He should live next door. It's too long of a drive to his place. Usually, I like taking drives. I like seeing the city and noticing changes and what's happening where, absorbing the vibe of my surroundings. Maybe eating ice cream while I drive. Not today. Today, I barely notice the stop lights as I drive, instinct and autopilot keeping me on the road.

Despite my brave words, I'm anxious and feeling the nausea that comes along with a mini panic over the idea that my whole future hangs on whether I can make this work.

I park behind our shop and practically sprint inside.

"What happened to you, Ada?" Jasmin says as I gasp for breath, moving my aviators up to the top of my head. "You weren't a victim of road rage, were you?"

Road rage? Ha. If I was involved in road rage I'd be the one raging. She should know that.

Her eyes are huge and both Pops and Marvin swivel from their seats on stools observing their project and look at me instead.

I pull myself up to my full height (marginal), grasp at all my calm (running on empty), and speak.

"I know you have your doubts about my working with BOOM Enterprises, Pops," I say calmly. "But they have a potential streaming service deal in the works and if they get it, then you'll have twice the budget to work on this Shelby with Marvin and the pair of you can take all the time you like. Plus, I'll have money to help Jasmin with launching her fashion career," I say, peeking at her. She's shooting me her "be quiet" glare, but I see her cheeks flushed with excitement. "I know that you think this is ridiculous, but you also like being generous and giving everything away and none of that will be possible if we run out of things to give."

Pops sucks his gums. From him, this is a hopeful sign. He's considering it.

"What's the catch?" he asks eventually.

Beside him, Marvin's eyes are pinging back and forth between Pops and me like he's watching Olympic beach volleyball.

I point right at him. "I need *his* help."

"My help?" Marvin runs a hand over his balding head. "Well, Ada, it's flattering that you think I have some kind of pull in the corporate world but —"

I cut him off. "It's your pull in Immigration that can help us."

His expression shifts from bemused to serious. "Tell me how."

So I lay it all out to him with Pops and Jasmin listening in. They both try to pretend they're working, but none of us is working. We're all hanging by a thread, wondering what Marvin will say.

I tell him about BOOM Enterprises. About the Silver Bullet. About my working relationship with Nicola — leaving out a few details, obviously. He doesn't need to know about why I call him

Fireworks, or how hot he looks mostly naked or right after I kiss him when the shock hasn't quite worn off. I tell him about the possible deal. The stipulations. And then about Nicola's parents.

By the time we get to that part, he's nodding.

"Okay," he says when I finish. "I can look into it. I owe your Pops a lot, and I guess the least I can do is see if there are any workarounds for his daughter."

I start to smile but he holds up a finger.

"Don't look too relieved. These things are legal in nature. And on top of that, I won't risk my retirement. T's will be crossed and I's will be dotted."

I nod earnestly.

"And sometimes there are catches," he warns.

"Like what?" I ask, biting my lip. Just what I need. More catches.

"Like if it turns out he's a landed immigrant and not a full citizen yet, we'll have to fast track that, and the way we do that might involve jumping through some hoops."

I swallow and nod as he stands up, purposeful in a way I haven't seen from him before. He's up and saying goodbye to Pops as I stumble over myself trying to thank him, and then he's gone, and the three of us are left looking at each other.

"You'd pretend to be this man's girlfriend for a tv show?" Pops asks, eyes narrowing.

"You picked up Mrs. Santiago's kids from school all of last semester because they were dealing with bullies on their walk home," I say.

"I thought you hated him."

"I thought you hated Casey Renos until I heard you lent him five hundred bucks for his medication." I say 'lent,' but it was a gift and we both know it.

"Sometimes you have to do the right thing. And sometimes you have to do the smart thing," Pops warns me.

"That's right, Pops," I say. "And this is both."

He rubs his chin, looking uncertain but I don't even flinch because there's no way he can be more uncertain right now than I am. I might look cool and collected on the outside but inside I feel like I'm being washed away by the waves of a tropical storm and there is no sunny sky in sight.

Chapter Twenty-Four

NICOLA

OVER THE PAST TWO DAYS, I've learned something about myself. I've learned that even if you try to do everything perfectly, it's still going to come crashing down on you.

The lawyer I found was pretty clear that we're all in a lot of trouble. The hospital wants me to know that both my parents require twenty-four-hour care from here on out, and that while their bills will be high, I should really be worried about the huge cost of getting my parents into a facility. They offer me a flyer for one nearby and when I call them there are spaces. But the lawyer says that the facility I put my parents in absolutely can't be in the United States and that I absolutely can't go back to Canada. I'd had to concentrate very hard on the mental image of Ada's frown to hold me together for that conversation.

The realtor I talked to says she can probably sell my home — after all, I need to cover this somehow — but the market is weak, and she isn't hopeful of the best price. It had been a memory of Ada pushing my chair back and kissing me without permission that got me through that meeting.

My mother has taken a step backward. She's heavily medicated and incommunicative. Visits to her make me feel like my heart is in my throat and I might puke it up. I've never spent so much time pretending I'm a smoker just to find a quiet place outside where I can cry with no one watching. No amount of memories can help with this, but I try. I fill my mind with memories of a pineapple bra and try like hell to drown in it.

Dad is worse than Mom. He doesn't want to stay in bed. He wants to be with Mom. He wants them to stop giving him medication. But his heart is all over the place. He's had three "incidents" as the doctor called them and the confusion is getting worse with every one. I don't know what that means and the doctor looks like he doesn't want to commit to an answer without more tests. Dad curses at us both in Serbian and tells me it's my fault. Which it is. So, yeah.

Basically, I'm screwed on every level.

I drive down the street, looking at every building as I go. It's here somewhere. I looked up the address online. And yeah, I shouldn't be coming to see Ada right now. Not with all the other problems I'm dealing with, but I owe her. I owe her because my mess has spilled over and ruined things for her, too. I owe her a goodbye and an explanation of why she'll have to let this drop — that there are no ways out for me. Not even if she frowns at all the right people.

My phone buzzes and I glance at the caller ID. Big Daddy Boom. This is the second time he's called me. I let it go to voicemail the first time and didn't listen to it. I'm not ready yet to tell him that I can't do this. That I'm out. That I can't even keep the commitments I already made to him. I choke a bit at the thought.

I'm Nicola Petrovic. I've never not kept a commitment I made. Until now. Until today. Fuck.

I find the place and when I get out of my truck I have to stop for a moment and just look, balancing my gift on one hip. It's amazing. Like a set for a movie, but it's real. The shop is low and both doors are flung open so that the busy street can watch the progress on two cars.

Flowering bushes grow on either side of the shop doors, untrimmed and trying to reach out for passersby like they might be carnivorous plants. They wave in the breeze. The shop — wow, it's a vlogger's dream. I've watched Ada's videos and I know it's beautiful, but she doesn't do it justice. The memorabilia on every wall is perfectly placed and stunning — more so because it's obvious that it wasn't chosen as decoration, but is merely the flotsam of a working shop that hasn't stopped since the 1950s. Rare parts are hanging from nails for when, one day, they'll be chosen for a project. There are old pop bottles on a high shelf with tubes hanging from them that are clearly used to bleed brakes. There are little oil cans so vintage that a picker would die to get them.

Inside the shop, Ada is in one bay beside a project half-sewn on her machine, working her phone like she's trying to diffuse a bomb, while a pair of older men are bent over a maroon Shelby Mustang in the other bay. They're laughing together, faces open and happy. Night and day different from the look of Ada's tense shoulders as she bites her lip. Beside her, further down her workbench, a younger woman is spinning back and forth on a stool, chewing the end of a pencil while she pours over a textbook. She's dressed like Ada — in bright colors and loud patterns — and one glance is enough to tell me this is her cousin Jasmin.

I make my way into the shop and pause just inside the door, hesitant to disrupt this family scene. And then my phone buzzes loudly enough in my pocket that all eyes turn to me.

"Nicola," Ada says, tapping her phone. The buzzing in my pocket stops. "I was just trying to call you."

"Good timing, then." My neck feels hot and I know a blush is creeping up my cheeks. "I ... um. This is for you."

I pass my gift to her and she takes it, face blank before an eyebrow lifts. She opens her mouth but it's her cousin who breezes past and grabs the bin I brought.

"Ooo! Pineapple! My favorite," she says and my face grows hotter.

"Mine, too."

I don't know why those words slipped out. They are treacherous when I'm here to say goodbye.

Jasmin looks up from the fruit. "You brought us pineapple and donuts and chocolate … in a plastic tote bin?"

I rip my eyes from Ada's face. It takes effort. But I manage to meet Jasmin's gaze. She has a knowing, almost teasing expression.

I swallow before I answer. "It's more practical. What are you going to do with a basket when the food is gone?"

"Bring those donuts over here," a tall black man says. This must be Pops. The grinning white guy beside him is definitely not.

I reach into my pocket and give Ada the last of the presents. She takes it, turns it around, and around and her eyebrows draw together in an accusatory look before darting to the white guy who immediately stops grinning, though his eyes stay huge.

"What's this?"

Her tone is unreadable. If I had to guess I'd say appalled — which seems like an odd reaction to a mood ring I bought from the stand beside the fruit cart. It was big and bright and I thought that maybe if she wore it and it worked, it might give me some warning about how she was feeling. I bought it more on a whim than anything.

"It's goodbye," I say, rubbing the back of my neck. "Goodbye and I'm sorry. I don't want you to waste valuable time trying to fix what can't be fixed."

"Well." She sounds hesitant. Ada never sounds hesitant.

She glances backward at the older man and her Pops who is halfway into a donut. All three of them are. And they're watching us like hawks, gathered around the tote bin with it set between them and us like a barrier between the audience and the players.

I ease my weight back on my heels. My body is telling me to run but I don't know why.

"Well," she says again and when my gaze tracks back to her, I see her visibly swallowing. Maybe saying goodbye is as hard for her as it is for me. She bites her lip, looking pained, and then she speaks so fast it's hard to catch it all. "So, this is my family." She gestures erratically at them. "Jasmin. Pops. And that's Marvin. He's an Immigration Officer." I flinch and she winces. "Or he was before retirement and that's why I was calling, because Marvin made some calls and called in some favors with a lawyer friend and some other friends in Immigration, and he thinks they might forgive your parents if you can get the hospital to sign letters stating they aren't competent to care for themselves and then they can fast track them to Landed Immigrants which means you can put them in a home here."

I look back and forth between her and the man, Marvin, who is eyeing me right back. My mouth has fallen open and I reach for words and nothing is coming. I have to almost shake myself before my voice finally rasps out.

"You did all this. For me."

Her cheeks are glowing and she won't meet my gaze. "I sent our design — well, mine, I guess — to Big Daddy Boom and I told him we're in. That we want the show."

"You did," I say slowly.

"Because you can do it if the stuff with your parents gets fixed." She finally meets my gaze and I'm nodding.

I should maybe be mad at her for doing that. I'm not, though, I'm unable to feel at all. I can't quite believe this could be real. That the legal problems could just ... go away? I look at Marvin.

"Is this real?"

He coughs uncomfortably and looks at Ada.

"Well, there is a small catch," she says and her bottom lip is trembling. I frown. I don't like to see her upset. How bad could this be that it has her worked up? And why is her cousin trying to hide a smirk behind a sprinkle-covered donut?

I raise a single eyebrow.

"Marvin says you're not a full citizen yet. That you're four years into being a Landed Immigrant."

"Yeah," I admit and my stomach is sinking. Does that mean all this just goes away? I didn't realize my hopes were up until I feel them sinking faster than a lead weight thrown overboard.

I shoot another look at Marvin, but now he's eating a donut, too, totally nonchalant. I frown. I don't understand. I look back at Ada and she's biting her lip again and fiddling with the mood ring I gave her.

"He says the case will be a lot stronger if you were married to a U.S. citizen."

I squint at her. Is she joking?

"That's not a real thing."

She folds her arms uncomfortably over her chest and looks behind her for the first time to where her father and his friend are both watching us with innocent expressions. I don't know if this is a real requirement or just something they've tacked on. I'm pretty damn sure they won't admit it one way or another. What I do know is that if I meet this requirement then that white guy eating my apology donuts could make my life possible again and Ada could get the deal she needs so badly. So I swallow my pride.

"Is this real? One hundred percent?"

Marvin finally speaks. "Nothing is ever one hundred percent but this is close enough. My contacts say we can get the ball rolling tomorrow."

"If I'm married by tomorrow?" I say, raising an eyebrow.

He shrugs like it isn't his problem that I have to come up

with a bride in twenty-four hours. I suppose it's possible. Amber was a weekend fling before our sudden wedding.

I look back at Ada as I inhale. I can't say no to her twice. I'll just have to try, I guess. This would be easier in Vegas.

Her face glistens with a sheen of sweat and I start to frown when she slips my ring on her finger — the third finger on her left hand and says, "What do you say, Nicola? Shall we make it official?"

Chapter Twenty-Five

"No," he says. Just that. Just "no," and then he turns on his heel and begins to walk away. He ... he can't be serious.

I hop up and chase after him and I swear I hear muffled chuckles from behind me, but they can laugh all they want. I'm not doing this for them. Not this time and —damn it — I'm just like my dad because I took one look at him breaking down and I couldn't walk away. Not when I could do something to help. It's crazy, right? To offer to marry someone because it will help them? Not because it's something you want or need, but just for them. I mean, it won't hurt our chances of landing that show, but we could do that while *pretending* to be together. We don't need to actually get married. But he needs this. And I've decided that I want to be the one to give it to him. Even if I can't quite explain to myself why that is.

I catch up to him in the parking lot and grab his belt. He spins around with a barked, "What?"

He looks furious. There's a vein pulsing in his neck and I

don't know why but it makes my own heart race faster to see it beat like that.

"You're being ridiculous," I say. "This solves all our problems."

I say "our" but I mean "your."

"This..." He looks incredulous as he shakes his head. He studies me intently, his dark eyebrows drawing down in a way that looks both threatening and ridiculously attractive. It's like he's trying to be certain it's really me. "This is messed up, Ada. Fuck."

I feel defensive even though it wasn't my idea. I mean, he's acting like I'm trying to trap him or something when actually I'm trying to help him. I cross my arms over my chest as I feel myself begin to flush.

"It's stupid, that's what it is," he says, his voice louder than I'd like. They can probably hear it in the garage. "Stupid. The dumbest idea I've ever heard and I can't believe you're acting like it's normal."

"Except it was pretty normal until a hundred years ago, right? People got married all the time because it made sense. For inheritances, and business interests, or because they were both trained in the same trade and could set up shop together. Or because they were the only two single people in a community and it cost less to live that way. The list goes on." I feel a little better with this excellent fact to hold onto. History. It's on my side for once.

"A hundred years ago," he hisses, taking a step toward me that should be menacing with how he's leaning in, but instead it's just freaking sexy. I can see the gleam in his blue eyes. I can see how wide his shoulders are in that old washed-too-often T-shirt and how they kind of bulge when he moves, even though he doesn't mean to show them off. My breathing is already erratic when he gets right in my face. "A lot of dumb shit was done a hundred years ago."

"Convenience marriages still happen now," I say, trying to stay cool. I mean, I'm not the white guy here so maybe he shouldn't be lecturing me on dumb shit that happened a hundred years ago, right? Or is that asking for too much? "Have you heard of India? There are tv shows dedicated to the subject."

"TV," he says, scoffing and waving a hand like it means nothing. "If I wanted to get married for citizenship, I would have done that a long time ago."

"And if you did, we wouldn't be talking now," I lean in very close, so close that I see the corner of his eye twitch. "I know you care about your parents. You told me you did. I've seen it. This is their one chance to be here with you."

He certainly flinches then, his hands coming up a little, open-palmed, defensive, as if he doesn't realize he's doing it. I step between them.

"You told me you cared more about your work than I did. That you wanted this exposure with BOOM more than me. So why does it feel like I'm the one standing here trying to convince you?"

"I —" He can't seem to get any more words out. He winces and grabs his neck with one hand like he might wring his own neck from behind. There's a look of intense discomfort on his face.

"I'm not exactly forcing something terrible on you," I say, gesturing with my hand at my phenomenal self. "I think most men would admit it's a gift to be offered this."

"Offered," he echoes and there's a dark hunger in his eyes that suddenly speeds my pulse up and out of control. Desire whirlwinds in my lower belly and I'm suddenly hot and wet for him and I need to remember that we're standing in a parking lot outside my family business. The family who are doubtless peering out at us.

"What I mean," I say precisely, "is that I'm willing to marry you, and give your parents the chance to stay, and give us both the fame and real money we need. Is that so terrible?"

"Like a real marriage."

"Yes."

"Like forever."

"As much as any other marriage, I suppose."

He draws in a long breath and I can feel it on my face and it's all I can do not to lean forward and kiss that worry away. He's gorgeous when he's riled up, his heavy-lashed lids are partly closed, and his blue eyes peer at me through them. The lines on his lean face are a little more etched, his nose somehow seems longer and straighter. His breath catches between his perfectly curved lips and I find my gaze catching there, too.

"And then what?" He breathes, and it's so quiet that I wouldn't hear him except that he's so close right now.

"And then what, what?"

"After we get married. What happens then?"

I grin. I might nearly have him. "Then we make great television and we spend the proceeds on our disastrous families."

He scoffs again. "What if I like it?"

"What are you asking?" I feel suddenly vulnerable when his fingers meet my waist and his gaze meets mine hot and intense.

"What if I marry you and I decide I like it? What if I decide I like all your scowls and the mean things you say?"

"I'm never mean, merely accurate," I hedge, but I don't know what to do with how my breath is sawing in my lungs suddenly or with how fucking loud my heart is hammering. Will you calm down for a damn moment and let me think?

"What if I decide I want to stay married to you?" he asks, leaning in so close he could almost kiss me. I swear I already taste him on my lips.

"What if you do?"

"Well, what will you do about that?"

It sounds like a challenge. I don't like backing down from challenges.

"There's not much you can throw at me that I can't take, Nicola Petrovic," I say cooly, and his low laugh cuts straight through me and into the warm inner parts of me who have already signed legal documents, dressed in white, stood at an altar, and are now lying seductively across a petal-strewn bed and are asking why the rest of me is so damn slow at catching up.

His jaw clenches like he's fighting an internal war. "I don't see how this is fair to you. What do you get out of it?"

"The show. The money."

He hums in the back of his throat. "What if you meet someone else?"

"What if I do? Anyone who gets married might meet someone else. The world is so full of people that the governments are panicking about it."

"What if you fall in love?" His voice is husky.

"What if I do?" I ask, and I look in his eyes as if to say, *what if it's with you?*

"Challenge accepted," he whispers, and then — to my utter surprise, he yanks me forward — almost too roughly — and takes my lips into his like he owns them, like it's up to him what they get to feel and taste and he's decided it will be all Nicola.

He's coffee and hazelnut and something sharp and basil-like. His rough, unshaven beard scratching my face and soft lips molding to mine. He's gentle, caressing tongue tangling up with me and fingers that are creeping up my side and then gently hitching me in a little closer and Oh. My. God. This is better than I imagined. It's better than last time. I might die or faint or whatever dramatic thing the girls are doing these days when a man kisses them almost to the point of orgasm.

When he pulls away everything protests, my suddenly empty arms try to catch him again and a needy grunt escapes me and I think he might be laughing when he takes my aviators, sets them down over my nose and whispers.

"Don't show those black turned-on eyes to anyone else but me, Pineapple."

Fuck. Him.

No, seriously, I think I might like to, though.

Instead, I stay cool as a chilled cola.

"City Hall isn't open all day. If you really mean business then we'd better find some witnesses and get over there."

"Oh, there have been witnesses," my cousin Jasmin says with a barely concealed laugh and I spin to see that she, and Pops, and Marvin have *all* followed us out of the shop and watched this entire thing and I'm speechless. I try to find words but I end up looking like a fish pulled up on the sand.

"I think I'd better drive." Jasmin flips her hair. "I don't trust you to do it when you look like that."

And thank goodness for the aviators because I don't want these eyes to show *everything* I have been thinking.

"I'll meet you there," Nicola says over his shoulder and I follow him with my eyes as he sprints over to his 7.3 diesel.

"At least he drives a nice truck," Pops mutters as we hurry to Jasmin's purple metal-flake Camaro. "There are rust spots in the front fender, though. Driver's side. Tell him I said so."

And on that cheery note, we all go to City Hall to watch me get married.

Chapter Twenty-Six

NICOLA

I DIDN'T EXPECT to get married once — certainly not twice — and not in a church either time. The beach with Amber was — very Amber. There had been a lot of beers with lime and her friends laughing and giving me sweaty high-fives while she giggled her way through the ceremony in a white lace dress she'd bought in some kind of sale years before "in case I ever need it" and I'd given her a diamond ring that I'd chosen because it was the only one in her size in the pawn shop I'd found on the way. Classy, right? I mean, it would have been romantic if we'd had the sticking kind of love. The kind that lasted for *me* past all the betrayal and drama, and the kind that lasted for *her* past the honeymoon.

But that's the thing about perspective. From one angle a thing might be beautiful and spontaneous and full of zest for life, but from another angle, it might be a train wreck that started the second Amber said, "If you want the American Dream you should maybe marry an American" and ended with me losing twenty pounds because I couldn't stomach food for weeks after she left me for Tyler. A dude with huge spacers in his ears who still called me "bro" even after he and my bride shacked up together — and I use that term literally because his "place" was an old travel trailer with a blanket wall out of doors for added living space.

She kept the ring. And her secrets. Including the one that explained why she married me only to throw me over while we were still technically on our honeymoon. I'm not great with women. I'm good at diagnostics, though, and since she's still with Tyler and now they have a pair of toddlers and an online channel on van living with small kids, my only conclusion is that I'm the reason it didn't work. Yeah, I follow them on social media. Judge away. Sometimes curiosity is a powerful thing.

But I like who I am. I mean, I don't like my current situation, but I like being the guy who notices everything and always does things the right way. I like being serious and dedicated and intense about things. And if happiness with a woman means giving up my gearhead ways and "embracing the chaos" — one of Amber's favorite phrases — then it's likely better that I stay alone.

Maybe people can't imagine what my life is like without a relationship or friends, but even before I was taking care of an opinionated older Serbian couple with health issues all day every day, I was caught up in trying to start an online business based around something I was making and selling. Anyone who has ever done that knows how all-consuming it is. When I'm not working on cars I'm researching my competition, I'm showing my face at events, I'm networking, I'm running online give-aways, editing clips, researching algorithms, analyzing data, and tending social media. I don't have enough hours in a day. Any day. And my life has been like that for years. I'm not lonely. I'm way, way, too busy to be lonely.

I think.

I thought.

The last few weeks have been different. I've felt it when Ada isn't there, like I've lost something but I can't remember what it is, and I know I just put it down a minute ago. Maybe that's friendship. What would I know? I've had very few friends in my life.

Anyways, here I am again, getting married in a rush to a woman who doesn't love me and is doing this for her own reasons.

I don't know why I bothered to try to rustle my father out of the hospital for this.

"He needs long-term care," the nurse objected. "You can't take him home."

"Just for an hour," I'd begged.

"No."

"What is all this? Why are you here?" My father had asked in Serbian — so sharp and harsh that the nurse jumped. "Does my son need me? Are you in trouble?"

"No trouble," I said, not meeting his eyes.

"No trouble? Then why are you here trying to break me out of prison when you wouldn't do it before?"

"Look," the nurse broke in, in English. "You can't rile him up. He needs rest."

My father rolled his eyes at her.

"These nurses are prison guards," he told me — in English, clearly to bother her.

"I'm getting married," I said in Serbian.

"To the firecracker?" His eyebrows went up.

"Yes."

"You move fast."

"Yes."

"Well, don't let me stop you." He lay back against his pillows, a smug look on his face, and the nurse's sigh of relief only increased his smugness. "You need a woman. To soften you."

"You talked to Ada on the phone and you think *she* will soften me?"

"I think she'll pulverize you. That's what you do with meat, you know. To soften it."

So, I don't get to bring my father to my rush second wedding. And by the time I get to City Hall, Ada looks like she might have had a similarly intense time of things. Her Pops is scowling, arms crossed over his chest. Jasmin is hovering, and Marvin is sipping a drink.

And no wonder my wedding party doesn't look thrilled. They all know what we're here for. Marriages based on money and desperation don't work. Only marriages based on love last, right? At least, that's how it looks from the outside. But for me, it kind of is love — love for my parents, at least. If I don't get married, then how am I going to take care of them?

But why is Ada doing this? It can't just be because it's practical. It can't be. I've seen her underwear. I've seen her shoes. She is not a practical person.

I swallow as I approach her.

Ava's holding a little slip of paper with a number on it and she's wearing some kind of filmy white top with tight white jeans — like an Ada version of wedding attire — and someone has put a white rose up in her hair. I think it must have been Jasmin because she's still fussing with it.

Ada's so gorgeous she'd put any other bride to shame. She doesn't need a veil or a big white dress to do that. But I don't dare care what she looks like right now. She could look like her Pops and I'd still be staring at her like I am right now, trying to puzzle out the *her* under this seemingly selfless act of marrying me so I can take care of my parents. We live in San Diego. She could go to the local hardware store and find ten other guys who need help getting legal so they can bring their folks here to take care of them. And I bet seven of those bastards would be better men than me. So why is she here?

"We're next," Jasmin says, snatching the little slip of paper from Ada and thrusting it at me. Behind her, Pops shoots me his best killing look but he fails — I guess he needs better connections with the voodoo community for that to work.

"I thought you'd left to get changed," Jasmin says irritably. She shoves a paper bag at me and inside is a Hawaiian shirt with a very light print so that it's almost white. "I bought that on the way. Wear it."

It looks — I kid you not — almost identical to what I wore to my first wedding.

"Not a chance," I say, jamming the bag into the nearest trash can.

She drops the roses to make a grab for it. "I paid for that! Where were you if you weren't getting changed?"

Four sets of eyes are all on me, waiting for a reply but it's only Ada's eyes I'm looking at and they're wide and scared, and her breathing is a little too fast. I realize suddenly that she hasn't spoken to me yet. That is so unlike her.

Impulsively, I grab her hand. It's cold, but she squeezes my hand so tightly that I'm glad I took it.

"I went to get my father," I say to her — not to them — to her. "But the hospital wouldn't let him out. I thought he should be here for this."

"Oh." The word is small but it carries so much understanding that it hits me in the chest and I don't know what to do with the warmth of it. I'll have to sort that out later. "I liked your dad."

Behind her, I see her Pops' frown melt into something thoughtful. I wonder what he'll make of my parents, if he ever meets them. Maybe this is all just too much.

"You don't have to do this," I say simply.

I don't like the uncertainty in her expression. I don't like how wide those eyes are. Ada is a lioness, not a fawn, and I shouldn't be doing anything that makes her skittish rather than furious and roaring.

She shakes her head and I think she's going to say something but then the number on the slip is called and she lets go of my hand and holds her chin high. The lioness is back and she's going to marry me. I feel like I should be full of love or at least lust or something but mostly I'm just feeling confused and grateful and I don't know what to do with any of it.

We're whisked through a flurry of signing papers and some awkward shots with Jasmin's cell phone camera and then we speak solemn vows before a fifty-something woman judge who looks flustered and smells of Greek salad and she has us fill out more papers before offering a genuine smile and waving us out the door.

It's a stranger wedding than my first one. Even less romantic, if that's possible. Wooden. Dead.

And yet.

Those vows did something stupid inside me. My first vows were ones we wrote ourselves. I think Amber promised me a happy thought every day and I promised her to go on a beer run whenever she needed it. They were stupid vows. Honestly, I'm not even sure we broke them. She probably does think happy thoughts every day and she hasn't asked me for beer, so ...

But the vows we spoke today are the old-school ones. The ones about loving, honoring, and cherishing. And I've always had this thing about keeping my commitments. I'm never late, because a scheduled date is a promise. I pay all my bills on time. I fulfill contracts to the letter. I read Terms and Conditions.

And when I say "to love, honor, and cherish," I choke.

Her eyes narrow in suspicion, but even after the words are said, they just keep ringing in my head and there's just no way that I can't try to honor these somehow. How do you love someone you hardly know? How do you honor someone who is a mystery? How do you cherish what is hardly even yours?

I don't know.

But I definitely cherish her speaking those vows back.

And I guess I honor the sacrifice she's made by binding herself to me.

I'm going to have to learn about love. It's not a thing I understand, I think. Unless there's a hint of it in how I feel relief when her Pops smiles at her like he's forgiven her for something, and how Jasmin promises her a pancake breakfast to celebrate.

We're hustled away almost before the ink is dry and it's a ballpoint pen we're using. Marvin has papers for us, too, from his immigration friends. I'm so rattled I don't even read them. I just nod and do what he says.

I keep looking at Ada, wondering what's going on behind her cool expression and her calm smile. She's giving me no indication. If only she'd scowl at me or sling an insult but she's so subdued that it makes me nervous enough that I start to feel sick.

She jokes with Marvin when the papers are all signed and then she turns to me and says, "I'll tell Big Daddy Boom so he can fast-track things with the relationship angle."

"Oh," I say because I don't know what else to say. It was beginning to feel almost real. Almost. And suddenly it's not again.

"I'll text you," she says, with a bright smile that doesn't meet her eyes.

"Oh," I say again, stupidly.

And then she's gone and I'm walking to the parking lot. And I feel — like someone stole something from me but I'm not sure what it is.

I basically sleepwalk to my truck. I take a call from my real estate agent. She's excited. She has a serious buyer for the house who wants to move on it *now*. I tell her to do whatever she needs to do to sell. I'm going to need that money. Because I get to keep my parents here now.

So I call one of the places the nurses got me flyers for, and before I know it, I'm over there touring their facility. I don't know what I'm looking at, but the staff seems clean and like they do this for a living, so I sign papers and call the hospital to make arrangements.

And by the time I have everything sorted and I'm ready to go home and go to bed, the real estate agent is calling again and I'm driving to her place to sign papers for the house. It's going to be a quick closing. I need to get all of our stuff packed and out by next week.

I hardly know what to think.

I guess I'm getting everything I need.

So why do I feel so fucking hollow?

Chapter Twenty-Seven

ADA

I DON'T HEAR from him the entire first afternoon of our marriage. Not that evening, either. And I am *not* going to be the first to text like some needy person.

Not a chance.

Pops watches me like a hawk and I don't know if he looks more relieved or more confused when Jasmin and Aunt Mary arrive that evening to make pancakes with us and still there's no husband making an appearance.

"Well," Aunt Mary says to the awkward silence. "I brought you some incense tied in green string for fertility. The Communal Presence says it's the best thing to bring luck to newlyweds."

Jasmin rolls her eyes. Aunt Mary has already regaled us on the other principles of her new cult, which sounds mostly harmless but a bit grabby for my liking.

"Pass the whipped cream," Jasmin says.

I take the incense like it's a snake about to bite me.

"Trust me," Aunt Mary says. "Having kids is the best thing you could ever do. You won't want to miss it."

I shoot a glance at Pops who has his fist tightened around his fork like he plans to reshape the metal with one hand. Aunt Mary always seems to forget that my mom died birthing me. That Pops lost the love of his life doing that thing that was maybe not so "worth it" to him.

But eventually, Pops says, "It's true," in a quiet way and then meets my eyes with a smile, and the tension melts and the rest of the breakfast-for-dinner passes in quiet conversation. Jasmin tells us about a new design for a handbag she's working on for school. Pops discusses the difficulty he's having tracking down an oil leak. We talk in abstract terms about the Big Daddy BOOM project and Aunt Mary relates basically everything back to her new cult's principles which is getting old fast.

"Tell us about your husband since he didn't show up," Aunt Mary presses. "Is he nice?"

The laugh slips out of me before I can stop it. "No."

"No?" She looks horrified.

"But I think he might be good."

There are grunts of approval for that.

"Is he hot?" she asks waggling an eyebrow. My Pops curses.

"He's swoony," Jasmin says. "Like seriously hot for a white guy. All muscle-y and perpetually unshaven with this face that's all angles, wearing close-fitting jeans and T-shirts. His hair is black and cropped pretty short but it lays down all neatly like he's posing for a magazine spread. If I do a men's line, then I one hundred percent want him for a model. He wears the most basic clothes but he slinks around everywhere like a cat and that makes his plain box store jeans and T-shirts look basically designer. He drips sex so hard."

"I don't know what that means," Pops says precisely. "But I know you shouldn't be saying it at my table."

Jasmin and Aunt Mary laugh and even I can't help my amused grin.

"Or saying it about my new son-in-law," he says more loudly, scowling, and with that, we all stop and stare at him. He's been so angry that I chose to do this that I didn't expect him to even acknowledge it. "What? I was there. It's not like it's a surprise."

"It had to be a bit of a surprise," Aunt Mary says gently. "Maybe even a shock?"

Pops shakes his head and sighs. "She's so much like her mother that sometimes I forget that she's also me." He looks at me and his eyes are almost apologetic when they catch mine. "Of course, she saw someone in need and decided to help without thinking about what it would cost her. Of course. Because that's what she was doing for that boy, even if he does "drip sex so hard" whatever that is supposed to mean."

I swallow but I don't break eye contact and eventually he grunts.

"Just tell him he's living here with you. I'm not letting you go live in some white boy's suburban home like some kind of trophy to prove how open-minded he is," Pops says and then he turns back to his pancakes and I meet my Aunt Mary's eyes to share the shock of this moment and then Jasmin bursts into giggles.

"You want him living here? With you? And mom's fertility incense?" she asks.

"Heaven help me," Pops says, standing suddenly, and turning to her sternly. "For that, you do the dishes."

"But I made supper."

And when he huffs and leaves to go back to the shop, the three of us laugh behind our hands, hoping he doesn't hear us through the door.

"You'd better get him here for dinner, Ada," Aunt Mary whispers. "If he's as hot as Jasmin says, then I deserve an eyeful."

"Bring a camera," Jasmin says waggling her eyebrows just

like Aunt Mary did a minute ago. "That butt is worth remembering."

Worth remembering or not, Nicola does not call that night. Or text. Not the next morning either.

Irritably, I go to his shop and use his door code. He hasn't been here, I don't think. I take some time and shoot some footage of me in front of the Silver Bullet talking about my design ideas and then I make a parts list for BOOM Enterprises and call Big Daddy Boom to tell him we're on track.

"This is great, Ada. Just perfect. But we're going to need more of the two of you together," he says. "Especially now that you've tied the knot! I hope you took pics of that, or even better — video! Our subscribers are going to eat it up!"

"I hope so," I say a little nervously.

"I'm going to send over some paperwork later today. Get Nicola to sign his and you sign yours and then we'll order those parts. I can't wait for more videos. You're both doing really excellent work."

Fueled by his optimism, I set up the body of the Silver Bullet on Nicola's rotisserie and take it behind his shop to sandblast it. It takes the whole afternoon and by the time I'm done I'm hot, sweaty, pleased with myself, but annoyed as anything at Nicola. What is he doing? Where is he? This is *his* shop and if he wasn't going to text his brand new wife, you'd think he'd at least show up here to work.

But I'm not going to be like that. I'm determined not to be a nag, and that means not texting him first or asking him where he is, or where he disappeared to last night.

Not even if my overactive imagination plays me scenarios of Nicola lounging in a hotel somewhere surrounded by bikini-clad ladies, or worse, writing another article about how my upholstery is "sufficient for a mid-range project" like he did last spring.

I'm so spun up by the time I get home that I cover both front seats of the project I'm working on and cut out the material for the rear bench seat and by midnight I'm out of work, out of steam, and my phone is out of power. I fall into bed too exhausted to be annoyed.

On the second morning of being someone's bride, I throw my ring in the trash can in my room.

Because if he can't take me seriously, then I'm not taking him seriously either. He has no gratitude for what I gave up for him — what I did for him.

Oh, and did you do it for recognition then, Ada? Well, obviously not. But that doesn't mean that *some* recognition would go to waste. A thank you, perhaps. A bare acknowledgment that something occurred. Maybe a sticky note in my mailbox that said, "You married me to help two old Serbians live."

I'm not going to get any of that, I realize. But I am a professional who is working her butt off and I need to go work on the Silver Bullet, so I get in my car, get coffee — just one, thanks for asking.

Because I don't expect him to be there. Just like he hasn't been there this whole time.

I tie a kerchief around my head — yeah, I mean business — sling my aviators low, and breeze into his shop, flicking on all the LED overhead lights.

And freeze.

He's lying almost entirely naked on a camping cot in the middle of his shop between the bay with the freshly sandblasted Silver Bullet and another project of his. There's just enough sleeping bag over his crotch area to pretend he's decent — spoiler alert, he's totally not.

And he's fucking gorgeous. Like gorgeous enough for fucking. I mean I knew that when I saw him in his fireworks undies before but I didn't get to watch him sleep like that and the softness in his mouth and the way his hand hangs over the side of his cot totally relaxed. It sends little flips and flops all through my abdomen centering around one part of me that is suddenly very vocally reminding me that I married this man and so far have nothing to show for it but could probably collect right now if I would stop staring and just strip down and join him.

I think I might be drooling. Nope. My imagination.

I am definitely getting wet, just not on my chin.

And then my hand loses all control and I drop the cup I'm holding and hot coffee splashes across the shop floor, scalding my leg in a pattern of mockery and spoiled daydreams.

I can't keep the pout out of my voice when I say, "Damn."

Chapter Twenty-Eight

NICOLA

I WAKE to a soft expletive and blink under bright lights and there she is.

My wife.

Fuck.

Every time I think that a little burst of panic erupts deep inside me, but it's nothing compared to that other feeling — the feeling of being stripped naked in front of those vows I took. The thought of trying to keep them is at once both electrifying and upsetting. I've been trying to shove it away from me since the moment their significance became real.

I sit up, rubbing my eyes. I didn't get enough sleep last night. Or the night before. I packed my entire house. Dumped most of it. Put some in storage. The buyers want it early if at all possible and now they'll get it early. My parents' things have been brought to Cedar Ridge — their new long-term care home. I hate it and all its sparkling perfection. Hate it nearly as much as my father did who let out a stream of curses in Serbian when I helped him to his room there. But he calmed down when he found out that he could visit my mom every day. Now that he's under proper care, the constraints have been lifted.

"You torture me," he told me and it broke my heart. "Why do you do this to me?"

"Because someone has to," I'd said shortly.

And then I'd given him his baseball card collection, his books of photos, and his favorite Western novels and gone back to packing and cleaning until I finally finished and realized I had nowhere to stay the night except my shop.

And here I am, being woken by the Goddess of Fury under the bright LED lights of my shop.

"'Morning," I say to her, still too muzzy with sleep to say much else. She's beautiful. Her scowl is brighter than the lights. I find myself smiling dreamily at it.

"I want answers," she says, and is she ... is she blushing?

I nod carefully. Of course, she wants answers. Everyone does. I saw paperwork in my inbox from Big Daddy Boom. He wants answers, too, though I haven't found the time to give them.

I reach for my phone which should be in my pocket. But ... oh. I had forgotten that I'd stripped naked to go to bed. I feel myself flush as I remember that I was out of clean clothes and I didn't want to sleep in what I was wearing.

I look down. A scrap of sleeping bag is working very hard to cover me up. It's not sufficient.

I look up, and a pair of dancing brown eyes is looking back, and I have to swallow at how they darken with interest. I guess this explains the blush. What would I do if our positions were reversed? If it were her here naked on this cot and me who had discovered her.

I swallow and suddenly the scrap of sleeping bag doesn't seem to be doing its job at all. I hitch it up around me to cover a bit more and she smirks from behind those dark glasses.

Dammit. She's caught me.

Basically naked.

With an erection just for her.

Well, I can't talk to her like this. I reach for my clothing on the floor beside me, but she's too quick. She kicks them away.

"I want answers, Nicola."

"To which questions?" I ask, tiredly. In the sleeping bag, my body is reminding me that it wants something, too, and it's not answers.

Her expression is entirely too serious. "Why haven't you called or texted me in two days? I'm your wife."

I make a waving motion with my hand. It's not that I don't think it's a good question. It's just that there's so much to explain and my head is foggy with the two hours — three? — of sleep I managed to wrangle. Maybe she'd agree to climb in here with me and we could sleep for a while and answer questions later.

"Don't brush me off," she says, bottom lip trembling slightly. "You owe me an explanation for this."

I make another grab for my clothes and she kicks them further away.

"I'm not letting you have those until you answer my questions."

There's something about the way she stands with her hand splayed out over her hip that riles me. Should I sit here submissively in my sleeping bag, huddled against her gaze, and answer her questions? Probably. But it's been a week. And I don't feel like it. What I feel like is riling up my wife a bit and reminding her that she did marry me, and that means she has *me* as a husband. Not some nice, meek man. Me. Thorny, problematic, and difficult as I may be.

Oh, yeah, and with a raging erection on top of all that.

So, instead, I drop the sleeping bag and leisurely stand.

"If you want to play it that way," I drawl. "You can have answers to *all* your questions."

I love the way her eyes widen as my sleeping bag falls and her gaze lands on me in all my naked glory. Her aviators betray her, slipping down her nose enough for me to see her eyes widen, slip down to where *all* of me is standing at full alert, and then fly back up to my face so they can take in my smirk.

"How's your blood pressure?" I ask.

"Just fine," she sniffs, pushing the aviators back up and trying to look cool as a glacier. But her cheeks are flushed and even from here, I can see her breath making her chest heave. I like that.

"I want answers, too," I say, stretching. Her glasses slip again and this time she snatches them off her face, fumbling adorably, and jamming them onto the top of her head. "What exactly does this marriage entail."

She has to swallow before she can answer, but she manages a light tone with a slight sting and I'm proud of her. That's some fine work under pressure.

"Oh, you know," she says, appearing breezy even though her breath hitches slightly, betraying her. "Marriage things. Like calling to tell me what's happening and not leaving me to guess for days at a time."

But I'm not letting her off that easily.

"Like sex?" I ask, lifting an eyebrow.

She licks her lips and her eyes dart down and I can't help my reaction to that or how I have to bite my lip when her eyes land on me.

"Ummm," she manages, which is pretty good, under the circumstances.

"I mean, if I'm committing to marriage things, then it's all the things, right?" I say slowly as her eyes run up and down my body. She's certainly not shy about taking her fill, though her eyes are big and her knuckles gripping an empty coffee cup have gone pale. The cup starts to crumple in her grip.

Honestly, I don't know where I find the confidence for this, but teasing Ada is like coffee in the morning. I've begun to crave it.

"I guess," she says.

A rumbling growl slips from my throat before I can stop it. But her reaction isn't nervous. Instead, she shifts her weight ... toward me.

I freeze. I was teasing. And despite my body's enthusiasm, I did not expect a warm response. I feel my breath hitch in my throat and my hands tremble slightly.

Confident, Nicola. Stay confident.

But when she crosses the floor all the way to me and reaches out to trail a finger from my collar bone down my chest, over one nipple, and then along my ribs and down to my hip bone — well, I'm body filler under her spatula. She can mold me, shape me, scrape me across the floor if she wants. I can't quite catch my breath again.

"I suppose sex would be agreeable," she says like it's brunch we're talking about and not our naked bodies pressed against each other. Like she's totally unaffected while I so very clearly ... am not. "But next time you text me if I'm not going to see you for hours, never mind days."

I clear my throat, "Yes."

She smirks, like she knows just exactly how she's flipped the tables on me, winding me up the way I was trying to do to her. Her fingertip is still on my hip. I feel desire surging down the length of me as every sense tries to concentrate on that fingertip.

I need to take back control of this situation as quickly as I can before she has me entirely in the grip of her pretty little fingertips. Ungh.

"Breakfast," I say huskily. "My treat. Let's celebrate. After all, we are partners now."

She laughs, low and husky. "Ah Nicola, you have no idea."

Chapter Twenty-Nine

ADA

I can't stop thinking of Nicola naked. Not even when I'm driving him to the breakfast place he likes — yeah, for some reason he insisted I drive — and I somehow almost blow a red light before his high-pitched screech brings me back to my senses. I suppose I could spend some time detailing how he looked or acting all shocked about his big dick, but seriously, if anyone has Big Dick Energy, it's Nicola so that's really no surprise, and frankly, I hate it when girls pretend to be surprised that men's anatomy acts as advertised. Yeah, it's big. Get over it, honey.

Was he gorgeous? Yes. But thousands of other men would look just as good naked. It's not how good he looks that's killing me. Nope — okay, it's nice, alright? There, I admitted it. But let's get back to the point. What stunned me about Nicola was that vulnerability in his eyes when I touched him. It was like I wasn't running my finger down his body but down his soul and I wanted to keep my finger there forever and just keep drinking all that Nicola in through his wide-open eyes.

If Nicola is a flavor it's black coffee. Bitter. Hot. Sharp. And it's my exact flavor. I want to drink it every day.

The fact that he's basically challenging me to fuck him and like it, only adds to that. He's pretending to be confident and strong but underneath I see all his uncertainty and desire and it's a heady caffeine-laden mix that I want to sip on all day long.

We get to the breakfast place without any real incident and order. It's a pretty little cafe where you eat outdoors at tiny black tables. I love it instantly and when Nicola suggests the pastries, I agree. They smell like heaven. There's an apple strudel drizzled with cream cheese frosting that might make my eyes go as wide as his were this morning. He has eggs. I appreciate that he's making an effort not to eat the devil gluten that turns him into a monster.

"What's going on with you?" I ask when we finally settle in to eat and drink coffee. Coffee. Like my hot Nicola. I take it black today just because.

"What do you mean?" He tries to shrug me off but I level a stare at him.

"Mr. I-do-everything-perfectly and I-care-more-than-you-do hasn't been to work in two days. I sandblasted the body of the Silver Bullet with your ground glass supplies and you didn't even send me an irritated text."

He flushes. And then it all pours out. His parents. His house. Resettling them. By the time he's done, he's shredding a napkin up into pieces small enough for an ant colony and I have to grab his hands to make him stop. When he meets my eyes he looks like a lost kid hoping a grown-up will help him find his way home.

"Nicola," I say gently. "Are you okay?"

"I ..." he runs his free hand over his face, but the hand I'm holding tightens like he doesn't want to let me go. "I don't think I am."

"I don't think you are either," I say grimly. "You just lost your family, sort of."

"Yeah." He looks away with red-rimmed eyes. He's trying not to cry, I think. It's a crazy look on a man as strong as him.

"And your home," I press.

"It was just a house," he says scornfully.

"You're sleeping on a camping cot in your garage," I say drily. "And you slept beside the Silver Bullet body and didn't notice that I'd sandblasted it."

He swallows. He knows as well as I do that it's a bad sign.

"Enough," I say firmly. "Wallowing doesn't suit you. Today, we work on the project. Tonight you come home with me and Pops."

"Pops?" he says, eyebrows raising.

"Not the sexiest roommate," I say keeping my detached tone. It's the only way I can keep from cracking at the distress I see in his face. I don't like seeing him upset. I don't like seeing him breaking apart. I think I can limit the damage if I take his care on myself. "Pops brews a good coffee, though. Just, please, I'm begging you, don't ask him for anything or he's gonna clean us out."

"About that," he says, looking awkward. "It seems like maybe you and Pops finances are intermingled."

"Yeah," I say, frowning. "I made the mistake of making our accounts joint when I was starting out my business."

"I was thinking," he says, "that maybe you'd like to have a joint account with me. And we can tuck away your show earnings there — if we get the show. Kind of like a haven for them. I won't touch them. They'll be safe. And you'll have a buffer between you and the bills. And until the show money gets there, my house money will be available for what you need."

Now I'm the one blinking back moisture in my eyes as his words hit me like a punch to the chest.

"You'd ... you'd open yourself up like that to me?" I ask and his eyes soften and warm for me in a way I've never seen before.

"I think there's not much I wouldn't do for you, Ada Ford," he says, and the way his blue eyes bore into me when he says it makes it sound like a challenge rather than just something a man says to a girl. It sounds like he wants me to push that to the limit and see how far it goes. I think I will.

I feel shockingly soft towards this man by the time we leave. Like something has been settled between us — some kind of understanding that involves having someone on which to lean. It's so new that I don't want to pressure it with names or definitive words, but it holds me and when I look at Nicola, I see something new in the curve of his shoulders and the way the corner of his mouth ticks up when he looks at me. It's something precious. I kind of can't believe it's mine.

We work all afternoon together and I'm actually not surprised that we work well together. That we tease and joke and laugh easily. That the metal work flies along perfectly. We film it all and send it to BOOM and post our own teasers to our channels and I think I'm actually enjoying this. I think I could maybe live like this with him. Is that crazy?

It's crazy, right?

We get pizza delivered so we can work into the evening and it's well past dark when we realize it's time to pack it in.

"We did well today," I tell Nicola with a grin.

He shrugs, "It was adequate."

And I freeze.

"What?" He freezes, too, like he thinks we're both in danger. "Did I leave the welding gas on?"

"You said the work on the Silver Bullet was adequate," I say, frowning as I search his face.

"Because it is," he says, with a shrug. "The job was done to an adequate level of quality."

"It looks *great*," I say, annoyed now.

"I've seen better." He pauses. "Why aren't you moving."

"Nicola Petrovic," I say, crossing my arms over my chest. "Do you know that you have described my work as 'adequate' in the articles you wrote for publication?"

He looks confused. "Well, yeah. It was adequate. So I said that. By the way, are you taking my name?"

"What?" I've never heard my voice in that register before. I could be a cartoon villain.

"Petrovic. It's a good name. Think about it."

"Good?" I echo. "That's a bit extreme, don't you think? Adequate might be more accurate."

"Fine. Adequate. It's a very adequate name that you'd look great in," he says, smiling so hard a dimple shows and then he hops in the passenger seat of my car like he belongs there.

This man. I swear.

Chapter Thirty

NICOLA

THIS MIGHT HAVE BEEN the best day I've had all year. Ada is so much more than adequate. She's great. Amazing. She has this hilarious way of settling her aviators over her nose right before she makes a particularly cutting joke and if her hands are full, she'll wait until they're empty so she can do the glasses thing first. She's crazy sharp. She anticipates all my moves before I make them, and her work setting up cameras and moving them around is pure professionalism. If we weren't already married, I might propose just so I can have her as a business partner.

It's tough to admit this, but Ada? Yeah, I could build an actual life with her. We're married after all. Is it so crazy to contemplate weaving something fresh with her? She might take some convincing, obviously. I might need to think about how to do that. But after today? *I'm* convinced. I've decided I want this. This easy working relationship. This constant teasing. This reliable other person who can actually accomplish things. This smoke show who looks just as amazing with a streak of dust across her face as she does dressed to go to a billionaire's house.

It's not until we're pulling into the parking lot of her family business — there are just three spaces in front of the shop, and one is already full with an ancient Jeep Wagoneer — that it hits me we're headed to her home. Where I'm going to stay with her. And I'd better get this night right if I want a long-term shot with this woman. I don't know where the landmines might be buried, but she will, and she'll be watching for the second I step on one.

I can feel the panic clawing up my throat, but I don't want to look scared. That would be decidedly unmanly. I should have thought this through before we arrived. I'm not the kind of guy girls bring home to their parents. Amber and her parents were estranged, so it never came up. Even though I've met Pops, I have no idea what to do if I see him again — *when* I see him again. After all, this is his house.

Ada must read some of that on my face because she opens her trunk as soon as she's out of the car and shoves a duffel at me. It's mine. I stare at her over it, feeling as stupid as I must look.

"I took the liberty of grabbing your bag for you. It feels too light. Did you have another one at the shop?"

She's *taking care of me.* That's … it melts me inside all over again. She's the sun and I'm the candy bar someone left on the dash of their car.

"No," I say gruffly, trying like hell not to reveal how much she's under my skin. I shove the bag under my arm and move to lead the way before I remember I have no idea where I'm going. "I left most of my stuff in storage for now."

"Even your clothes?" She asks with a raised eyebrow. "How are you supposed to work with clients if you have no clothes?"

"It didn't seem to be a problem for you when you wandered in the shop this morning," I say.

She frowns, and because I've been with her all day, I know this frown.

"Just say it," I tease. "You don't need the aviators down first. You can try a zinger without a shield up."

If anything, it makes her scowl harder. Achievement unlocked. I've discovered the next level Ada scowl. And it's just as amazing as I thought it would be.

I laugh, but I don't laugh for long. The tension swallows the laughter.

"Are you sure you want me here?"

"If that's you trying to escape because now I know that 'adequate' for you means, 'fucking amazing' to anyone else and the secret is out that you're my biggest fan, then think again, buddy."

I feel the heat in my cheeks. She knows.

But then she laughs like she's joking and she leads me around the back and up an outdoor staircase — recently painted, I note — to a landing above. I guess she still doesn't realize exactly how obsessed I've been with her even before our disastrous, or maybe fortuitous? — journey into the woods of northern California together. If she had any idea how long I've been checking her out with sidelong glances, she might make me pay for it.

"We're here," she says and when she opens the door, I swallow and follow her.

Pops is there, sitting at a table playing solitaire and nursing what looks like a beer and smells more like vinegar.

"Kombucha? At this hour?" Ada asks him, striding over to press a kiss to his forehead. She doesn't get to see his faint smile because he erases it before she can.

"It helps with digestion," Pops says and then fixes me with a long look. I rub the back of my neck and look away. It gives me a chance to take in Ada and Pops' apartment.

The entrance emerges straight into the small kitchen fitted with post-war cabinets which have been painted white recently. You can tell because they didn't remove the hardware to paint them and the paint is lumpy over the hinges. A tiny single kitchen sink and barely enough Formica counter to prepare sandwiches make up the rest of the kitchen.

Pops is sitting at a round wooden table that someone painted pineapple yellow — any guesses on who? — that's surrounded by four chairs also painted, but this time a very pale turquoise. There are tea towels with roosters on them hanging from the handle of the oven door, and a broom and trash can are in one corner. It's tidy and ancient.

To the left, the kitchen opens through a double doorway to a living room the exact same size fitted with mid-century olive-green couches that I'm pretty sure have been sitting in those exact spots since they were purchased. Above the couch is a macrame owl hanging on the wall and staring at me with its wooden bead eyes.

"It used to be two apartments," Pops says, seeing me looking. "Each one had a kitchen slash living space, a bedroom, and a bathroom. My dad opened the wall between and made them one big apartment. It's where I grew up, where I moved *my* new bride when I got married, and where I brought Ada home from the hospital."

I nod. I never know what to say in these kinds of family situations. "Sorry for your loss?" Or, "such a nice place to grow up?" But is it? I don't know. It feels very ... ingrown ... to me to live where your parents lived and their parents lived. But maybe that's just because I've moved to two different countries in my lifetime and left everything over and over again. Like I did yesterday when I finished packing up my house. Maybe staying in one place for a few generations would be a nice relief from that.

"Where are your parents?" Pops asks.

"Don't bother him about his parents," Ada scolds him. "You know perfectly well he had to put them in a long-term care facility. Look at his face. It's got these worry lines because you had to go and bring it up."

She presses a finger to my forehead between my eyes and I startle.

"See?" She frowns at her father.

He spreads his hands wide like he's trying to make peace. "I'm just asking which one. Maybe I want to visit."

"Cedar Ridge," I say woodenly. It still doesn't feel real. "But Mom won't move there until she's well enough, so for now it's just Dad."

He nods.

"You are the one who said you wanted him living here," Ada reminds her father, opening the fridge and holding up a soda to me with a question in her eyes. I wave a hand, dismissing the offer, my eyes jumping back and forth between her and her father. He's the one who wanted me here?

I suddenly feel less comfortable than before. I definitely shouldn't have come. There's a very nice camping cot with my name on it at the shop.

"I'll just take the couch then," I say calmly and start to walk toward the double doors but I have to stop when Pops stands up suddenly, blocking my way.

"No," he says shaking his head. "You're married now. There are responsibilities to being a husband."

I nod. "Don't worry. I will work hard. Provide for her. Be there in emergencies."

"You don't need to make those promises," Ada complains from beside the sink. She's washing up some dishes with the kind of speed that suggests this is a timed race. "I can look after myself. I don't need a man to do it."

Pops shakes his head and the amused look on his face makes me frown. What's so funny? I just promised to do everything a father wants for his daughter, right? So he can't be laughing at me and he'd better not be laughing at Ada and her bold declarations or I'll set him straight pretty fast. If she wants to be independent, I'm not going to take that away. Besides, she's been taking care of him all this time so she clearly does look after things on her own.

"Being there in emergencies is fine," Pops says, looking skeptically at me. "But a wife needs her husband to be there all the time."

"Pops," Ada warns. She's drying her hands now.

"Okay." This is the awkward conversation I never wanted. "Don't worry. I'll be here when she gets up in the morning. We're working together, after all, and we have a lot to do."

"And what?" Pops asks, arms crossed over his chest. "She sleeps alone at night in a cold bed?"

I feel my mouth drop open.

"Pops!" Ada protests, but she takes my duffel bag from my hands and strides briskly to the tiny hall off the kitchen, and opens one of the doors. The other door is already ajar and inside I see a pedestal sink, which means she's taken my bag to her bedroom.

You know that phrase "broke into a cold sweat"? I had no idea that it meant an immediate thing. I feel like I have a personal sprinkler system installed in my body.

I swallow awkwardly.

"Sorry, what?" I ask, my Canadian raising creeping to the forefront. I'm apologizing to him for his ridiculous behavior. Damn you, Canadian school teachers! Was that the thing you had to drill into me? It couldn't just be adding "U's" to every other word?

Pops hands are on his hips and his eyes bore into mine. "You married my daughter. She did that for you so you could keep your parents around. Admirable. But you aren't going to use her more than that."

"I don't plan to —" I begin but he talks right over me.

"She is your wife and you'll treat her like a wife with all the privileges that come with that. You'll make sure she's happy. You'll be around. You'll eat pancakes with her family."

I run a hand over my face. Is he planning to monitor all of this? My cheeks flame at the thought of going into that bedroom with Ada with her father out here knowing ... damn it. I just need him to stop. Like right now. No. Five minutes ago.

I raise a hand and deliver my best glare. It's a good one. I know. It usually silences people.

"It's taken care of. No need to deliver a speech. Your daughter will have the husband she needs."

Wow. Did I just promise that? I feel ill. Not because I dislike the idea of eating breakfasts with Ada and cuddling in her bed. I mean, I could really get used to that. But there have been so many changes and adding this one more thing makes me miss my lonely cot in the shop where I could moan miserably if I wanted to with no one to hear.

I'm suddenly very tired.

I don't bother to say good night to him or anything else. I just stalk into the room Ada went into and close the door behind me, spinning, before I even look at the room, to set my forehead against the wall and breathe out a long sigh.

I feel a small hand rest on my back.

"You should have married the dentist." My words come out muffled. Probably just because I'm close to the wall. Not because there's any emotion going on here.

"Sure, Fireworks," she says in a soothing tone like she's trying to talk me off a ledge.

"I think it shouldn't have to be said out loud, but obviously there will be no sex."

Her hand on my back freezes.

"Your dad is out there!" I'm annoyed. She didn't have expectations, did she? Because if she did, she probably should have done something about him first, like a dog you warn people about before they come over. "Don't touch his food dish or he'll bite." In this case, it could be, "Don't walk toward the living room or he'll decide to monitor your physical relationship with his daughter."

Her whisper in my ear is a hiss. "Who says there won't be sex?"

Now I'm the one to freeze. Apparently, my concerns have not been shared with the regions of my body responsible for sex and they have decided this is good news and that they should stand by for instructions.

"But not tonight," Ada says gently, taking my hand in hers and turning me so I can see her bedroom.

It's pretty, of course. Just like her. Tidy and organized and decorated in bright colors and patterns. She leads me to her huge bed — is it king-sized? — pulls me down to sit on the edge of it, and pulls my hoodie and shirt over my head in one smooth movement. I watch her every move utterly stunned. She said no sex, but she's undressing me, her fingers grazing my skin and leaving tiny trails of goosebumps, her eyes bright and delighted by what she sees.

I swallow, willing myself not to touch her back. If I do, I won't be able to stop touching and there is *no way* I am fucking her in her family home with her father out there.

She smirks at me like she knows exactly what I'm thinking as she yanks off my shoes and socks, and then shoves me backward so that I collapse into her soft bed full of pillows and brightly colored patchwork quilts.

I have to swallow again. "Ada, I —"

"Shhh," she whispers as her fingers fumble with the button and zipper on my jeans.

My whole body is flushing, I think. Her soft touches along my abdomen as she works to open my belt and fly are like some kind of hypnotism. I gasp as she shucks my jeans off and it's pretty obvious that despite my protests, my body wants her and wants her very badly.

"You need sleep," she says, tossing my jeans on the floor and pulling her quilts over me.

And I know I shouldn't be disappointed because seriously I am *not* having sex with her in her father's house — yeah, keep telling yourself that, Nicola — but I still kind of feel sad. Even when my eyes drift shut and my body feels heavy, I still am. Until I feel her warmth as she tucks herself around my back and slings an arm over my side. I catch her hand in mine, glorying in the soft warmth of it, and with that gentle clasp, I finally find enough peace to fall asleep.

Chapter Thirty-One

ADA

IT'S GOT to be fattening to eat pancakes every day, right? And yet, somehow I can't make myself care. Nicola has lived with us for five days. Five days of pancake breakfasts that Pops supervises with a Marine Corps patented stare while I try to tell them both that Nicola should have fruit instead because he's gluten intolerant. Five days of working from the minute breakfast is over to the minute we fall in bed at night. We did take time to open that joint checking account and Nicola made me keys for literally everything he owns — a truck and a storage unit. He's taking this marriage seriously. I didn't really expect that.

Mostly, we work on the Silver Bullet. The project is going well — the body is in primer now and the parts order arrived yesterday. Each of us tries to carve out a few hours in the morning for our own projects before we move to our shared project. It's frenetic and exhausting.

But in the middle of it all, there are glorious moments. That first night cuddled with Nicola, I barely slept. I've never had a man sleeping in my bed before and it turns out, I love it. He's warm and herbal-scented and his breath and heartbeat lull me. I get to press my cheeks to his naked skin and he doesn't complain. I get to weave my fingers between his and hold on tight. If I wake in the night, I don't listen for trouble like I used to, or toss and turn, worried about debts. Instead, I sink into the soft flesh of Nicola Petrovic and breathe him in, and it's like some kind of tranquility drug. I'm a complete addict. I cannot get enough. Sometimes, when I have a second, I daydream about what a daytime nap would be like with him, and my heart flutters hummingbird-wild with just the thought of it.

And there are the showers. We aren't showering together, so get your mind out of my bathroom. Well, we aren't yet. But just hearing him in there is winding up my levels of frustration. Through the wall, I can hear the sound of the water catching on him and the sudsy soaping going on in there. I can hear his electric shaver going — yes, he does shave. He just doesn't shave all the way, settling for buzzing it down to the lowest setting on his electric buzzer. It grows back by lunch. I can hear the swish of his towel when he gets out. And just when I think I'm going to start drooling, he usually pads out in bare feet with a towel slung around his hips, and I just want to reach out with one finger and tuuuug and see what happens. Not that I haven't seen what's under that towel before, but now it's on my mind *all the time.*

I drew a pattern for seat upholstery yesterday and when it was done I had to tear it up into itty bitty pieces. Unconsciously, I'd shaped the pattern exactly like *him,* if you know what I mean. I still blush whenever I look at the diamond pattern I went with instead.

There's also the fact that apparently, he has old-fashioned manners. He waits respectfully for me to be ready before he eats. He holds doors open. He folds his clothing and keeps them neatly to one side of the room. As he's leaving a room, he asks if he can get me anything. It's considerate. I think Pops thinks it's an act he's putting on for him, but I know Nicola. He doesn't put on acts.

And there are the looks. His gaze is so heated whenever he looks at me that we could use it in place of the shop plasma cutter. And he's looking at me *all the time.* I can't so much as grab a shop towel without seeing his eyes running over me like an invisible caress. I think I caught him breathing me in the other day when we were waiting in line at a fast food place together. It's unsettling and distracting and so damn sexy that I might spontaneously combust.

I'm dying here.

"Ada," he says whenever he catches my gaze on him, saying my name so slowly that it's like he's caressing *it*, too.

Combined, these things are slowly killing me. But worst of all, he hasn't laid hands on me. Oh, he holds my hands. He lets me hold him and cuddle him, but he keeps his calloused fingers all to himself. Apparently, he was serious about not having sex with me in my father's house. Or maybe he's never going to have sex with me at all. He's just going to ignore the evidence of his attraction that I see every time I look for it. Some people do that, right? They live lives of self-discipline that exclude all sex. Is that what Nicola is going to do — even though we got married? It is, after all, a marriage with a purpose, and sex is not it. I try not to think about that last option, try to persuade myself it's merely the first because when I think of him living with me for years and *not* putting those hands all over me, little whines tend to escape me and people are noticing.

"It's sinful to be that hot," Jasmin whispers to me on the third day as she pretends to be working. Nicola has come to pick me up to bring me to the *Knockin' Rods* shop but he's distracted by a strange engine noise in the Shelby that Pops needs help with and they both have their heads under the hood, mirror images of one another as they squabble over how to diagnose it.

"Like, as in literally a sin that God will be mad about?" I

whisper back. "I don't see how. Wouldn't it be his fault for creating that man in the first place?"

"That's exactly what I mean," Jasmin hisses back. "He's like a test or something. Like a perfectly sinful temptation sent to make sure you stay on the straight and narrow."

"Trust me," I whisper back, eyes running down Nicola's long legs and lingering on his ass. "I'm feeling extremely straight right now."

"Have you already done ... you know ..." She waggles her eyebrows. "Because if you haven't, then you should get on that."

"He's my husband." I roll my eyes. "We can do whatever we want."

"Then why haven't you?" She sounds actually hurt by this, like it's physically painful to think about Nicola not being with me. Actually, I'd better not dwell on that because it totally is.

"Stop whispering about my husband and tell me about the handbag design. Is it working out?"

I managed to turn her to more productive conversation, but at the same time I agree. I should get on that. After all, he's my husband and it's considered normal for wives to want to be with their husbands, right? But also, he could just as easily slip out of my life as he slipped in and I'll have lost my chance to be with him. Maybe even forever. *That* seems like a sin.

Somehow, he feels forbidden to me because if he wanted this, too, wouldn't he have already made a move? Wouldn't his hands have roamed while we cuddled in bed, or "oops" he could come into the room and the towel could fall, or "oops" maybe in the shop he'd press up against me without realizing it as we studied the same thing on the Silver Bullet and I'd feel his hard cock pressed against my butt and I'd gasp dramatically and next thing I knew he'd be spinning me around and pressing me against the wall and ... Or maybe those are just my fantasies.

Which is why it's the fifth day of us living together — the seventh day of our marriage, if you're asking, that he suddenly disappears. No text. No heads up. He's just gone while I'm assembling the front end with the new parts we have and the recently sandblasted and painted frame and axle. I mean, I can do this myself but we're supposed to do it together and I think the camera is picking up on my annoyance.

I text him.

Something wrong with your parents?

If there is, I'll feel bad for being annoyed with him. I drop my work, agitated, and make my way over to where I left the boxes with the BOOM branded products. In all the chaos I still haven't unpacked them and I feel a sudden urge to do something violent like pop bubble wrap and cut into boxes.

No, he texts back.

Okay then. I'm definitely annoyed and I'm allowed to be. I rip the boxes open and begin to sort through. There are T-shirts and mug cozies and coasters and stickers and at the very bottom, there's a large white box.

Where are you? I text him.

I open the box as I wait for an answer. It's … is this a box of one thousand individually wrapped bright orange condoms with the BOOM logo printed on them?

Exactly *how* were they planning for us to display this particular product? My face is so hot that I could cook our breakfast pancakes on it. I sift through the box and find a packing list, running my finger down. Oh. One box of decals. The product number is only one digit different. There's been a mix-up.

I stare at the condoms. They're mocking me in all their orange boldness. "You'll never need to use us," they say.

Annoyed, I cross the shop to where Nicola has parked his truck in the other bay and I toss the box in his backseat. Nicola can figure them out. Maybe they'll give him some ideas. Or at least maybe they just won't mock him like they're mocking me.

My phone buzzes. *Cool your engine, Pineapple. I'll just be a few minutes.*

My engine is most certainly not cool. I get back to work, assembling with maybe more energy than is strictly necessary. I'm feeling flushed and irritated when the shop door finally opens and he announces himself.

"Impatient much?" His eyes are twinkling. He looks impossibly good in the natural light that comes through his clouded glass shop doors. His smile quirks in the corners, forming dimples I can only barely see behind his scruff. I'd like to put my fingerprints right into the divots they make.

I wipe my face with the back of my wrist, hoping it's not as dirty as my hands.

"I'm only impatient when I've been left to do a job on my own that was meant for two," I say pointedly. The cameras are still rolling but I don't think he can wait for me to shut them off. The excitement is rolling off him like waves. "Just tell me."

His grin deepens — rare for my serious Nicola.

"I have a present for you."

"A present?" I scowl suspiciously. I know this one. People give presents when they want something from me. Usually donuts. "It's not a donut is it?"

"Of course not," he says. "I'm off those."

He's not. I saw him eat one yesterday and he still gets cranky when he eats them. Same with the pancakes my Pops makes.

"Wash your hands and I'll show you," he says and there's a challenge in his voice.

"How about you show me and I'll decide whether it's worth washing up for." I don't like backing down easily but he just stands there, unwilling to bend, watching me like he enjoys the view. I enjoy what I see, too. I don't mind standing here, watching. I slip my aviators up onto my head so that I can watch even better and his expression twists so that he can disguise a laugh.

"Trust me," he says, licking his lips. "It's worth it."

The lip lick does me in, but I don't dare let him know that. I settle for a dignified hand washing, trying not to betray how much that lip lick turns me on.

When I get back, he looks at me blankly like he doesn't know what I'm doing here.

"Can I help you?" he asks.

"You said you had something for me?" I cross my arms over my chest and raise an eyebrow at him. I like how his eyes linger where my arms are crossed.

It makes his eyes brighter and his throat bob. "Close your eyes, Pineapple."

I do — reluctantly. But not until I get both my aviators and my scowl well in place. The moment they close, I feel him take my hand, and then ... he slips something on my finger. He must have found his mood ring in the trash where I threw it. Oops.

I can feel myself flushing and I'm trying to think of how to apologize. I've hurt his feelings. Is this why he hasn't touched me yet?

He interrupts my sudden freak-out and his voice is surprisingly warm and deep. "It was my grandmother's. In the old country. My parents were saving it for me. I got it resized to the size of that mood ring when I saw that it fit your finger."

My eyes fly open and I'm so stunned that my aviators fall off my nose and Nicola has to catch them with a quick snatch. He puts them delicately on top of my head for me.

Our eyes meet and there's something in his gaze that looks like ... expectation. Hope, maybe? It makes my heart speed up. He's feeling something. For me. For us.

"This is ... it's ..."

"A moonstone," he says, looking shy. Shy! My heart flips over. Nicola shy is apparently my kryptonite. It makes my mouth dry. "Apparently, in the old days, they used just about any stone. It didn't have to be a diamond."

"It's beautiful," I say, staring at him instead of the ring. And I think I might be talking about him, too.

"Maybe you should look at it," he says, but he doesn't sound upset that I'm not looking. His gaze has darkened, thickened into something deeper.

I finally glance down at the shimmering white stone. Little hints of milk blue and blush want to show through the white. It *is* beautiful. It looks magnificent against my skin.

"It's yours now," he says running his hand uncomfortably through his hair. It makes all the muscles in that arm and shoulder pop and I'm staring at how they move before I realize it.

I start to bite my lip.

I suck in a breath.

I want to press my face to the smooth warmth of his arm. I want to scatter little hot kisses along it. I want to taste him — forbidden or not.

And then he crosses to me so suddenly it's like he's a predator pouncing and he catches my surprised lips in his, and I'm thinking about five nights spent crushed against him, about warm skin and hot desires. I'm thinking of him standing right here in nothing but his skin. I'm thinking of how his body responded to my attention. And then I'm not thinking at all, as I lose myself in his kiss.

It's all Nicola. It's insistent and sweet, gentle but wanting, bitter and delicious, and I want more and more of it. I suck softly on his bottom lip, tasting him in all his black-coffee splendor. I'm memorizing the warmth and feel of his mouth as he curves it against mine, as he lets out a half-strangled moan into my mouth, memorizing how he moves as if arguing his case for affection. As if he needs to convince me it's a good idea.

I encourage him with a sigh of my own, with my hands reaching up to tangle in his hair. I press up on my toes as his hands wrap around my hips. His fingertips dig into the softness he finds, kneading slightly as if he can convince me to soften for him, to open up to his offering, to loosen all my tension and let him deep within.

He can, actually, if only he knew it.

"Do you like it?" he whispers into my kiss, his lips grazing mine with each syllable. "Do you want this?"

"Yes," I say into his mouth and he catches my yes with my lips and twists his tongue through it and somehow that makes it the sexiest thing I've ever said. He's intoxicating me, making me want him more and more with every teasing kiss, every gasp of breath. I'm tangled up in him. I'm unraveling and opening, unfurling all my ragged edges. Does he even know what he does to me?

Maybe he does know it, because he pulls back, lips swollen with my kisses, and lets me go, and just as I stumble forward to catch him back, he leans toward the first camera and slowly, agonizingly slowly. He shuts it off.

"What we're about to do, Ada Ford," he says slowly, drawing out every word. "Is only for us."

"*What* are we about to do, Nicola Petrovic?" I ask, a little breathlessly. "Because it had better involve fucking me very adequately, or I'm giving back this ring of yours."

Chapter Thirty-Two

HE LOOKS at me with purpose in his eyes, but I don't think he realizes how shy he looks when he bends over the next camera and looks up through his eyelashes at me. It's so devastating. So heart-stoppingly gorgeous. I have to swallow as he moves to cover the lens with a cap as he turns it off.

There's only one more. He's behind it when he slides his shirt off, eyes still stuck on me like they don't dare release me.

He's beautiful without his shirt, the light hair of his body forming modest trails. My eyes run over him greedily as if I can hold onto the sight of him and keep it all for myself.

My breath is uneven in my ears.

He sets his shirt aside and licks his lips and I know he's nervous and excited just like me because over the hammering of my heart, I hear his breath gasping through his lungs as he turns and bolts the shop door.

"Confidence suits you, Fireworks," I drawl. Trying so hard to maintain my illusion of cool calm while inside I'm melting, melting, melting.

He saunters over to his truck and leans against it like he's waiting for me to join him, like he knows all he has to do is stand in one spot, and eventually I'll come to him one way or another.

"My ring suits you, Ada Ford Petrovic," he says, smirking. "It suits you so well that I don't think you should wear anything else."

It's a dare, I can see that by how his lip curls, but I can also see that he wants it badly by how his jeans are suddenly way too tight.

I love it.

I love it so much.

I slip my shirt off slowly, making him watch me drag it over my skin, reveling in how his fists clench tightly before he seems to force them to loosen. I'm wearing my same pineapple bra he first saw me in and the sight of it again lights his face with a smile.

"I didn't agree to the last name," I say. But I really don't care. He can call me anything he wants, just as long as he stops teasing me and lets me feel his touch.

I walk toward him, and if I exaggerate my hip sway just a little, can anyone blame me? The way his face goes pink as he watches it is worth the extra time it takes to tease him.

"You will," he says a little bit huskily.

I'm right in front of him now and he leans forward and wraps his forearms under my bottom and lifts, and suddenly I'm off my feet and in his arms and I can't quite catch my breath as he hitches me against him and breathes into my hair like I'm life.

He holds me like I'm precious, like I'm breakable, like I'm all the water he has on a desert island and something about the vulnerability of it drives down into me and spirals in so deep that I know I can never hurt this man — never will, if I can help it. I want to guard all his secrets for him. I want to help carry him the way he's carrying me.

We're moving. I know we are, but I don't realize where he's

taking me until he opens the rear doors of his crew cab and sits me on the edge of the seat. He takes a moment to study my breasts which are right in front of his face and his expression screws up in adorable concentration.

"Solving a puzzle, Nicola?" I tease, but my hands have found the back of his head, and my fingertips, it would seem, are obsessed with the light, soft hairs on the back of his neck, and they can't seem to stop trailing through it again and again with soft, light caresses.

"Yes," he says in a manly growl.

"Do tell," I tease as my finger tips trace his collarbone and I smile my cat-ate-the-canary smile because this right here is making me happy in all the ways. My heart is happy, my mind is happy, even my mouth is happy as I lean in to press it to his forehead.

He has to clear his throat to talk, pausing just for a moment to press a gentle kiss to my brow, and I love it. I made Nicola Petrovic clear his throat. Mr. Control. My smile widens.

"I'm trying to figure out how to put both of them in my mouth at once."

I laugh then and the problem he's solving bounces enough that he makes an "uhh" sound and his eyes roll involuntarily. He laughs at himself ruefully and then leans down and I don't know what he's going to do until I feel my shoes being pulled off.

"Ada," he says as his fingers trail up my legs, skimming along the seams of my jeans and making my breath hitch.

"Yes?" I ask and I'm more breathless than I'd like. Those fingers pause and I pout, catching his eye to be sure he sees. Why stop there? It's still inches from the goal. I don't like it.

"I'd like to give you some constructive criticism." No one has ever said that to me before with so much sex in their voice.

"Wait," I say still pouting. "You're stopping to give me critique? Can't you just write an article for *Sex Today* about my adequate kissing technique and leave it at that?"

"Kissing? Oh no, it's much worse than that," he says, leaning in and even when I lean back in annoyance, he keeps leaning forward until he catches the lobe of my ear and he sucks it. And somehow the way his nose tickles my skin while he does that finds an ancient path right from my earlobe to my innermost parts and I clench so tight that I have to clench my jaw, too, to keep from making an embarrassing sound.

I place a hand on his chest and push him slightly back — sad to lose the intimacy of his caress even as I enjoy teasing him — and his smile is both devious and smoldering.

"Exactly what are you criticizing?" I ask, crossing my arms over my chest in a way that makes his breath hitch. I love that.

He reaches up and slips one of the straps of my bra off. It floats down my arm in a way that's so sensual that I almost shiver, but I won't give him the satisfaction. Not even when I see his gaze stuck on my parted lips.

"What?" I press.

He laughs deep in his throat. "Your shower technique."

"As you've never seen me shower, I don't think you've much grounds on which to criticize," I say, breathless, maybe, but undefeated.

He leans forward, slips my second strap down, and reverently kisses my shoulder.

"Perfect," he whispers.

"What's perfect?" My voice is barely louder than a breath.

"Your body is perfect, Ada. Absolutely perfect."

That pulls a gasp from me, because *nothing* is perfect to Nicola.

"Are you sure you don't mean 'adequate?'" I ask with a lifted brow but if he does much more of this to me my brain will melt and there won't be anymore fun comebacks.

He nods, looking a little stunned as he kisses his way down my arm, nuzzling his nose into the sensitive crook of my elbow before sliding a wet tongue to my wrist. He laughs again as if I am a secret he's keeping to himself.

"Can we get back to the critique," I ask, but my voice is choked and I can barely manage the words.

"It's the length I take issue with," he murmurs. "It's so long that it just builds and builds in my mind until all I can think of is you under that water washing this perfect body, and then I want to be the one to wash it, to slide my fingers all soapy and slick over every inch of you — and I do mean every inch, Ada."

He punctuates that with kicking off his boots, hitching my hips up in his grip, and sliding me backward along the seat so he can crawl up into the cab of the truck and hover over me. And he gently places a fingertip on the tip of my nose and slides it downward so that it meets my lips where I greet it with a kiss, slides over the peak of my chin, trails down my neck, gently circles the hollow of my collarbone, and moves further down to skim between my breasts and in a long, soft line to fall into my bellybutton and then slip from there under the waistband of my jeans and lower, yet, sliding under my lace panties and further still to where my body parts for him. His touch is feather-light and I ache for it as he stops to open my jeans and slide them from my hips and legs and toss them aside.

He's distracted for a moment, kissing the inside of my knee like it's better than those stupid powder donuts he loves, but a moment later his fingertip is back to my belly button and he's tracing his line again, down, down.

"It's too long, but it's also too short," he says, sternly. "Too short because it's not enough time for me to find any relief as I wait for you."

"I'll work on that," I say breathlessly and he huffs a laugh, bending to press a kiss to my belly button.

"Keep talking like that and I'm going to lose it right here," he says into my skin.

The thought of that makes my breathing hitch and my

eyelashes flutter. My body wants to be swept away by him. My mind, however, still wants answers.

"You touch me like you want me," I say, taking my aviators off my head and settling them up on top of his.

His mouth falls open like I've crowned him as king or something and his words gust out all tumbling over each other.

"I've always wanted you, from the second I first saw you," he says, and as if to punctuate, "saw you" that's the exact second that his finger slides into the spot where my folds meet and I hiss at the touch.

A tremulous smile plays on the corners of his lips for a moment as he stokes me long and slow, speaking in a low, deep voice that sounds like a pained confession.

"Why do you think I wrote those fucking articles about you. So many of them. I thought for sure you realized. That I was obsessed with seeing your work, with talking about it, with the idea of being near the person who made it."

And I want to answer him in some clever way but the things he's doing with the tips of his fingers under the veil of my lace underthings are so ridiculously intimate, so intensely pleasure-laden that I can't quite think of what to say. He leans forward, slowly, as if he's asking with his body if he can kiss me, which is kind of a silly thing to do when he's already making love to me with his clever fingers. I answer by curling up to meet him halfway and catching his face between my hands so I can kiss him as senseless as he has me.

"I thought you hated me," I say when I break away, breathless.

"I don't hate you," he sounds like he's choking on his words. I open his belt and his jeans and because he doesn't stop me or pause in what he's doing for me, I reach into the side access on his boxer briefs and I slip him out where I can play, too, running my fingers over him, learning his curve and length, enjoying the way he feels fitted into my hand.

"You're obsessed with me," I say, still stunned by this.

"Yes." The word is a gasp and I love the agonized look on his face when he says it. "I think I am."

I draw him close again with my hands, gentle but desperate, letting my nose nuzzle his as I find the angle I like and arch my back up so I can kiss him.

He moans into my kiss, and one of his hands breaks free, coming up to tangle in my hair as the other curls under my lower back to press me up to him and I feel like I can't get enough of his skin on mine, I can't cover enough ground with my hands and my lips.

We're on his rough truck seat and I find I don't care. We could be on the concrete floor and I wouldn't care. I just want all of him and I want it right now.

"It's entirely possible," I gasp, when our kiss lessens, "that I've become obsessed with you, too."

And I guess my words are also powerful, because they darken his eyes and make his expression go wild.

"Ada," he gasps, and I shimmy out of my little lace underthings as he buries his face in my neck and kisses me with sharp, needy kisses down the line of my clavicle until his nose grazes between my breasts and he lets out a sigh of contentment that fills me up the way nothing else ever has.

"I promised you so many things," he says from between them, kissing them sweetly between his sentences, first one then the other. "I promised to honor you."

He kisses them like he honors them, pulling the edge of one bra cup back just enough to sneak a mischievous kiss under it.

"I promised to cherish you."

He gets a hand behind me and I feel the catch of my bra release, and then he slips it aside and the sound in the back of his throat makes me bite my lip as I watch him go slack-jawed as he takes me in. The slack expression doesn't last long, it morphs into a satisfied grin and then he lowers his face over me, arms braced against the seat backs as he catches the tip of one breast in his mouth and slides his tongue over me. I want to memorize the sound that comes out of him when he does that. It's ... intoxicatingly intimate, like I'm the one touching his exposed parts instead of the other way around.

When he pulls up he pauses long enough to meet my eyes.

"And I promised to love you."

He can't quite hold my gaze. He flushes hot and seeks refuge in kissing my other breast.

I draw my leg up far enough that I can hook my toes in the waistbands of his jeans and boxers and pull them both down together with one powerful motion.

That makes him look up at me and laugh.

"That's ... do you practice that?"

"Yes, all the time," I say, blank-faced. "I just have a few friends who come by and I practice with them. I'm competing in the nationals this summer."

He laughs again and I love what it does to him, how all his muscles flex and his head bows into my belly. I slip my hands up under his arms to his upper back and try to pull him up to meet me at face level again. I'm not quite done with kisses.

"Ada," he gasps, looking up at me with a boyish grin. "Let me kiss you."

"Why do you think I'm pulling you up here?" I ask, teasing.

"No, I mean ..." Is it possible that he has gone redder? His face is furrowed with concentration. "Let me kiss your sweet pussy."

"No," I growl, narrowing my eyes at him.

"No?" The way his dimple pops with his amused surprise softens my expression along with it. "I think you'll like it."

"I'm sure I will. Some other time. I swear, Nicola Petrovic, you have been married to me for seven days and in that time I have not been properly fucked and I want you to get up here right now and fix that."

And I can't tell if he's laughing or dying of shock or over-whelmed with attraction. I'm not sure he can tell. He seems to almost choke on that, his eyes are so wide but it only takes a moment before he reaches up, slips my aviators down onto his nose, and looks over them at me.

"Yes, ma'am."

Chapter Thirty-Three

NICOLA

I THINK I might love her. No, seriously, I know everyone says that in the throes of passion, but I think I might actually love her. My heart did a flip when she pulled me up by the shoulders and demanded that I fuck her. And it was already treading on thin ice after seeing her naked — God in heaven, you've made a gorgeous woman here. I can't decide if I love her pouting lips or those breasts the most. I keep alternating between the two like someone might show up right now and demand an answer and I'll have to say I don't know and then Ada will be whisked away and given to a more decisive man.

Her words from our first night in her bedroom have been ringing in my head all week. "Who says there won't be sex," she had said. And after that, it was all I could think about.

She'd lean over something and I'd dream about kissing her neck, long and soft and pleading until she turned around and pulled me to her.

She'd look up flushed from a task and I'd wonder if she'd look up like that after brushing hot kisses down my body.

She'd smile one of her subtle almost-there smiles over the project and I'd wonder if she'd smile like that in pride over laying me out and devastating me.

That we're here now, finally drinking each other in — it's almost too much. I have to keep reminding myself to breathe, reminding myself to think of what she might need so that I don't lose myself entirely in her beauty, in the feel of her soft skin, in the intoxicating way her murmurs drug me and make me glassy-eyed with desire and pleasure.

I've never wanted anyone more than I want her right now. I've never wanted *anything* and for me, that's bigger. There's always been something I wanted more than a woman. Not now. Not ever again.

She's changed me with the touch of her delicate fingers, changed me with the vulnerable look in those big brown eyes. I'm never going to be the same Nicola ever again and I don't mind. The old Nicola can slink away. He can go enjoy his cars and his ambitions. This new Nicola belongs entirely to Ada now.

I know exactly the moment that I became hers. It probably should have been with the wedding vows and the signed papers. But it wasn't anything so appropriate.

It was when she put the aviators on *my* head.

Her aviators. To me they practically *are* her and she put them on me. Conquerors raise their flag over the nations they've claimed and taken for themselves. Ada put her flag on me and I am conquered and now all that's left is for her to enjoy the plunder. And fuck, I hope she takes her sweet time and devastates all of it.

I guess I've been looking at her stunned by love for too long because she growls in her throat and it draws a laugh from me. She's so perfect. I adore her growls. I love them almost as much as the angry pout she's giving me right now because she seriously has zero patience. No chill.

I lean down and snatch her pout away with a kiss. It's fun to do. I could keep annoying her all night just so I could steal another pout away. But I won't. No, because I like her dazed smile and her love-drugged heaviness even more. It matches mine. And it tastes of pineapples and a future we don't really understand yet.

But I'm not worried about the future right now. Not when the present is so immediate.

I cup my hand around her pretty face and shuffle so I can get an elbow on one side to brace myself over her on the seat — have I mentioned it's awkward to have sex in the backseat of a truck? —and then I gently press the whole length of myself to her and my eyelids flutter at the feeling of as much of our skin as possible touching, at the silky warmth of her underneath me, pressed against every part of me, at how our legs tangle together. I can hardly think. I nuzzle into her neck and press kisses as I try to catch my breath enough to form a thought.

It's not working. I'm lost in her. Lost in the thrum of her pulse in her neck, in her pretty little sighs, in how she arches her body to press her pelvis right into mine to hurry me up.

"Impatient," I whisper in her ear.

"Tardy," she whispers back.

"Demanding," It's hard to make out the word when my accent is this thick. I can't help it. I can barely handle English when my senses are this inflamed.

"Hot fuck that's sexy," she says and it bursts the bubble for a moment and sends me laughing and the laughing makes our bodies slide against each other.

I let out a shuddering moan and freeze, pushing up to meet her eyes in horror.

"Oh no."

"Oh no, what?" she asks, lips quirking in amusement. "Is this as far as you know how to go? It's okay, I can talk you through it like I talked you through the wifi camera set up."

I give her a dry look but I can't hold it because I have to admit that I really am a moron. I seriously forgot about this. "I umm ... it's been ages since I had sex with anyone. Amber ..."

"Wait, you haven't had sex with anyone since Amber?" she asks and there's a kind of tenderness in her voice that makes it okay for me to shake my head no.

To my surprise, she reaches up and draws my face down to her breasts. For something so drenched in eroticism, it's also strangely comforting. I breathe her in for a moment.

"I've pushed you too hard," she whispers. "I'm sorry. I should have gone slower."

I pull my head up. I should get a gold medal or something for that because I'm pretty sure most men wouldn't have the strength.

"No, I just ... I don't have a condom ... or anything." I don't know what the "or anything" will be but I say it to pad my words.

Her suppressed smirk only makes me flush harder. If she's laughing at me she has every right.

"Well, Mr. I-don't-have-a-condom, rest assured that you don't really need one with your wife who has practically been a nun most of her adult life." Oh wow. She's blushing. I love it so much that I lean down to kiss one flushed cheek and then the other. "But I'm also not quite ready to add 'mother' to the lengthy list of things I'm responsible to be at the moment, so maybe you could reach into that box beside your right hand and see what you find."

I frown in confusion, but I can follow instructions.

"Is this ... how many condoms do you think we need?" I ask, holding up a bright orange packet. "And why are they this color?"

She laughs then, big and full and it moves her body against me again and I bite my lip and moan.

I guess that works for her, too, because her voice is husky and low when she says, "It was a packing error. They're supposed to be BOOM branded decals."

I rip open the packet and try not to think about how industrial this blaze orange condom looks as I fit it in place.

"A decal would be a lot less useful," I say and her answering laugh is too much.

I lean in to kiss her, to steal her laugh like I stole her pouts.

Our kiss is long and slow and perfect and when she nips at my bottom lip, I gently ease myself to her entrance and tease her until she sucks my tongue into her mouth and I slide the rest of myself into her with it.

Our shared gasp is almost enough to make me come. It's just the knowledge that I'm sharing this with her, that the tingles racing up and down my spine might be racing up and down hers, too, that the pleasure forming hot and jagged in my cock and zinging up into my abdomen may very well be mirrored within her body, that when I taste her and I want to keep tasting her forever, she might feel that same way about me. I groan into her kiss and I think I feel something hot on my cheeks. I don't even realize what it is until I feel her soft fingers come up and wipe it away. I feel the bite of shame when she breaks our kiss, but it's only to whisper into my ear.

"I don't think there's anything more *fucking* manly than being so obsessed with your wife that you get emotional when you enter her."

And I don't know why these crazy moments of compassion she offers me do this to me — maybe it's because they're like rainbows in the clouds of her usual frowns — but it's almost too much and I have to turn my attention to the slide and flow of our bodies against each other, just to shield myself from how intense this emotion is, how cataclysmic. I'm not the same man anymore — can't be. A volcano has spilled over my village. A hurricane has ripped through my island. An avalanche has come down on my home. I'm devastated and reformed and most certainly not the same.

I turn carefully to place myself under her and draw her up onto my chest so I can run my hands over every part and whisper praise to her. I want her pleasure. I want her enjoyment.

The smile she gives me is radiant, a thing of angels and sunshine and pineapples on the beach. Maybe those things don't go together. Maybe my brain is broken. It must be because it can think of nothing clearly except for her.

I take her aviators off my head and place them on hers, with an affectionate smile as she braces herself with her tiny hands against my broad chest so she can work her pleasure on me. I love every slide and gasp, every ebb and flow of my Ada. I'm trying to make myself last, to enjoy every bit of her as my hands run down her back and cup her hips, as they feather down her thighs and then trace a light touch to where our bodies meet — a marvel still, no matter how common a thing it may be. When I've explored that spot enough, I trace her body upward to where her glorious breasts dance. I cup them in each palm, and to my surprise, she arches her back at this, and her mouth falls open with pleasure, and I arch my back to come up and steal her surprise from her lips. She breaks, falling heavily into me as her body clenches around me in a shocking kind of rhythm that is almost too much. I barely hold on as she surfs the wave of her pleasure and finally comes down to me, her breath harsh and ragged.

My eyes half close in the sheer pleasure of this.

And I can't help myself, I cradle her to my chest, the precious girl she is, and I whisper to her in Serbian. "My girl, my good girl, I love you."

"What does that mean?" she asks when she can speak again. Asks with a smile as she pulls herself up enough to press the tip of her nose to mine.

"I will show you," I say thickly and I gently turn her again so that she is under me, so I can use my strength and gentleness to wring one more from her. I kiss her with feather kisses — her forehead, then her cheek, then her jaw, smoothing her skin where I have kissed with tender hands, and by the time I get to her collarbone she is coming for me all over again, and this time, as she releases the power of her pleasure, I let go of the brakes and let mine come with it.

We gasp together, heave together. I think that's me making a strangled sound in my throat, but I'm not listening to it, I'm listening to her quiet happy sounds. I'm living right inside them. I never want to let them go.

Chapter Thirty-Four

ADA

I LIE in his arms in an uncomfortable truck cab but I feel only his skin beneath me and the soft curls of his chest hair against my cheek. I sigh, spent with pleasure, absolutely content in this moment. I don't trust gifts and he's given me two in a row — a family ring and now the gift of his delight. There's something about giving your whole self to someone else that feels hard to define. Because it's more than giving pleasure, though wow. That was ... an exceptional experience. It's more than giving attention and focus, though even that is a rare gift. It's giving that intimacy, I think, that kind of access to another soul where they're bare and unhidden, open to be somehow touched by you. And souls are funny things. They're like drying paint. Touch them and you leave your prints indelibly in the hardened result. I've touched his paint and he's touched mine. His prints are on me now, forever.

Knowing it gives me a little shiver. I have always loved owning things. Partly because I've owned so little and so much of what I have owned has been given away that now, even a shell found at the beach or my knock-off sunglasses are special things to me. Special because they're *mine*. Maybe I don't own Nicola. But I own this tiny piece of him, and I want to hoard it inside my chest forever.

His hands cradle me, one tangled into my hair, one resting comfortably on the curve of my waist. I press up so I can look at his swollen kissed lips and his dreamy smile.

"You must respect the hell out of me," he says lightly.

"Why is that?"

He's almost shy when he says, "Because you lit right up for me."

And I *did* didn't I? For the first time, I've taken my pleasure *with* someone and it was utterly amazing. I'm not sure what to say to that. Is there anything that won't make this awkward?

"Are you okay, sweetheart?" he asks and the "sweetheart" sends a little breathless stab into me. His naked affection is almost too much.

"I'm wondering what this means," I say, biting my lip.

He pauses and I think he might be considering playing dumb. Asking me what I mean by "this." He doesn't in the end. Instead, he leans forward and kisses the tip of my nose.

"What do you want it to mean?"

I don't know how to answer that. I don't quite know what I want beyond more sex just like this. I think I want him. But won't it scare him if I admit it? It's so new. And we're so fresh. On the one hand, he admitted while he made love to me that he made vows to love me. But on the other hand, it was in the heat of the moment, and from what I can tell, there are a lot of people who don't take those vows very seriously. Admitting that I might want him for more than convenience — would that spook him? Would I find him living on a cot in this garage again?

"I can feel your heart racing," he murmurs, his voice deeper when I both hear it and feel the rumble of it through our naked skin.

He reaches up and smooths the hair at my temple with the backs of his fingers before craning up to place a gentle kiss there. The motion stiffens his whole body and brings contact between us in sharp detail all along our bodies. I gasp at the sudden joy of it.

His whisper only makes it worse. "Tell me what you want, wife. What should this mean?"

I want to say, "Could you love me?" I want to say, "Can we try to be really married for years and years and maybe even wildly in love?"

But it all sounds ridiculous, so I settle for, "I want it to mean there will be more sex."

He laughs and I love his laugh against me. I want it forever. I lean in and kiss his laughing lips, not gently, not sweetly, but with all my desires dripping out, all my wants making me forceful and demanding. I want to take another bit of him. I want to leave more prints.

He breaks away enough to laugh, "What, right now?"

But then he tucks me to him, wrapping his huge arms around my shoulders and waist so that I fold neatly into his chest. He presses my head down with his cheek and when it's curled against his chest he presses his chin over it and his voice rumbles into me like a harmonic that will break apart stone. It's going to shatter me all through and leave me in tiny Nicola-shaped shards.

"I'm not going anywhere, sweetheart. We don't have to rush and you don't need to panic. No one can give me away, or collect me on your debts, or spend me to nothing. Do you understand?"

I nod even though I don't understand.

"You get to decide what to do with me," he says eventually. "Just you. No one else."

He says it in a funny way, half like a promise, but also half like a goodbye and I don't know what it means, only that it makes me want to cheer him up. I rise gently from his embrace and look into his unguarded eyes. I should tell him how I'm feeling, even if I don't quite know, right? He's left it wide open for me. I can do this. I take in a big breath, not sure how I'll say it, only that it needs to be said, and as I open my mouth, his phone buzzes. Loudly.

His eyes go wide.

"My parents," he says, shifting smoothly to slip out from under me and set me on the seat while he scrambles naked out the door to try to find his pants. I hear more buzzing as he curses, looking, and then he's standing again and very coolly answering his phone as if nothing has happened.

And the moment is gone. I want it back, but it's slipped away.

I swallow, feeling ridiculous now to be seated in the back seat of a dusty truck in nothing but my skin.

With my face flaming, I hop out and start to gather my own things.

I'm shimmying back into my panties and jeans when I catch sight of him in his boxers watching me. He leans casually against the truck, phone to his ear, gaze hungry as it takes me in. When our eyes meet, his smile is slow and almost sad, as if he's lost something.

"Yes, we're both here," he says and his voice sounds heavy and his accent is thick. "I'm afraid a video call won't work right now, we are having ... technical difficulties."

He looks down at the phone in his palm, then quickly up again, lips falling open when he sees I'm putting my bra back on. He makes an exaggerated pained expression at me until I start to laugh and then he wipes it away immediately and speaks with cool professionalism.

"I'm putting you on speaker, Ada Ford, Adam Boomhower."

"Ada!" Adam's voice booms through the speaker and I catch

Nicola's eye and we're both big-eyed as we try to maintain a professional demeanor — in our underwear, having just had amazing sex.

"I'm so glad I caught you both!" Big Daddy BOOM says, his enthusiasm pouring through the phone speaker. "It's been a crazy day."

I meet Nicola's eyes again. Crazy is an understatement. And I love this. I love us teamed up, sharing this secret along with everything else.

"The possible deal with the streaming service fell through."

I feel my heart drop with those words and I see my disappointment mirrored in Nicola's eyes and somehow that makes it worse.

"So we've been working like crazy over here to think of another way to make this work," Adam says. "And my daughter Gracie — I'm not sure if you know about her. She runs our marketing department for BOOM Enterprises. Genius girl. The best. Anyway, she suggested that since we were wanting to expand our empire beyond just our channel and make kind of our own motorsports streaming service focused just on motorsports, that perhaps we could pilot that with your show. We want to call it, "Married to Design" and offer it as a show under the BOOM Enterprises umbrella, which would mean that for now, our channel — BOOM Enterprises — which we're going to call "BOOM Off Roading" under the banner — and your channel, Married by Design would be the first two streaming shows offered in our service. This isn't the big deal that other streaming service show would have been, but it's a sure thing. I can pay you an advance this week. If we can hash out the details."

It's ... well, it's a genius idea. I'm disappointed that we didn't get that other show. That would have rocketed us into a great place. But this is still better than nothing and that other show was never a sure thing.

"The thing is, we will need to keep the bulk of what you're filming for the channel now," Adam says, laying it out for us. We'll have to shut down our own channels and feed everything under his. This new joint enterprise will replace both of our former streaming careers. He'll pay us well, and he'll work to sort out our shop situation so that we can work together in the same space, but we'll still be doing our own filming — though he wants to think about bringing on a camera person — and we'll have to wrap up any projects in the works and clear our schedule for BOOM content by next month at the latest. And finish the Silver Bullet.

By the time he's laid out the project, I feel overwhelmed. It's a lot of work. It's going to pay — he's even being pretty generous with what he offers up front — but we lose control. We lose the platforms we've been building ourselves. We lose independence. And we have to decide as soon as possible.

"I need to know right away," Adam says. "We're investing a ton of money into building the site and the app and we're going to be recruiting the very best to make shows for the streaming service, but this is a highly competitive space and things move fast. I need to know in twenty-four hours if you're in or if we're scrapping this idea and recruiting someone else. I want you guys. You're perfect. Viewers will eat up your content. But it's all or nothing. I'm not going to invest unless you're fully invested. Let me know by tomorrow night."

And then he hangs up just like that, leaving us stunned and staring at each other.

Still in our underwear.

"We have a big decision to make," I say, scrambling to dress, as if being clothed will somehow make this easier.

It's not until I'm fully dressed that I realize Nicola hasn't moved, that he's still in his boxers, leaning against his truck box, looking like some sort of Diesel-powered god with his chariot. I mean, the engine in that thing is called a "Powerstroke" if that isn't sexual then I don't know what is.

"*You* have a big decision to make," he says when I still and face him.

"Does that mean you've already decided?" I ask, confused.

"Pineapples, when you asked me to marry you and I said yes, the decision was already made for me. I'm all in with you. In life. In business."

I don't know what to do with that. He looks serious. His brows knit together like he is. His glower is back on his face, full force.

"Just like that?" I ask, challenging him. "Just like that, you decide and it's all being bet on this one thing?"

"Oh," he says with mock surprise and I don't like him teasing me right now because this is too serious of a moment for teasing. "Have you never seen people gamble before? Let me fill you in. They put their money on a thing all at once. Just like that. They say "all in" and all the money goes to that one turn of the card or spin of the wheel."

"I'm aware of how gambling works," I say dryly. "I just wasn't aware that you thought that's what this is."

My words come out more snappish than I meant them to.

"Ada," he says as I pull my top on and pull my aviators down.

I feel safer already. I ignore him because I'm annoyed. It's not just that he's teasing me. It's that he's telling me he's decided to gamble his whole future on us and it's too much pressure. I already have too many people relying on me. I can't have one more.

"Ada," he repeats, hands spread open like he's trying to calm an unreasonable zoo animal. It makes me even more annoyed.

"So you're betting it all on me?" I say, crossing my arms over my chest. "You're betting everything you have on this? That's ridiculous."

His frown matches mine now as he spits back, "Why shouldn't I? I've built a successful creative business, Ada. I immigrated to another country and I built a life for myself there. I've bet everything before and I've won. I say this is a good bet. The best bet, maybe." His face softens and it seems like he's conceding something to me as he says, "When I bet on a thing I don't just sit around and wait for it to pay off, Ada. I do the work. I rig the game. I make sure I win."

But it's not enough to calm my fears and I want him to make me certain, to prove beyond a doubt that I can trust him when I've seen again and again that I can't trust anyone. It's a terrible thing to expect of someone else — unfair. And yet, I find myself saying the exact thing that I shouldn't.

"Like you did with your parents?"

His face falls and his hand forms a fist and trembles and then he looks up at me again, like I've broken something inside him. He's still in his boxers, only now he doesn't look like a Power-stroke god leaning against his chariot. He looks like a boxer who has taken a hit and is dangling on the ropes.

"Ouch," he says distinctly, and I feel myself flush at how he's called me out. And then slowly, deliberately, he says, "I married you to win with them. Are you saying that wasn't a big enough sacrifice? That I don't know how to make the hard choices?"

"Sacrifice?" My eyes are wide and I scoff. "Nice one. That landed below the belt."

And now neither of us knows what to do. And it's ridiculous. Because seriously, we both have what we want, don't we? His parents are taken care of. If we agree to Big Daddy Boom, then my debts are still taken care of. We work well together. We love each other's company and we just had mind-blowingly good sex. What is there to be mad about?

But I can't stop being angry that he called marriage to me a sacrifice and I guess he can't stop being mad that I said he couldn't fix his parent situation on his own.

We dress in silence. We drive home in silence. We walk in the door in silence.

I don't know what it means that he's still with me, going home to bed with me, if he's this mad. I don't want him to run away but I don't understand why he isn't storming off somewhere or at least screaming at me or making sharp, mean digs.

He opens his mouth when we get in the door, face flushed, and I brace myself, but before he can speak I hear a throat clear and see my Pops sitting at the kitchen table drinking tea with Marvin. There's a duffel bag at his feet.

"I'm going to go stay with Marvin for a bit," he says.

Nicola's mouth snaps shut with a click.

"Why?" I ask and all the annoyance and hostility I feel right now toward Nicola is in my voice.

My Pops raises an eyebrow. "Well, if I didn't have a reason before I do now, hmm? Is that any way to speak to your old man?"

"Sorry, Pops," I say, looking down. He's right. I need to keep my hostility where it belongs.

"Marvin's lonely," Pops says. "You know how it's been since Evelyn died."

"Yeah," Marvin says. He doesn't sound lonely. His eyes are twinkling. If he ever decides to be a betting man he's going to lose a ton of money unless someone tells him he has no poker face.

"Just for a few weeks," Pops says and then stands leaving the tea mugs where they are. "I'll let you wash up."

"O-kaaay," I say, uncertainly. Clearly, he's manufacturing a reason to leave us to ourselves. But I don't understand why that would be. Is it consideration? Because we're married? Is this his way of giving us a honeymoon?

I watch him leave with a furrowed brow. It's not until the door closes and I hear Marvin's car start down below that I open the door and call out to them.

"What's going on?"

He didn't kiss me goodbye. He always kisses me goodbye.

He looks up from the trunk of Marvin's car where he's stowing his duffel bag. Marvin looks up, too, wide-eyed and guilty.

"I sold the garage,' Pops says, slamming the trunk and practically running to the passenger side of the car.

"You what?" I ask, feeling like I'm going to fall right over the railing. "You sold *this shop?* Our *family* shop? The one thing we still had?"

"That's the one," he calls back.

"My *home?*"

"You're married now," he calls out the window as Marvin starts to drive. Wisely. I'm already halfway down the stairs and picking up speed. "You'll find a new place together!"

And then Marvin hits the accelerator and the car squeals down the lane and away leaving squiggly rubber tread marks on the ground.

They cut off abruptly. Just like my sense of security.

NICOLA

HE SOLD HER SHOP. I stumble down to the bottom of the stairs behind her and I don't know what to say. I sold my house. I can't take her to my home and tell her it will be okay. I don't know what to do.

There's no guarantee that her dad will put any of that money toward their debts. She might end up with no home and no shop and all the debts she's had all along.

She's standing there in the middle of the back lane just staring after Marvin's car and something inside me solidifies. Who cares if she hurt me? She wasn't all wrong. I don't always win. Doesn't this prove that?

I stride across the gravel and stand there beside her.

"It's a shitty thing to do," I say, watching the last hint of Marvin's car vanish.

"Maybe you should sleep at your shop tonight," she says, and her voice is ice cold, her eyes like root beer slush.

I don't know what to say. I mean, I know I need to say something but everything sounds stupid in my head. I run a hand through my hair and let out a long breath but before I've thought of anything my phone buzzes.

It's the hospital.

I take the call under Ada's eagle eye.

"Mr. Petrovic? Your mother has had a change in care."

"How bad is it?" I bark. I don't mean to do it. The stress is a bit high over here.

"How soon can you be here?"

"Tell me what's happened."

"It's our policy to communicate these things in person."

"Are you ... can I talk to her?" It's a long shot. She wasn't verbal before. I doubt she is now. But I have a sick feeling in my guts that tells me this is worse than it sounds.

"Please, come here quickly," the polite woman tells me.

I disconnect the phone.

"I ..." I start to try to explain but I'm not sure how to tell Ada that I'm about to leave her with her home ripped out from under her.

"I heard," she says, and ... is that compassion in her tone. "You'd better go."

"I'm coming back here afterward," I say miserably. "Be here?"

She shrugs like she's not ready to commit to that.

"Please?"

She nods and I think maybe she's crying under her aviators. Fuck. I can't be in two places at once. It's not possible. And the way that the hospital administrator was talking on the phone ... it's bad. I know it is. It's a coma or ... I can't fill in the blank. I can't say it even in my mind.

I should tell Ada I love her. Or that I'll find a way to fix this. But I can't find words. I just shake my head, mutter a Serbian curse and leave. I'm in my truck and driving before I realize I didn't even say goodbye.

It's almost four in the morning before I ease my truck back into that parking space. I'm exhausted.

It turns out a "change in care" doesn't mean something worse. My mother, it seems, had a change for the better. So much so, that she was asking for me. If she stays this good — if she can swallow her own food — then they'll move her over to Cedar Ridge with my dad. I'm more thrilled than I can explain as I tell her about my wedding. About moving her and dad. She seems happy enough. Still mostly out of it, like a child hearing a story about someone who has nothing to do with them — but she's okay. She's speaking and eating. She's not dead — which I was one hundred percent sure was the case after that call.

"A mix-up," is what the horrified nurse told me when I ran in, out of breath and feeling like I might vomit. "There is another woman with the same last name who ... well, her family needed a call, too."

I feel worse for the other family. Were they told things had improved only to drive in and find out the truth? Yikes.

It's the middle of the night, but I go to see my dad next and have to sweet talk the front desk clerk to let me sneak in and see him. Somehow he caught wind of what happened with mom and wouldn't stop calling my cell until I came.

"I need to see her. Tonight," he insists.

"It will have to be in the morning. Visiting hours at the hospital are over," I say, rubbing my forehead and hoping I'll get some sleep before then.

We're both speaking in Serbian. It's easier that way. Since the heart incident, dad finds English more taxing.

"Visiting hours are over here, too." He's practically bristling. I have to put a hand on his arm to keep him from jumping out of his bed a second time in as many minutes. "That didn't stop you from sneaking in."

"Security is tighter at the hospital, Dad."

"Then why do you have us in this budget place? Better to be

in the hospital!"

"I thought you were glad I snuck in."

We go round and round for a while.

"You need to bring your wife to meet us," he tells me. "Not bringing her is a disgrace."

"Mmmhmm," I agree.

"I mean it. Bring her, or I'll find my own way to see her. You don't get married and then don't introduce your wife to your parents. Or are you ashamed of us? Were you waiting for us to be prisoners of nurses and doctors before you wed so you would not have to bear the shame of admitting we raised you?"

"Of course not, Dad."

I'm wrung out like a rag by the time I'm discovered and the nurses ask me to go home. Thank goodness for the interruption. My dad is so pleased that mom is coming to Cedar Ridge that he can't calm down. It's like he's been given a second life.

When I get back to Ada's, I'm exhausted. Exhausted and envious of my father and his good news. Of a man who knows he's loved and is excited to see his wife again.

Me? I sit in the kitchen in the dark. I try to think of how I can tell her what a fool I am. That she's the best thing that ever happened to me. That if it were my choice she'd always come first. I'm not good at saying these things. They sound like lies when I do and I'm more afraid she'll think I'm lying than that she won't know how I feel.

I don't know how long I'm sitting there with my head in my hands before she walks in and flicks on the light. I can see her bare feet. She painted her toenails peach. I love it. I love everything about her.

"Is your mom okay?" she asks softly from the doorway. Her voice is burred with concern. Is that for me?

I don't look up. Not yet. Not before it starts, because I know it's going to start and honestly, I'm too short on either sleep or coffee to be ready for what's next.

"Yes."

I hear her take a deep breath — here we go — and when it comes out raised. I laugh into my hands. I called it. Who says I'm bad at betting? I'm amazing at it.

"Nicola Petrovic," her voice is firm like she's a cop who pulled me over for doing donuts on the highway, not a super hot girl in silky shorts with a huge ribbon tie in the front and an itty bitty crop tank. "Being married to me is not a sacrifice. In fact, you're pretty damn lucky that I took you. I'm a smart, ambitious, hard-working woman, who has built her own business selling things she creates. I look after my family. I make my own way in life. I have a sense of humor. And I'm fucking gorgeous in the right light. It won't cost you a thing to be with me. Not a thing. You should feel lucky, Mr. Sacrifice. I am way too good for you."

I look up and now I really am laughing. "You think you have to tell me that, Ada?"

She crosses her arms over her chest, flushing. "Don't laugh at me. I wouldn't have to tell you if you hadn't forgotten."

"You think I forgot?" I repeat, low and yes — maybe teasing. But I'm thinking of all the ways I can show her that I *do* cherish her, even if I'm not good at showing it. That was one of the things, right? Cherish. I swallow and I see her eyes trace my Adam's apple as it bobs.

She's not distracted. "You wouldn't have said being married to me was a *sacrifice* if you hadn't forgotten. So I'm here to remind you just how good you have it."

Her lip juts out when she's mad. It's incredibly kissable. I'm mesmerized by the thought. Would it taste as cherry red as it looks? I should know. I was kissing her just hours ago, but somehow I've forgotten that detail. I might need reminding.

I push her a little, reveling in how she always pushes back. "And now what? You think I'm going to leave you?"

She thrusts her chin out defiantly.

Oh. Oh, God, she does. She thinks I'll pick up and leave. My chest heaves at the thought of that, and I'm on my feet before I realize it, the chair I was sitting in kicking back and clattering to the floor.

"I'm not going to fucking leave you, Ada," I growl. "I'm not going to walk out or sell everything you care about, or leave you in debt and feeling desperate."

Her lower lip is trembling. It makes me madder. Not at her. At me. Fuck, I'm an idiot.

"I'm not," I say sternly. No more trembling lips. She deserves better. "Do you know what I fucking am going to do?"

"I don't have a clue what you're planning to do, Nicola Petrovic," she says, throwing it at me like a challenge. Her hands are on those pretty curving hips. I want to kiss the spot where they kick out from her waist. On either side. And then in the middle, and then work my way lower. "Why don't you tell me?

I take a step forward, looming, I guess. I don't really mean to, but I'm kind of built for looming.

"Yes, let me tell you," I say slowly in my most seductive voice. I don't know if it works. I've never had reason to use it before. "First thing tomorrow, I have to take care of something with my parents, but immediately after that, I'm going to find us a new home."

"Us?" She sounds suspicious.

"Yes. My wife lives with me. Those are the rules."

"There are no rules," she says coldly, holding her hand up so she can study her fingernails as if I'm not even looming.

I take another step forward, to redouble my loom. I could touch her now. She could touch me. I want to shiver at the thought of that.

"There are if I say there are, and I say there are," I've never heard this throaty tone from myself before. This girl does things to me. "Rule one. My wife lives with me. Rule two. She wants for nothing."

"Nothing?" she asks and there's a pleading tone to her voice. It does something animal to me. Makes me want to bow down to her. To offer her anything she'll take.

I'm breathless for a moment. Desire rips across me like harsh winds kicking up dust in a dry field.

"Nothing," I finally manage to say. I lift her chin with one finger so I can look into her eyes. Her eyes darken and her gaze catches mine like metal shavings to a magnet. I can't look away and I can't breathe while I look. I'm dizzy with her. With the nearness. With the imagining. Dammit, with the lust. I've never been so crazy before and I don't want it to stop.

"I'm going to take that deal with BOOM," I gasp out. "I'm going to give them everything I've built. And I'm going to take their money and make you a home somewhere. One no one can ever take from you."

"And then what?" she asks breathlessly.

"And then I'm going to be your family. Not the kind of family that leaves you. The kind of family that stays. The kind of family willing to fight with you at five in the morning after spending an entire night awake — because it's worth it."

"It's worth it?" She's breathless now, too.

I let my hands find her waist and lift her to the countertop so I can stand between her legs. She's breathing heavily. I can't help myself, I pull the wide ribbon on her shorts and the bow unravels. Satin ribbon slips over her thighs to either side. It's like unwrapping a present. I have to close my eyes and swallow at the thought.

"That's rule three," I say in a gasp. "We fight when it's worth it."

Her eyes are half-lidded now, too, but she rallies, lifting her chin. Her hands snake forward to grab my waist and pull me in toward her so she can wrap her legs around my back. I swallow a groan.

"I think we'd better get all these rules out of your system. You know I'm not going to keep any of them, right?"

"That's fine. They aren't rules for you. They're rules for me," I say, and I lean down so I can nip her lower lip lightly, teasingly.

"Then I think you'd better tell me rule four," she says, shuffling forward until her breasts are flush with my chest. When I look down, I see a little path between them. Without thinking, I slide one of the tiny straps of her tank top down.

It falls, revealing most of her breast on that side. She hardly seems to care.

"Rule four is, kiss like you mean it," I say and then I lean in and kiss her, cradling her face between my hands.

I stretch down to kiss the top of her exposed breast and she lets me. If she's angry with me, she's not angry enough not to want this. I'm so hard the cupboard hurts as I press into it. I want her like I want sleep right now. So basically I want her very, very badly, in case that wasn't clear.

I feel punch drunk. Like so much has happened that I can take anything now. I can beat the land speed record at Bonneville. I can race a six-second quarter mile with a stock car. I can drop an axle to the perfect geometry every single time.

"That's a silly rule," she says, catching my mouth in hers for a biting kiss while she reaches a hand up to tug on the hair at the nape of my neck. "You always kiss like you mean it. Pick a new one."

"Fine," I say, kissing her just under the ear. She's perfection. She's my undoing. I groan into her skin before I can go on. "My rule four is, 'She always comes first.'"

She pulls back and gifts me with a scowl. "I didn't feel like your top priority today."

I laugh into her neck and wrap my hands around her hips, fingers splayed out to grip as much of her sweet bottom as I can. I tug her in close to my body and hold her tight.

"I wasn't talking about priorities, Pineapple. I was talking about *coming*. And I'm pretty sure I've delivered on that so far."

She laughs, now, flushed but still a little pouty when she says, "Is this how you apologize?"

"Is this how you accept my apology?" My voice is rough and tangled, the language slurring on it as my need for her bubbles up from somewhere deeper than speech.

I don't wait for a response. I kiss her with hungry lips, my tongue slipping past her lips to stroke her tongue, to remind her how good it can feel when she lets me inside. To remind her how good it can be when our bodies intertwine instead of standing so far apart. I trace my hands up her back and thread my fingers through her hair, wrapping my thumbs around and under her jaw so I can cradle her close.

I pull back long enough to look at her with heavy-lidded eyes, my jaw slack with desire, my breath trembling.

She likes it. I see the moment my thirst for her becomes her thirst for me and then she grabs my shirt and yanks me to her chest so she can kiss me as her legs clamp tightly around my waist.

When she's done I can barely think. I shiver in her arms, cheek pressed to hers, eyes closed tight as I let go of her with one hand to steady myself against the counter. It's almost too much. I'm swept away by her. I barely hear her whispered, "Yes."

I repeat it as I turn my face so my lips can caress her cheek with my answering, "Yes?"

"I'm not sure I believe these rules," she teases me, breathlessly, her hand finding my cock and startling a rough gasp out of me. She wraps that hand around me through the cloth of my jeans so she can slide up and down, teasing me with her touch even while the zipper of my jeans threads the pleasure with the sharp bite of pain.

"You're making it hard to keep rule four." My accent is so thick that even I can barely understand myself.

"It's gonna have to be hard if you want to keep that rule," she says, laughing now, and I'm too stunned to have a clever comeback.

"Does this mean you forgive me?" I ask.

"That depends," she whispers, her breath hot against my neck. I might come just like this, with her hand wrapped around me and her heaving chest right against mine.

"On what?" My heart is racing. God have mercy, she's perfection in feminine form.

She pulls back and she looks so serious that I have to swallow. I feel a furrow forming on my brow. Her eyes meet mine and then she smirks before she forces her face into dead seriousness. "On whether you keep rule four."

My answering laugh seems to please her.

"Ada," I gasp, remembering I had something I had to say to her.

"Nicola." The way she says my name makes me have to form a fist and clench it to hold back the pleasure already rippling through me.

"Not like that, don't say it like that, or it's going to be too much," I beg her. I never beg. Except with her.

"Nicola," she says again, this time lower and with more growl. It makes my cock twitch violently and she laughs. "I like this game."

"Dammit, woman," I gasp. "I just want to tell you that I plan to be a good husband to you. Always. I'm not just some passing thing."

"You know what a really good husband would do?" she whispers in my ear.

Somewhere, the sun is coming up. Rude. I'm not done here. Its intrusive rays are penetrating through the blinds.

"Tell me," I gasp.

"Keep rule four," she whispers. "Right. Fucking. Now."

It's all the invitation I need.

Chapter Thirty-Six

ADA

HE LIFTS me while I'm still whispering commands into his ear, and carries me to my bedroom. I thought that was a thing that people only did in stories, but this is now the second time he's lifting me to bring me where he wants me and I am enjoying it. I may never walk again if he plans to carry me like this. It makes me feel treasured. Makes me feel wanted.

I'm a ball of nerves inside — mostly over having my life upended by my father and also being incredibly anxious over making the right decision with this BOOM thing. I don't like handing control over to anyone. Not even someone who is willing to pay me a lot of money for that control. But I'm not in a financial position to say no and the tangle of the two is making me ill.

But this right now — Nicola kissing me, apologizing, making intoxicating promises? This is pushing all that into the background. Would this be what it would be like to just surrender to my marriage with him? To stop trying to look for his hidden motives or the proof that he wants out but to just enjoy it?

I'm not sure I have it in me to let go of control here, too.

"What happens when you tire of me?" I whisper as he carries me through the doors. I have to ask this now. Now, before this gets even more real.

"I won't."

"You *will*," I insist. "You'll get bored. You'll try to give me away."

"How could I possibly give you away?" he asks, leaning back against the doorframe so he can hold me out from him enough to see my face in the hazy light of dawn. "You can't give a person away."

I huff a bitter laugh. "Yes, you can. That's why Jasmin is here all the time. Her mother gave her to us when she grew bored. Like a dog who's too energetic for your city apartment. People do it to their spouses all the time. Usually, they give them to the kids, or back to their own families, or to a group of girlfriends, or party friends they spend time together with as couples. That's what Pops did just now when he left me to you. He gave me away."

Understanding dawns in his eyes and something softens in his face.

"I'm not the kind of man who willingly gives up what is his," he sounds possessive. Some girls wouldn't like that. For me, it's all I've ever wanted. To *have* something. Someone. Forever.

"And if you grow bored?" I press, biting my lip. His eyes linger on it, and I can tell he wants to go to bed now, but we have to talk like this first. We have to or I can't.

"Boredom is for the weak," he says.

"And if you are weak?"

"Then you will make me strong," he murmurs, pressing his forehead to mine. "We'll refuse to run from each other. Instead, we'll run toward each other. We'll refuse not to talk, not to fight, not to do what it takes."

It's beguiling. I've never wanted anything so much as this. I tighten the grip of my legs around him. I want to open them, open myself, right down to the soul, give him everything and more. I want to be able to do that. I don't know why my grip won't loosen so I can.

"You talk like you're planning to fall in love with me," I say and even this much feels like an admission — an admission that I want it, want him, so desperately that I'm hoping he will fall first and drag me under with him.

"Who says I haven't?" His voice is breathy, almost desperate and when he curls forward to catch my mouth I moan into it and his lower lip falls open as he huffs a sound that's half pain and half disbelief.

"Just give me a chance," he begs when I pull back. "Just let me show you how it can be. Just that."

I nod, clinging to him. You're not supposed to make someone else be *it* for you. I know that. You're supposed to find that in yourself. But what if the *it* isn't in you? What if your *only* option is to find it in someone else? Is it really so bad to ask them to give you what you can't give yourself?

"Just let me unravel you," he whispers into my hair as if he can read my thoughts. He leaves the doorframe and takes us to the bed.

I'm clenched tightly around him. I let go enough that he can place me on the quilt and extract himself enough to shrug out of his clothes. I bite my lip as he undresses slowly, never breaking eye contact with me.

"Trust me," he mouths.

He's revealing himself inch by inch. Just like he does in this strange marriage of ours. This partnering of two people toward a single goal. Well, a dual goal, I guess, and one that seems to get further away by the day. I try not to worry about that.

"Hey," he says softly and I realize he's stripped naked and standing there before me like a present to be enjoyed. He's unconsciously confident, like he knows anyone looking at his naked body could only ever be pleased with what they saw. "Let me take your worries, sweetheart. That's rule number five."

"Oh it is, is it?" I huff a laugh, but I have to lean backward as he sinks to all fours on the bed and crawls toward and then over me. "So many rules."

He leans in so closely that his lips brush mine when he speaks. "Rule number five. Bed is for sex, nothing else. No clothes, no worries."

He leans around to catch the remaining strap of my tank top in his teeth and pull it free. His wink is both playful and ridiculous.

"What about sleep?" I ask him dryly. "I require that to survive. Can I do that in bed, too?"

"Not right now. We can revisit the details later," he says, looking down at my shorts with dark eyes as he bites his lip. I think he's wondering if he can take them off with his teeth, too.

I'm going to give him a chance, I think. A chance to show me how being in love with him could be. If I just let myself fall.

He presses a kiss between my freed breasts and then slides his lips down to my belly button and lower until they snag on my shorts. He catches their hem in his teeth and pulls gently downward. I like this game. I kick my hips up so the shorts will slide free and I gasp as the tip of his nose runs down my pubic bone and slips across more sensitive areas before he has the shorts — and my tangled panties with them — past my hips and down to my knees. I extract my foot carefully and he leans to one side so he can nuzzle my calf with his cheek as it pulls free. Laughing, he finally uses his hands to throw the last shred of our clothing over his shoulder.

It might be too late for him to fall first. I might be falling right now.

I move to sit, so I can get closer to him, but he reaches a long arm up and presses me back into the pillows.

"I made you very specific promises," he murmurs and that murmur has some kind of echo effect like when you play a clear note next to an instrument and, unbidden, the instrument hums the same note? Well, Nicola whispering about promises does that same thing to my core, making me hum in response to him.

He presses a kiss to the inside of my knee and then my thigh and sighs happily as he works his way up my leg and I am sighing with him, enjoying this teasing journey as much as he is.

His hand on my chest splays out, fingers fanning over it and I reach one hand up to lay my palm over his, fingers threading between his much larger ones.

"I promised that you come first," he whispers and when his breath spreads across my thigh like that, it's so hot that I see no reason he won't fulfill that promise.

"I respect that," I say.

And he remembers. I can tell he remembers because he gasps at that and his kiss moves to the crease of my hip where it meets my leg. He sucks lightly on the skin there and my tiny mew of satisfaction gets an answering growl.

"I respect the hell out of you, too, Pineapple."

"Mmhmm." I hardly know what I'm saying, only that his kisses are intoxicating to my skin, making me tingle with desire while I relax under his warm touch. I hardly know what I'm thinking, never mind doing. I just don't want it to stop.

"Which is why I should maybe confess something," he says as he sinks down so that his face is between my thighs.

My heart is already racing so hard that it's surely in overdrive. I might die like this. So excited that my heart races to the very end of me.

"Confess what?" I ask, biting my lip, meeting his sharp desire-filled gaze. My free hand tightens in his hair and he smiles, his dimple popping into view.

He leans forward just enough to lick me, quick and teasing and I gasp, pulling slightly away at the sudden intensity of it, but his hand holds me against the covers as he meets my eyes again. His accent is so thick right now that he's hard to understand. But not so hard that I miss what he says next.

"Confess that I've already completely fallen in love with you."

"You have?" I gasp. I can't think. I can't respond properly.

It's worse when he answers by lowering his mouth again and using his tongue to caress me with a gentle ardor in place of words. By the time he's through, by the time he gives me a second to speak at all, he's already kept his rule four.

"Rule Six," he growls as he moves up my body, kissing my belly and breasts, stopping to suck on them reverently like they are holy things, one and then the other. "Rule six is once you fall in love, you never look back."

"Then don't look back," I order.

"I wasn't planning on it," he whispers into my ears as he finally lays himself out over me, all his skin touching all my skin, our harsh breaths gasping together, our beating hearts like battling drums.

I twitch inside at the feel of him so soon after my orgasm, at the pleasure just touching him gives me, but then he kills me as he pulls up for just a moment and leans over the bed to grab his pants. In the back pocket is a BOOM condom.

"You were planning for something," I say with mock sternness.

He laughs and I take the condom from him so I can slip it on him myself, enjoy the feeling of the whole length of him in my hand. He's delicious. I want to drink him down. Maybe I will next time.

He mutters something in Serbian as he draws himself from my grasp and then slips himself gently, confidently into me.

"Translation?" I ask as I lean in to catch his lips in mine and I kiss him hard and long as his first strokes open me wide and send my mind spinning dizzily away.

"I said that I *was* planning on something," he says brokenly into my hair and his breath is coming in stilted gasps. "I was planning on loving you always."

And when he rises so that I can see his face, he's biting his lip, eyes glazed with desire, and I can't help it. I pull him down, kiss him roughly and then pivot with my hips, and understanding, he lets me roll him over me and take the reins so I can move fast and intent, focused and determined as I draw his pleasure from him.

I lean down to give quick kisses to his chest, his arms, his neck, like I'm choosing savory delicacies, until he catches my face in his hands and lowers it down gently to his, opens my lips with his kiss and with a trembling gasp, he comes as he's kissing me, his hips bucking and reaching as if he can have more of me in that moment if he only tries, and just the thought of that is enough to send me over the edge again until I'm a gasping, spent, sated woman lying in the arms of her lover.

He says something in Serbian and then immediately translates it, his words broken and tangled. "Sleep with me?"

I nod tiredly into his neck and I've never slept like this before, with someone I'm falling in love with actually still inside my body. And he's so good. He's a morning stroll on a sunny beach. He's hot coffee and cinnamon rolls on a crisp fall day. He's completing a huge project perfectly and on time. He's someone wrapping a blanket around all the parts of you that shiver.

And I think that maybe he might be mine.

Chapter Thirty-Seven

NICOLA

I WAKE to tangled legs and arms and her breath heavy on my chest and my heart is more tangled up in her than my limbs can ever be. I'm drowsy in her embrace and yet energized by it. I've been with Ada Ford twice now and I want to say that it feels like I'm on the world's most wild rollercoaster. I climb up and up, crash down so hard that I think there's no possible recovery, and just when I'm gasping, the car starts climbing again to even greater heights. But it's not. It's not that.

It's like going on a journey that turns out to lead to the inside of yourself. And finding there's a waterfall, or mountains, or something impossibly deep and tall you didn't know existed, even though it's a part of you. Being with her is like a new dawn every time — one that reaches light further, and further out so that I'm suddenly seeing things I didn't know were possible. Maybe they aren't possible without her. Maybe they don't even exist, unless she's there, shining her light on them.

She reaches inside me somehow and twists and I'm all brand new. She's passion and strong-willed determination. She's scowls and laughter and sharp remarks. She's the tour guide to a better Nicola and I'm trying to negotiate a lifetime pass.

I've fallen for her. Irrevocably.

The words seem weak.

Okay, I'm in love with her. Completely. Is that stronger?

It's a sudden thing, sure. Sudden, like finding rescuers on your beach when you're on a desert island. Sudden, like falling from a height only to be caught by a ring of men holding a huge blanket - does that happen outside of kids' cartoons? Sudden, like getting a call that you've inherited a fortune and just need to sign the papers. Sudden can be good if it's the right thing.

And this is the right thing.

I'm a fool in many ways, but one thing I've always been good at is seeing an opportunity. And when I see one, I never hesitate. I grab it with both hands and hold on tight so it can't be ripped away again.

With Ada, I'm going to hold on with both hands and my teeth.

And yes, I love the excitement of her quick mind, but do you know what else I love? I love the soft moments. I love her acts of compassion and tenderness to me. I love how she holds on to her family even when things are messed up.

I run an idle hand along the skin of her back, soaking her in and thinking. It's afternoon by the look of the sun in the sky. We need to respond to Adam Boomhower's proposal, and I need to get to the hospital to arrange things for my mom. But if I want to hold on to Ada, I'd better make sure she wants to hold on to me.

I cup her face with my hand and breathe in deep, memorizing this moment of her heavy with sleep, trusting me enough to relax completely in my arms. I'll make this beautiful woman a home so that all her frowns have a place to live forever alongside the smiles I plan to tease out of her. As soon as I wrap up these urgent things, I'll turn my mind to that.

"Nicola," her sleep-filled voice sends a thrill shooting down my spine. She turns her face muzzily into me and my hand trembles slightly as it caresses her hair.

Don't lose this, Nicola, I beg myself. Don't lose this.

"Good afternoon, sweetheart," I murmur and I kiss the top of her head.

"Afternoon?" She presses up, startled and she's beautiful with wide root beer eyes and a slight flush to her glowing skin. I lean up to press a kiss to her cheek, ridiculously happy to have this sleepy Ada moment. "What time is it?"

She presses up on her arms and I get the sight of her naked breasts — perfectly shaped, have I mentioned that? My eyes skim down her rib cage right to where she's pressed against me and I groan at the feeling of her hips thrust into mine as she looks for her clock. I know as well as she does that there is no time right now for us to fall back into bed together. We've slept away the morning, and with it, all the time we had, but my body doesn't know, and it is sending me shooting requests to please stop stalling. I can tell the moment she feels me hardening under her because she looks down with a wry expression.

"I see someone is already up."

I feel strangely shy at that. And somehow vulnerable in a way I never have been before. I can't quite find words and I don't know if my face is accidentally giving it all away — my sudden shift of heart so it aligns with hers — while I grasp for something clever to say to hide behind. Nothing is coming to me and I think she does see it because her expression softens, and she leans her pretty face down long enough to kiss me.

I try to put what I'm feeling into the kiss — tenderness. Longing. Some undefined thing that's sweeping over me that I don't quite understand and that makes my eyes moist and my throat choke. Love, you idiot. I'm pretty sure that one is love.

When she breaks the kiss she's breathless and smiling shyly like maybe she could feel it, too.

"You have to get to the hospital," she says and I nod. "And we have to call Big Daddy Boom."

I nod again. She smirks at me like she can see I'm too overwhelmed with her to make proper thoughts. My eyes keep drifting to her pretty breasts. My hands must have drifted down to her hips while I was kissing her. They're lingering there now.

She leans down to press her forehead to mine. "You aren't going to get any of it done if your mind keeps going to that."

I think I might flush. "What do you recommend?"

Words. Excellent. I'm making progress.

"Go and shower. I'll get a video call set up with the BOOM people."

I nod but I can't help it. I stay where I am to watch her as she stands and shows her glorious body to me. She dresses slowly and I think she's purposefully teasing me and I'm hard enough to pound rivets in by the time she's done. She spreads lip gloss on, puts her aviators on her head, and winks at me before she leaves — and is that an extra hip sway she threw into her walk just for me? I growl at the sight of it and have to run a hand over my face before I can make it to the shower.

I have to shower under cold water. It's hardly enough to resolve things, but at least I'm presentable when I make my way to the kitchen.

Ada waves to me and I see she's talking to Tanner on a video call.

"He's going to be thrilled," Tanner is saying with a big gappy grin. Behind him, there are beaches and palm trees. He's moving with the camera phone and then he finds Adam who is bent over a car engine messing with the distributor.

"Oh, Tanner!" He says with a huge grin, a smear of grease on his face — and how can you fault a man for being a billionaire when he still gets greasy working on cars? "And is that Ada and Nicola? Excellent! This is good news, right?"

"It is," Ada says. "We'd like to sign on with you."

I can hear the hitch in her voice. I understand it because I feel the same way. This is a huge gamble and we're the ones who lose everything if it doesn't pay off. I should have been talking to her about this before my shower instead of being distracted by her body. I clench my jaw at myself. Unacceptable, Nicola. Now here we are, making the decision and I can tell she's nervous as hell about it.

I do the only thing that remains and take her hand under the table. She grips it like she's trying to choke the life out of it.

"I'm so stoked about that!" Adam says. "I have the perfect place for the show! I've been thinking about it all night. We could do it right here in my San Diego beach house! You can live here and my shop can be for the show."

To illustrate, he grabs the camera from Tanner and holds it back to show his shop and then strides out the door so we can see the hulking monstrosity of his "beach house" which is actually a mansion. Behind him, Tanner is grinning, arms spread over his ragged BOOM T-shirt and safari hat tugged low on his head. He looks like a stray dog that wandered in and took up residence. And so will we, if we work and live there.

I glance at Ada and know immediately that she's freaking out. She has a tight, professional smile on her face but sweat has broken out across her forehead and her eyes are glassy.

"That's so generous," I say firmly into the camera and Adam's smile swells even bigger. I think he loves giving gifts. He's like Ada's dad that way, only wealthy. But I know Ada now. I know her well enough to know she doesn't like that kind of gift.

I clear my throat. "But part of our charm is that we're regular, self-made people. Would you consider letting us run the show out of our own shop?"

Adam thinks about it. "Not the *Knockin' Rods* shop, right? That's a rental. I don't want to have your setup change suddenly if the landlord decides to do something else with the property.

Consistency will be key so that our subscribers form a connection with the place."

"I understand," I say and I have to swallow now, because if we don't use my shop and we don't use his, where are we going to go? Ada's family shop would have been perfect. I see on her face that she's thinking the same thing. But her Pops has made that impossible.

Adam is not one to be deterred. "Okay, I'll send over the papers and we'll get things signed up and taken care of and then we'll figure out the shop space afterward. Get me a proposal asap for that. This is going to be a fantastic partnership! Tanner will call you to set up a dinner here to celebrate in the next few days before I leave town. Buckle up, you two! We're going to take the motorsports world by storm!"

And then he's off the line leaving Ada and I looking at a blank screen.

"Well," she says.

Our phones buzz at the same time. It's the contract coming in by email. Wow. He really was eager to get started. There's also a link to the hidden BOOM Motorsports site where our videos filmed so far have been edited, branded, and set up for streaming. There are two of them. One is the extraction. One is what we've done on the car so far. They've taken stills of the two of us — flattering ones — and cut them out, put a colorful background behind them, and a huge title. We look like stars.

I exchange big-eyed glances with Ada.

"What. The. Hell."

"It's good, right," she says and I think she might be hyperventilating. "If we're giving up our own income streams then we need this to succeed and they have us set up for success."

"I guess we toss the dice," I say grimly as I digitally sign the document and send over the information for our joint bank account.

Usually, this kind of thing takes time. When I submit online freelance articles, it can take weeks to iron out details, sign contracts, and get paid. With BOOM it's like an overly eager AI is taking care of things. The moment both of our signatures are on the documents, I get two more emails. One tells me that a huge sum of money has been deposited into our joint account. The other is from Adam Boomhower welcoming us to the team and telling us that the big site launch is next week, and to be sure to wear our BOOM branded products for the next video. He'd better not mean *all* of them.

Even that joke feels weak in the face of all this. It's happening so quickly that I can barely catch my breath.

"Ada," I say, wanting to set her mind at ease. "How are you doing with this?"

But the moment the words are out of my mouth the phone rings and all I catch is her falsely-sunny smile before she bolts into the bathroom and I hear the shower running.

I lean my head against the bathroom door when the call is over.

"Ada?"

"Was that the hospital?" she calls over the sound of the shower.

"Yeah, my mom is doing really well but I have to go help them transfer her."

"Okay," she calls out.

"Do you want to come with me?"

There's a pause and then a squeak and then the door opens a crack and a sliver of her face appears through the open door.

"Really?" She sounds uncertain.

"Only if you want to."

"I do." She bites her lip. "Can I shower first?"

I nod.

This is the first time I've been at her place without either her or Pops here, I realize when she closes the door. It feels clandestine.

Nervously, I make my way down the stairs to the shop below. Going in there where the cars are, feels safer somehow. Like I won't accidentally tread on anything secret.

Marvin's project is gone, leaving Pop's bay empty. The pit yawns wide from the center of his bay. I'm not even sure those things are legal anymore. A complete hazard. But an easy answer for back in the day when lifts were hard to come by. You can service the entire underside of a vehicle with ease from one. I might even prefer them, odd as that might sound. I just have to be careful not to break my neck in this one.

There's a free bay in the middle that's currently cluttered with tool carts and smaller projects.

I wander over to Ada's side of the shop. A pair of bucket seats sit to one side, clearly finished, and waiting to be reinstalled. Something is cut out and pieced on the table beside her sewing machine. Sample blocks are hung on the wall, pieces of one material or another sewn in tuck and roll, or diamond patterns, or other stitching options. Her desk is just a huge sheet of plexiglass over a wooden table with papers sandwiched between the surface and the table below. Some are nostalgia papers: ancient ownerships, old flyers, even posters. Some are newer things — a series of important phone numbers. An event badge.

And then I see it. There, on the wall, someone has cut out and pinned the articles I wrote about her.

I read one. And then I hear a voice reading over my shoulder.

"'The interior was done by 'Pin Up Stitchin'' whose hurried work suited the ramshackle look the rat rod was affecting.'"

"It was hurried," I say, looking over my shoulder at her raised eyebrow and crossed arms. What woman looks this great straight out of the shower? "Didn't you have to complete it in three weeks?"

"Doing work quickly and doing 'hurried work' are two different things. One implies a rush. The other implies shoddy craftsmanship." She fixes me in place with an indifferent look and tosses her head. "How about this one?"

"'Not the best work I've seen from Pin Up Stitchin' but suitable for a daily driver,'" I read. "Not a word of a lie. I've seen at least a dozen cars you did better."

She barks a laugh. "Really, Nicola? You aren't going to take any of it back?"

I turn, finally, and lean backward so that the table props me up as I take her hands and offer her my most charming half-smile.

"Pineapple, I'm no liar and I don't say things I don't mean. I meant it when I said this wasn't your best work. Just like I meant it when I said I was falling in love with you."

Her breath hitches.

"I don't plan to apologize," I say in a husky tone. "But I also don't plan to write anything else about you."

She frowns.

"It would be a conflict of interest. Because I find I'm suddenly very interested ... in you, in case that wasn't clear."

And that makes her finally crack a grin and shake her head. "You are the worst, Nicola Petrovic."

I smile. "Of course I am. It's part of my charm. Now, come meet my parents and see if you dislike them, too."

Chapter Thirty-Eight

ADA

THE LAST TWENTY-FOUR hours with Nicola have been some of the most turbulent of my life — and that's saying something when it's coming from someone who has watched her dad give away all the grocery money at least a dozen times.

Sex with him is unreal. I love it entirely. It's like he's learning me and with everything he learns, he slides deeper inside me — metaphorically, of course, but I stand by that metaphor. If I were going to custom order a lover, he would be what I ended up with. Who would have thought it possible when our marriage was built on solving life problems, not on passionate love?

I don't know if it makes it worse or better that I can do with him what I've done with no one else. It complicates everything, layers in emotions and wants I didn't expect to factor in at all.

The thing is, he's still Nicola. Delightfully acidic, difficult, gorgeous Nicola. He almost hurts to look at sometimes, he's so beautiful, and then he goes and ruins it by standing by his insulting articles about me, or saying he's gambling all his happiness on me.

I don't think he's lying to me. I think he's really falling in love. I think he's really committing to be my husband forever, even though I married him out of compassion for his situation and a common need to make a living.

And I'm not exactly in a position to turn my nose up at what we have. I'm homeless — or will be in thirty days. I've just burned my professional bridges to set out on a new course. I have — in essence — lit my entire life on fire and am sitting here calmly watching it burn. I'm in a fight with Pops even if he won't admit it by picking up his cell phone.

And in the middle of all this, is Nicola — with his addictive, mind-numbing sex, and kisses that should be controlled substances, and touches that should surely be considered criminal for how they seem to fuck me before he even slips his cock into my body. Okay, that's crass to put it like that, but how do you describe feeling like every stolen glance at him is like an intimate touch leaving little ripples of pleasure coursing through you? How every squabble or exchange of comments that should sting, ends up making you feel like you're a hair away from coming. We've had sex twice, sure, but every other thing we do feels like sex, too. It's ...indecent? But no, that's the wrong word. It's the opposite of indecent. It's the most decent thing to ever have taken place. Or something. Look, I upholster the cars, I don't write the words.

I just know it's messing with my head because I'm afraid of slipping. If I let myself fall for Nicola like he's falling for me, then the tiny bit of control I'm still clinging to will go whipping away and I'll be entirely anchorless. He doesn't seem to care that he's jumped into an abyss of which neither of us can see the bottom. In fact, he wants to pull me in with him. And I'm too scared. I want to see the bottom. I want to know how this is supposed to end, and what's going to be expected of me. And right now I don't have the slightest inkling.

I learn very quickly that Nicola is a wonderful son. Watching him help his mother settle and then going with him to get his father — there's commitment there. Kindness. His expression is full of gruff frowns, but his hands are tender as he guides and reassures them again and again that all will be well. Would he be this kind of a father, too? There's gentleness in all his movements. Softness shades his tone as he speaks to them — almost entirely in Serbian.

They smile at me. I greet them in English. They nod and speak to him in Serbian.

"Speak to her in English," he chides. "She doesn't speak Serbian."

A stream of words floods back at him from them both. His mother is doing much better, it would seem.

"English!" He barks at his father, mock offense on his face.

His father leans in and grabs my cheek in a pinch. I try to pull back, but boy, the grip on that man!

"You'll be good for him," his father says to me. "Make him fight for something for once. Everything comes too easy for him."

I feel my brows lifting and my eyes widen. Too *easy*? If I've seen anything from Nicola since I married him, it's that his life is a struggle. A lesser man would have quit by now.

I'm relieved when Nicola's dad finally relinquishes my cheek and returns to berating his son in their mother tongue.

Nicola is quiet when we leave.

"They like you," is what he says, but he's deep in thought. "They say I married well."

He spares me a shy glance and my heart shivers, and all at once, I realize that this family is now my family, too. More people relying on me. Me, who hasn't been able to keep up with the family I am already responsible for. My marriage is about more than a husband I want to roll into bed with day and night. It's also about these two — it was for them in the first place.

When my phone pings with a message from Tanner —

dinner with Big Daddy Boom tomorrow night — I'm practically sweating.

"Look, don't panic," Nicola says, but he's absent, as if his mind is elsewhere. "It will be fine. You looked stunning last time in that yellow dress."

I offer him a half-hearted smile and try to call my Pops. No answer. He's avoiding me.

I look at the accounts we share. He has not settled our debt. He's not going to either, I don't think. He's probably giving it away to someone. Probably.

I text Jasmin and it takes her forever to reply and when she finally does it's with, *Ugh. Drama with Mom. Coffee tomorrow?*

I text my agreement but it doesn't feel soon enough. I'm unsettled. I'm anxious. I feel like the world is too tight and I can't breathe.

Nicola drives me to the shop and despite our hours of rest this morning, I can tell he's tired. His responses are slow, his smiles slower, his brain drifts away on whatever winds are taking it. We wear BOOM T-shirts and start to tear down the engine of the truck for the rebuild.

"I think we should revise the paint scheme you picked," he says as we work. "I don't like the powder blue. It's not a Ford original color."

"Maybe not," I say, annoyed that his first real words to me are to pick something apart, "but it's the best color for the truck. It practically screams 'beach hot rod.'"

"The color should be period correct."

"They didn't have the good colors at the time," I argue, and if maybe I turn my wrench a little too hard and he has to dodge it, well, I didn't mean it.

"Yes, but this truck isn't about us," he argues and he sounds so damn reasonable.

But that's the thing. Of course it isn't about me. Nothing is, is it? My life as a daughter isn't about me. It's usually about Pops giving things away to anyone who *isn't* me. My home isn't about me, it is in fact, not my home anymore. My business is no longer about me. As of this moment, it belongs to BOOM Enterprises. And even this marriage which I was starting to like — it's not about me, either. It was about saving an older couple from dying alone. Which is noble and good, but for once I just want one thing to be about me.

Is that selfish? Probably.

Do I care? Not at all.

"It's the color I picked when you were too busy to help," I say sharply. "And it's the color I like. I already have fabric ordered for the upholstery and paint ordered based on those samples, and I'm not changing it just because you roll in here and suddenly have an opinion."

"Well, using an original Ford color would just be more authentic, no?" He says it like it's undeniable.

"No," I say, crossing my arms over my chest.

The look on his face is stunned, like he can't fathom that someone would have an alternate opinion. I sigh. I'm too tired for this.

"Fine. Whatever you want," I say in defeat. After all, everything else has been ripped away. Why not this, too?

We work in silence after that. Drive home in silence. Wash up in silence. Eat in silence. It's not until we're done eating, both slumped in our chairs, exhausted, running on fumes, that he fumbles for my hand on the table — missing it the first couple of times, before he finally captures it — and then holds it until my gaze catches on his.

"I'm sorry," he says. "I don't know what I did, but I'm sorry."

I'm tired, too, but not so tired that I'll let this slip. "You belittled my opinions and tried to override my choices."

"I'm sorry," he repeats and he truly looks contrite.

I nod my head, accepting his apology. But I wasn't really

mad about that. I was mad that my life is out of control and his apology can't fix that.

"Let me sleep with you tonight?" he asks and his eyes are so open and vulnerable that it would take an even colder, harder heart than mine to say no.

He seems to realize how conflicted I am, how torn. Or maybe he's just so tired that he can't do more than place a gentle, chaste kiss on my shoulder before he curls around me and sinks into sleep.

But I lie there, awake for a long time, trying to think about what choices I have left and what I should do about them. I like Nicola. I want him. But do I like him and want him enough to allow myself to slip into love when it has the potential to cost me so much? I'm not sure, and thinking about it with him lying so close to me feels like its own kind of torture.

Chapter Thirty-Nine

ADA

THE NEXT DAY is fraught with tension. Every time I look up, Nicola is watching me with something warring in his eyes. He offers me small, gentle smiles that are so unlike his sharp, opinionated self that I'm not sure what to do with them. It makes me think of someone trying to earn the trust of a wild animal, slowly offering tiny tidbits until the creature comes right up to them, and allows them to stroke it. He's doing this with me. Trying to draw me in.

It wouldn't be so confusing if it didn't also feel like foreplay, as if every heated glance he sends my way isn't also a promise of what's coming later. And it's not that I don't want what's coming later, it's that I'm not sure how far to let this go.

Question: is it ethical to let your husband fall in love with you? What about if you won't let yourself fall in love with him back?

These questions haunt me until Nicola's phone rings and he has to leave urgently.

"My parents," he says as he kisses me goodbye.

I've been kissed goodbye. He did it as naturally as waving to someone you know. I'm not sure what to make of that.

Fortunately, coffee with Jasmin interrupts my worries. I meet her close to her dorms, happy for a reprieve from everything — even my home.

"He bought her a house," Jasmin says as we sit at a round wooden table so carved and re-carved with the scratched names of patrons, bands, and wild declarations of love that it's practically a cultural monument.

We're both drinking frothy, overpriced coffee drinks. Jasmin got extra whip and extra syrup because I guess her guts aren't in knots like mine are.

"Who bought who a house?" I ask.

Her eyes are so intense that it's freaking me out. I don't know whether I should be excited for her or wary.

"Your Pops bought my mom a house. It's why he sold the shop and your apartment," she says and I can tell from her expression that she's maybe as much of a jumble of emotion as I am after all.

She doesn't know whether to be hopeful and pleased or stressed and I can hear that little note of begging in her voice. She's hoping I won't disown her for this — as if either of us could have prevented it or caused it.

"She's leaving the cult and the boyfriend. She's going to go there. He's moving in with her and so is Marvin, for reasons unknown. They're going to help her unbrainwash or whatever it is you do with people who have been in cults too long."

"Deprogram," I say, shocked.

"Yes, that."

"Does she need that?"

Jasmin shrugs. "Maybe she needed it fifteen years ago. How would I know? I don't know what normal parents are like."

"So all the money from our last asset ..."

"Went to my mom." She looks down and picks at her clothes. She knows I'm ripping apart inside.

Honestly, I can hardly breathe. We could stay out from under the debt with the Boom money — me and Nicola. But that means me asking him to use *our* money on my Pops debt. I feel like I'm choking. I feel like it's swallowing me up.

Does it count as using someone if you're married to them? It feels like it does.

Will he blame me for it? He's infatuated now. How will he feel when his money is being soaked up like spilled water on one of those magic rags they peddle on the shopping channel?

"Say something, Ada," Jasmin begs, still not looking at me.

And I could fucking scream at my Pops right now for putting us here. I would gladly shove all that debt in his face and tell him to deal with it.

But this isn't Jasmin's fault. And damn it, I don't want to lose one of the last people I have.

"Will you come to eat with me and Nicola one night?" I ask her softly. "I miss you."

Her eyes spring up and look at me and I see her mouth work and then she shakes her head minutely like she knows just like I do that we don't have to say anything. That we can just be cousins and friends without having to forever wear the decisions of our parents.

"Does this mean you're staying married?" she asks eventually when our coffees are half gone.

"Of course," I say. "I promised I would."

We drink the rest of them before she asks, "But do you love him? Can you stay married to someone you aren't in love with?"

"Of course I can," I say firmly. "Our marriage isn't about us."

That makes her frown. "Maybe it should be."

I have to blink back tears at the sound of someone saying my thoughts back to me. At the thought that it even *could* be that way. But it's silly to be emotional about it because of course our marriage can't just be about us, and this latest development only makes that possibility more unlikely.

When we're finished I try calling Pops. He still isn't picking up.

I'm about to try Nicola when I get a call from a number I don't know. I pick up.

"Is this Ada Ford?" an unknown voice asks.

"Yes?" I answer, uncertain if I want to admit it.

"Nicola Petrovic gave us your number in case of emergencies."

My heart is in my throat. Nicola.

I barely get out the words. "Is he hurt?"

For someone I don't love, the thought of him hurt is affecting me enormously. I clutch at my chest, as I listen.

"No, this is Cedar Ridge. We're calling because he made you the secondary contact for his parents and we can't get a hold of him by phone. His father is ... agitated ... and we hoped Nicola could come in to help."

"Yes, of course," I say. But wasn't that where he was going this morning? What was he doing if it wasn't helping them? Did he lie to me?

But after I hang up, Nicola isn't answering either. I try to text him, but after five minutes of staring at my screen, I sigh and get in the car.

I literally just told Jasmin that my marriage isn't about me. That it's about so much more. If there's one thing I understand, it's putting family first.

I drive to Cedar Ridge.

"Where's Nicola," is the greeting I receive when the harried staff hustles me into Nicola's mom's room. It's his father speaking. He is in her bed with her, arms crossed over his chest, face red and furious looking.

"We need him to leave her room for a while," the nurse whispers to me. "Neither of them have eaten since yesterday. We need them to eat and take their meds but when he's here, they won't."

I nod. Suddenly, Pops selling everything we own doesn't seem so bad. At least he feeds himself. Mostly.

I watch them, and I swallow because there are two things I realize in that moment and they both hit me hard.

First, that the reason Nicola's dad won't leave is because his wife is asleep and holding his hand, and he doesn't want to let go. And isn't that real love? Not letting go even when the other person doesn't know that's what you're doing? It's what Nicola's doing with me. Holding on, even while my heart is still asleep?

Second, I realize with unsettling certainty that I'm not going to walk away without resolving this. That I'm going to take on these two people's troubles as if they're my own. And if I'm going to do the work of a wife — then why can't I enjoy the good parts of it, too? If I'm going to show up for the difficult parts, am I really protecting myself at all by refusing to show up for the good parts? For the falling in love part?

"They called me instead," I tell his father. "They're worried about you."

"They should be!" His father nods firmly. "You should have seen the trouble I caused when I was younger. I won't be moved against my will. Not even by pretty girls in sunglasses."

I push my aviators up on top of my head and give him a long look. "You aren't going to get on my good side by calling me pretty."

He laughs. "See? I told Nicola to marry a firecracker. No point in marrying one without a spine! Choose a girl with some life in her."

"If you like women with life in them then you're going to have to let the nurses feed and care for your wife," I say dryly.

He looks around guiltily. "Last time I left her, they kept her from me for weeks."

I put a hand on my hip. "But this time your room is right down the hall."

"Don't put your hand on your hip! I'm not a child."

"Don't talk like a child and I won't treat you like one," I shoot back.

He looks at me for a long minute before he laughs and gently sets his wife's hand down, scooting to the edge of the bed.

"Fine, I will go. But you have to walk with me."

I nod, chuckling. "I think I'm looking into my future here. Were you as strong-willed as Nicola when you were his age?"

"Of course! Where do you think he got it from? That and his taste for fine women."

By the time I get him settled, I'm feeling better about things. Maybe I can do this. Maybe it wouldn't be such a bad thing to jump with him, even if we don't see the bottom, even if we can't predict the journey.

I try to call him, but there's still no answer.

I pick up my phone to try texting again, but there's a buzz and a notification. I open my email without even looking at it. It's an alert. From the bank. To let me know that my account is now two dollars in the negative. The joint account that I opened with Nicola just this week. The one that had all our shared BOOM money in it.

Panic hits me like a drag car at the end of the quarter mile.

Desperate, I text Nicola.

Have you looked at our joint account?

Nothing.

I try to call again.

Voicemail.

My heart is in my throat. Fear, gripping me tightly, I race

home. It's almost time to get dressed to go to the BOOM party and I don't know where my husband is, our collective money is gone, and my father has spent his money not on our debts but on a house for my aunt.

I blow a stop sign without realizing it until I'm two blocks away, that's how freaked out I am. I think the radio is playing. I can't hear a note. My mind is roaring. Little black dots dance across my vision, mocking me for being such a fool.

Minutes ago, I was deciding it would be safe to fall in love. *Safe.* Ha. As if anything for me is ever safe.

I pull into our shop lot with squealing tires, narrowly missing the huge car-hauler unloading a car at our shop. The driver runs toward me while I'm still hopping out of my car.

"Are you Nicola Petrovic?" he asks me.

"Do I look like a Nicola?" I ask, but I can't put the bite into it that I'd like to, because I feel bewildered. What is *this* now?

"Well, the name ends in an "a" so I was thinking it was probably a girl's name," the driver says. He's white. Sixties. What was once likely a hearty beer belly is now a drooping victim of whatever diet his wife has put him on. Like most older white guys, his skin is mottling with age.

Even so, I bark a laugh. That had been my line what feels like a million years ago.

"I'm married to Nicola Petrovic," I say, feeling flustered.

"What a relief!" he says, grinning now like I've made his day. I don't have time for him, but judging by how he keeps pace with me as I go to open the shop doors, I'm going to have to make time for him. "I was worried there would be no one here for the delivery."

"I don't think we ordered anything. There must be some mistake," I say, but I'm feeling ill as I look past him to what's on his car hauler.

It's a '32 Ford three-window coupe. A barn find by the look of it. From here, it looks immaculate.

Our signing bonus with BOOM Industries was big. But if Nicola bought this car, even with it in need of restoration — which it likely is, even if it's as nice as it looks — he'd have had to use not just all of the BOOM money, but a big chunk of what he made when he sold his house.

"Are you sure it's for Nicola Petrovic?" I ask. My lips feel numb. Is this what it feels like to have a stroke?

"Yep, says so right here," the guy says. "It rolls and the brakes work. We can roll her right into that empty bay."

I follow his gaze to Pops's empty bay. The one I found Nicola looking over this morning when he was pretending to read the articles he wrote about me. When he refused to apologize for them. Just like I bet he won't apologize for this, either.

Maybe he'll say, "You have to admit it's a good investment, no?" like there's no room for argument. Just like this morning.

I feel cold right through.

"Can I deny delivery?" I ask, breathlessly.

The driver huffs like I've offended him. "Sure you can, if you want to pay a two hundred dollar surcharge and reschedule delivery. You'll have to pay another two hundred dollars a day if you want us to store it for you, though. We aren't a storage company. We're pure haulage."

I meet his eyes. I know I should ask other questions, like when this order was placed, or where it's coming from, or anything really, but I don't have the heart to do it. I scrawl my signature on his papers and help him roll this sweet gem of an old lady into the shop.

We do it with care. It's not the car's fault that she's spelling the end of my marriage and any trust I ever had in another human. It's not her fault that she's fully shattered my world the way some moron shattered her rear glass.

I feel like I might throw up.

And when the delivery man pulls away and I'm left trembling behind the closed door of the shop, I do. Right into the trash can. It doesn't help. I just feel like I might do it again in a minute.

I thought I was safe with him. I thought he'd never do this to me. I believed all his damn promises.

But I'd always believed Pops, too.

And look where that got me.

Chapter Forty

NICOLA

"Trust me, Nicola," Pops says for what feels like the hundredth time, "It's better this way. Give her some space. She's an independent woman. She doesn't want to be crowded."

"I'm not crowding her. I'm her ride for dinner."

"You're *my* ride for dinner."

"And mine," Marvin reminds me from the back. The three of us are driving in my F-350 Diesel.

"I still don't understand why either of you is invited for dinner," I say with a scowl at my phone. It died hours ago, and still, I keep checking it like it might magically come to life again.

"Speaking of that, I have good news," Marvin says casually.

"I hope that the good news is that you have a change of clothes for me so I don't arrive to a celebration dinner dusty and sweaty." I can't keep the grumble out of my voice.

When Pops grabbed me after our meeting this morning and asked me to move some things with him, he didn't take no for an answer, and by the time I realized I should call Ada and tell her what was happening, my phone was dead and we were already on the road.

"Let me use yours," I begged him.

"I don't have one right now," he had said breezily. "Those things are bad for you anyway. They distract you from what really matters."

"Ada's been trying to call you on it for days," I said, aghast. "Why would you get rid of the only way she has to contact you?"

He'd looked out the window for a while before shrugging. "Fine. I didn't pay the bill. I called you this morning on a pay phone. I'll talk to Ada."

"How did you get my number?" I asked but he didn't bother to answer.

I'd run a hand over my face at that point, frustrated, but locked into this plan to help her father. Besides, we'd had more important things to discuss — and places to go — after that, and when it was all through, we still had to pick up Marvin.

"Tell me *you* have a phone," I'd said to him.

"Of course I do." The man's smile was always perfectly at ease. "Just give me the number and I'll type it in."

Which was when I realized that I didn't know her number by heart. That I was used to just tapping her name on my phone. Turns out Pops didn't know it, either. Or wouldn't admit to it. So now, I get to look guiltily at my dead phone while I drive two squabbling old men to a dinner to which they were never invited.

Marvin clears his throat and I meet his eyes in the rearview mirror.

"Everything is settled," he says. "Your parents are legal. You're all set. Here," he hands a business card forward and I take it. It has "US Citizenship and Immigration Services" on it along with a name and a number and an extension scrawled in pen. "Meet him on Monday at 10 am at his office and he'll square away the rest of the details, but you're set."

"Just like that?" I ask, stunned, and I don't know whether I'm thrilled or irritated that this can be no big deal for some people while it's life or death for me. I think I might be shaking a little. "Thank you."

"Of course."

And then my eyes narrow. "I didn't actually have to marry Ada to make this happen, did I?"

He shrugs. "Didn't hurt."

"But it didn't help either, did it?" I press.

"Didn't hurt." His expression is blank. This is the most I'm getting out of him.

I swivel to look at Pops. "And you're fine with that? Your daughter marries a man who is practically a stranger and maybe for no reason and you're fine with it?"

"You're not a stranger. You've known each other for years," Pops says with a shrug.

"At events. In tiny glimpses."

"She watches your show. She reads all your articles. Clearly she likes you."

"She hates me! She read them because she hates what I write!"

He shrugs again. "Looked like love to me."

"But there was no good reason to force her hand." I feel like the only sane person arguing here.

"There were plenty of reasons." Now her Pops looks annoyed. "First of all, she was in debt."

"Because of you."

He keeps talking like he hasn't heard me. "And she needed someone to help her figure that out. Second of all, she's too choosy. Too afraid to take a gamble on someone in case they let her down."

I pinch the bridge of my nose. "I wonder why that would be."

"Third, she didn't realize until you that she could be with

someone to help *them* and until she realized that, I wasn't very supportive of her being with someone. Selfishness is a great sin."

I just stare at him when he says that. It explains too much about this pair.

"It's for the best," her dad says as we turn in to stop in front of the gates of Big Daddy Boom's beach mansion.

I sigh in resignation. "Neither of you have told me yet why you're coming to this party."

"Oh. Yes," Marvin says from the back seat. "Adam Boomhower is my cousin. He says you make a lovely couple, by the way."

And my hands are tied. I can't very well choke the man who could still pull the plug on this deal for my parents. Instead, I grab my dead phone and tap it to my forehead as I find a parking spot and settle the truck into it.

I am screwed.

I am so, so screwed.

Fuck.

Chapter Forty-One

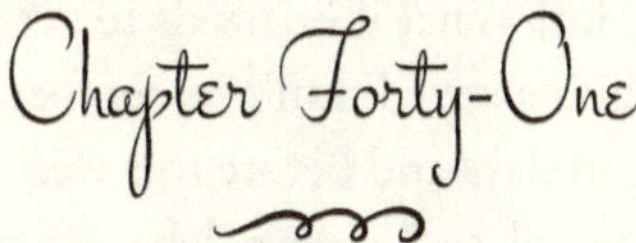

ADA

WHAT DO I DO NOW? Seriously. What.

I'm committed to this marriage. I can't just up and leave it, first of all, because of those two old people in Cedar Ridge who are counting on me. And second of all because I literally just signed papers with BOOM Enterprises this morning and if I don't make good on this husband-wife channel then my entire career is sunk. I'll be starting out again with nothing and I can't do that. Not with debts hanging over my head and no home.

Wow. I feel sick again just thinking about it.

I dress mechanically. Do my hair and makeup by rote. Throw my good-luck aviators — for all those good those traitors are — on top of my head, and stomp out to my hotrod.

No one is answering texts except Tanner who helpfully lets me know about an accident that might interfere with my route to the beach mansion and offers another route as an alternative. Nice guy. You'd think this was his home city instead of mine.

We can't wait for you to get here! he texts to me. *This party is lit!*

I have no idea where Nicola is. He might be in a hospital somewhere. He might be dead. He sure as hell wasn't where he said he was going to be — taking care of his aging parents.

I could wait around for him. Should I? What if something bad happened to him? What if he needs to get let into the apartment? Did I give him a key? I don't remember. We haven't been apart for this long in days and before this week, Pops was always pottering around the place. I wage a debate in my head before an idea occurs to me.

Any sign of Nicola? I text Tanner. *We got some wires crossed.*

He can make of that what he will.

Yeah! He just arrived, Tanner texts me back.

Oh, he did, did he? He arrived at the party without me? Without so much as a text. I do not know this man I am married to, and frankly, I'm not sure I want to.

A huge part of me is in the back of my mind screaming that I do know him. That I maybe know him better than anyone else, including his first wife who might end up being married to him longer than me if I don't rein this in, but I tell that part of myself to be quiet.

We like him! It insists. We might even love him.

Shut up, I demand, revving my engine.

We'll definitely never find anyone like him in bed again.

Yes, but do we make decisions for that reason, Ada? I hope not. I hope we can be clear-headed. I hope we can remember that it's a bad idea to base our life choices on a man who just swindled all our money just like Pops has again and again. We thought we were escaping only to end up trapped.

And why do I keep calling myself *we*?

I drive like a saint even if I feel like the fires of hell are consuming me inside, and when I reach Big Daddy Boom's beach house, I'm cool, pristine, and classy as I slip my car into the line of vehicles parked around his circular driveway.

This is no one's fault but Nicola's, I tell myself as I step out of the car and freshen my lip gloss. I won't take it out on anyone else. I won't let them know.

But I should let him know.

I fire off a text to him.

I know the money is missing. And now this car shows up at the shop. You told me you'd never do this to me, but you did.

My heart might be breaking, but I'm smiling as I knock on the door and am greeted by Tanner.

"Ada!" He says, grinning ear to ear. "I'm so glad you made it! I told Big Daddy Boom you were on your way. We're eating BBQ on the patio out back."

Of course they are. They always are. Five guys are drinking energy drinks and laughing to one end of the patio when we emerge out the back. And even though the sun is setting in beautiful crocus purples and yellows, even though the chrome waves are splashing onto a dusky beach, I'm too upset to care, too wound up to absorb even a moment of their beauty. The balmy sea breeze does nothing to unwind me. The calling birds do nothing to put me at ease.

At the other end of the patio, a man in chef's whites is slaving over a smoker, a series of salads set in dishes of ice in front of him. He's grinning ear-to-ear as he chats to a woman not much younger than me. Her blonde hair falls in ringlets down her back. She fusses over something he shows her like they're siblings, but I know her. That's Gracie Boomhower, Adam's daughter. She's online famous and beautiful and just about the sweetest, if her online profile is to be trusted.

And there's her husband, Jasper, drinking a beer silently to one side as my Pops and Marvin talk to him. Pops? Here? With *Marvin?*

But I can't care about that. I'm looking for Nicola. I feel like an assassin or a secret agent or something, so set on my target that everything else in the room is just an obstacle. Where could he be?

My text window to him is still open and he still hasn't responded. I glance down for long enough to dash off one last text.

Please talk to me before we're both at this party together.

Before I even hear the text send, Adam Boomhower appears and sweeps me into a hug.

"Ada! You made it! I was just telling your Pops how excited I am to be working with you."

"Yes," I say, so stunned that I don't know what to do when Adam draws back.

"Drink?" he asks and I gratefully take the ginger ale he's offering. Sure. A canned drink. At a party with its own private chef. Why not?

"I can't believe you invited my Pops," I finally manage. "That's so generous."

"No, Ada!" he says, expansive in how he turns us, so he's talking not just to me but to the whole room. "You two are the generous ones! I'm so happy to hear that my cousin Marvin is able to spend time with your family. He's been so lonely here on his own."

"Your cousin," I gasp. Oh. Oh, this might explain a few things. Like how Adam Boomhower needed me to be married and then suddenly his cousin was there, suggesting it could solve all of our problems.

I feel the blood draining from my face. What will Nicola think when he finds out?

But then I'm kicking myself. What do I care? I'm not the one who has taken advantage of this situation. I'm not the one who *still* isn't here when I said I would be.

The knot in my throat is getting tighter. I don't know if I can do this — smile and pretend I'm doing well when my whole life is crashing down around me.

"We all practically feel like family these days, don't we, Gracie?" Adam asks his daughter. Looking back and forth between the two of us like we're ten and he hopes we'll go play nicely together and maybe make friendship bracelets.

She smiles warmly, willing to play his game. "Sure. Your show is a perfect addition to the BOOM Motorsports streaming service, Ada. And I'm certain Jasper's dad is going to love the truck."

"It's been hard to keep it from him for this long," Adam says, leaning in toward me like we're sharing a secret even though he's saying it to the whole patio.

"Has it ever!" Gracie agrees. "Jasper's had to invent wild excuses to cover us."

There's a noncommital grunt from her husband.

"But all that aside," Adam says, stepping in a way that angles his body out and completes a rough circle that was forming so that it seems like he's gathering us in, and just with that move, I find everyone *is* gathering inward. He's like that. Magnetic. Where he goes people follow. "What we're going to do here is so more than that. We're building a whole media empire and we're building it on the BOOM foundation and every brick we add from outside only makes that foundation stronger. I love the values you and Nicola bring to the channel, Ada. Family first! You both care enormously for your parents. Isn't that right, Pops Ford?" My dad lifts his drink in salute and Adam grins wider. "Strong, healthy relationships, Ada — look at this beautiful family you're building together with Nicola! And this kind of humble honor that you two have ... well, it's that kind of thing that I so enjoy to see."

I feel my heart sinking because after today, I don't feel like I'm in a strong, healthy relationship, but everyone has quieted now and they're watching us. Still no Nicola. Wherever he is, it's not here helping me with that 'healthy relationship.' I try for a smile.

"Humble honor?" I say, thinking it's the most likely to at least have a shade of truth to it.

"Well, I offered you a house and a shop — top of the line — and your husband turned me down!"

"Oh, the beach house," I say a little breathlessly. "It was very generous of you."

"Not that," he says. "The other one. The one that fit your working-people vibe more. I said I'd pay for it and he wouldn't hear of it. That kind of humility and pride — well, you just don't see that in modern young people and I am just so impressed!"

I want to cry. We'd been offered a shop and a home and Nicola had said no? Really? Where *is* he?

I tap into my phone, trying to hide that I'm doing it by smiling widely at Big Daddy Boom.

"That sounds like Nicola," I say.

What have you done?

But still no answer.

"I can see why you love him," Adam says, grinning widely.

"Yes," I'm speaking between gritted teeth. Love him? I might strangle him. And those two things are *not* compatible, no matter how much my favorite authors keep trying to jam that down my throat.

"Well, no need to stand on ceremony here. This isn't a photo shoot." Adam laughs as if he's told a joke. "That's tomorrow. We'll pull the Silver Bullet in its current state over to your new digs and do a full shoot tomorrow, right Jasper?"

He nods to his son-in-law who smiles indulgently but keeps his mouth shut. Probably a wise move around Big Daddy Boom. But I'm panicking. We have no new digs. Certainly not in time for tomorrow.

"Tonight is just for fun. In fact, I think Gracie and I even have to jet for a bit. We're interviewing a lovely girl who drag races and we think she'd be a great addition to the streaming service. How do you feel about the name *What a Drag!* for her show?" he asks me.

"It's very unique," I admit, but I feel relieved when Gracie looks at her phone and gasps.

"Oh, we are late, Dad," she says. "We'd better go."

And I can't help it. I melt a bit when her husband leans in for a kiss and a tender look before he lets her go. It's like a knife to my heart. The only person I could imagine myself being like that with has betrayed me. Utterly. I sure hope that barn-find car is worth it.

"Have fun, everyone!" Big Daddy Boom calls over his shoulder as he leaves, but I'm not in the mood for fun.

I look down at my phone. My messages are still unanswered.

Furious, I type in, *If I don't get an answer from you in five minutes.*

But I stop. Am I really the ultimatum girl? What if there's an honestly good reason he isn't answering?

I look up, biting my lip, and there he is.

Barefoot.

He's coming up off the sand beach, a drink in one hand and his phone in the other. He's scowling at the screen.

I erase what I was typing and type something else instead.

People who love each other don't betray each other.

He looks up but when his eyes finally meet mine, and they reveal nothing. Instead, he smiles at me a little hopefully.

Hopefully?

Like he hasn't broken my heart.

I swallow down a wave of sadness. What is it about me that makes everyone think I'm open to being used? Do I have a huge welcome mat rolled out on the doorstep of my heart?

I feel my eyes watering as I look at him and his are suddenly sober, shifting from hopeful to confused.

Confused.

Like there's no way he could possibly guess why I'm upset. I guess the welcome mat also has a flashing sign that says "Use Me" in fluorescent lights.

I suck in a shuddering breath as Tanner steps between us and shoves a paper plate at me.

"BBQ?" he asks, smiling, and I can't.

I can't take the plate. My hands won't move. I don't even know how to say no. Maybe this is the stroke. Maybe it just had a delayed timer on it or something. Maybe I'm about to start sobbing right here in the middle of this celebration, and they'll can the show because I'm too unhinged to work with.

I think I might be hyperventilating at the thought.

Tanner's mouth falls open and his brows raise. He's sussed it out. I'm insane.

And then a big hand gently takes his plate of BBQ and sets it on the table beside us, and the same hand claps on Tanner's shoulder and gently turns him aside.

"Thanks, man. That's very generous," Nicola says in a thickly accented voice. "But I've got it from here."

And then, as my eyes are still swimming so hard I can't see him, he puts that same hand spread wide between my shoulder blades and gently steers me off the patio, and out onto the beach, out of earshot, as if we're just two newlyweds looking at the ocean together.

I feel like I'm going to throw up.

"I didn't expect you to take it like this," he says quietly.

"You didn't?" I say, and I can't help myself. Some of my spirit is rising to the surface again. A tiny mini-figure Ada willing to fight for life-size Ada and her rights to at least be *told* about life decisions.

"I thought that maybe you'd be excited. I thought it was what you wanted."

"You thought draining our joint bank account was what I wanted?" I ask, and now I am crying and I'm furious with myself for crying because I'm not sad, I'm angry. Okay, maybe I'm sad, too. Or devastated. Or … I'm out of words. It's like my emotions are soda at a serve yourself station and a seven-year-old is in charge of filling my cup. Everything is pouring in there with no rhyme or reason at all. I'm swamp water. That's my emotion right now.

"I thought you'd want it for this," he pleads. "We'll make the money back. It's worth it. It's just ... the thought of it going to someone else when it has so much history..."

"Oh, I know all about the history," I say viciously, thinking about that barn find three-window coupe. It *is* the find of a lifetime. But there will always be finds of a lifetime. There will always be fucking *history*.

"I suppose you do." He looks nervous. He runs his hand through his hair with a pained expression on his face as he looks out to the ocean.

"Look," I say, "I'm not going to break our marriage apart."

Suddenly his eyes are on me again, panic writ large in them.

"I know your parents need it."

"My parents," he says stupidly but his breath is coming too fast now, too, like I've reversed our roles somehow. Ha.

"Yeah, the ones you were supposedly taking care of this morning when actually you were going behind my back." He opens his mouth to speak but I don't let him get a word in. "And I won't sink things for them because they're important. I know that. And frankly, I put every egg I have into the BOOM basket, so I can't afford to sink that, either." I draw myself up and fix him with my most level glare. "So, we stay married. We do our job. But when we aren't working, you stay far away from me, Nicola Petrovic. No joint bank account. No sharing a bed or even a house. This marriage is for everyone else, but it's not for us. Not anymore."

And then I spin in the sand and I run back to the house, and right past the gaping bros with their energy drinks, right out to my car so I can speed away in a satisfying squeal of tires.

Chapter Forty-Two

NICOLA

"This marriage is for everyone else, not for us."

Her words are still ringing in my head.

Shit.

I thought she'd be happy. Or at least less stressed. Maybe she'd finally realize that I really love her and that I'd do anything for her. Which is stupid, I guess, because somehow I've stepped in it again, as only someone whose longest relationship was two weeks and who spends most of his time with his aging foreign parents really can.

My cheeks are hot as I stare stupidly at my dead phone.

I think I'm realizing that charging it is an A-1 priority.

I follow the trail she left in the sand back to the patio where the guys are having some kind of competition to jump off the roof without breaking a leg. The only ones on the ground are the chef who is cheering them on with no conscience, and Adam's son-in-law Jasper.

"Hey man," Jasper says with a nod to me.

"Hey."

"Your girl went that way." He nods at the door and when I hesitate he clears his throat awkwardly. "Need something?"

"A phone charger," I say with a wryly embarrassed look. "I think I've missed some things."

He laughs and I'm not sure why until he reaches into a plastic bin and pulls out a BOOM phone charger — bright orange and branded, complete with a plug-in for the cigarette lighter in my truck.

"You wouldn't believe the things Adam brands."

"Oh," I say, shaking my head as I unwrap the charger from the cellophane wrap. "I think I would."

He snorts and looks at me, and I know he knows exactly what I mean but he's not going to say it if I'm not, and trust me ... I'm not.

He claps me on the shoulder as he says, "Keep the charger. I'll see you both tomorrow at the shoot."

I nod, grateful, and then I'm hurrying to my truck, my anxiety at odds with the delighted whooping behind me as I shove the charger into the port, start my truck, and wait for my phone to boot up.

The moment it does, her texts flood my screen and I feel the blood rushing from my face. I swallow back nausea.

Fuck.

No, no. no.

Fuck it all.

She thinks I bought a car? With our money?

Something is spiraling in my chest dragging my heart down to hell.

Her face on the beach comes flashing back in my mind. Did I specify how I spent ... I didn't, did I? Somehow, I thought she'd figured it out. But what she's figured out is all wrong and she's going to take off and leave me because of it, ban me from her life over a misunderstanding.

I curse, palming my face as I try not to panic.

I could be mad about her assumptions. I could throw them in her face or silently let her go so I don't injure my pride. I could decide it's my job to let her call the shots and to respect the distance she's put between us.

But I'm not that guy. Maybe I like things to be perfect. Maybe that makes me overly judgmental. But do you know what it doesn't make me? Stupid.

I know exactly what this could be and I'm not going to just sit there while the ball rockets around jumping from number to number on the roulette wheel. I'm going to go put a magnet in the right spot and do my damndest to win this bet.

I'm in the truck and my foot's on the accelerator before I finish thinking, and I'm racing down the streets, heart in my throat, jaw clenched so hard that soon *I* might wish she'd married that dentist so he can fix my poor worn teeth.

It takes a decade to reach her home — or so it feels. Our home, if I'm being honest. Because this is the only home I want.

Her car is here.

That's a good sign.

The door is locked, which is not.

I bang on the door. No answer.

I try a call. Still nothing.

She's going to freeze me out, isn't she?

I put my forehead against the trim and I breathe hard as I try to think. There's a scuffling sound behind the door and I know it's her. I know it. And what, she's going to wait in there until I slump off and make a home somewhere else? Alone? Without her?

Nope, not happening.

I sit down on the step, my back to the door, and I text her instead. One last gamble.

I don't know what car you're talking about.

Her answering text is lightning fast.

You don't know about the car that was shipped to Nicola Petrovic that I signed for just over an hour ago?

No.

The '1932 three-window barn-find in mint condition?

Sounds gorgeous. Still no.

The car that definitely drained your bank account and our joint one?

Don't see how it could, when I already took all the money for something else.

The door behind me creaks and I scramble to my feet.

I feel like a kid caught breaking windows by throwing rocks. She's there in the open doorway, arms folded over her chest, aviators down, but even with them down I can tell she's been crying and I hate it. I feel like I'm powerless to stop it.

"Listen," I say, sounding stupid even to myself. "I didn't realize you thought I'd drained our bank accounts and bought a car. I didn't. I don't know where the car came from, but look."

I pull up the pictures on my phone and hold them out to show her.

"I went to the bank today with your Pops. I wanted it to be a surprise, so I lied and said I was helping my parents. I bought out your debt with the money I got selling my house and we closed those accounts."

She looks at me then and I can't see her eyes and it's killing me, so I reach out, certain she'll stop me, but still hopeful. Still painfully hopeful. I draw the aviators from her nose and put them up on top of her head. I do it slowly, like I'm sure she'll stop me. It feels agonizingly intimate and yet she lets me. And her big eyes are open and aching. I want to take all the ache away.

"Is this true?" she asks, and I nod. Her tone turns plaintive, like she's begging me to give her reasons to keep listening to me. "But it doesn't explain the rest. Why is our account empty?"

"Because your Pops told me who he was selling your family shop to. He was selling it to Adam Boomhower. Adam was buying it for a set. For us, because Marvin warned him we'd turn down his beach house. He was saving it as a surprise to give us tonight. So I talked to them both and I made a different deal. I put a downpayment down with our BOOM money. The deal is in the works with Adam, and it's gonna close first, but then he'll sell the shop back to us. In your name, Ada. Because it's your family's shop, and I saw what it was doing to you to let it go."

She swallows like she doesn't know what to say and I see her arguing with herself internally. It's all over her face that she's looking for reasons to reject this.

"But you did it behind my back," she says.

"We ran into Adam at the bank. It was complete coincidence. I was in the middle of explaining to Pops why he couldn't sell your home. I was going to call you. But my phone was dead and I'd forgotten the charger, and apparently, your Pops doesn't 'do' things like phones anymore."

She barks a laugh. I know it's accidental because she covers her mouth like she can take it back.

"What happens now?" I ask her and I hope she knows I'm spread out in front of her. That she can do whatever she wills with me. I think my heavy accent must tell her that. I can barely get the words out in English.

"This is the part where someone feels betrayed and they go storming off nursing a broken heart. And they're inconsolable. And they find out who they are without the other person," she tells me, and I'm drowning in those root beer eyes. I don't want them to be telling me goodbye.

"It doesn't have to be," I plead.

She swallows but she's still telling her story. "And a month goes by. And then they realize they can't live without the other person."

I nod now. "So what, you're leaving? You need time to clear your head?"

I hate this. I want her right here where I can love her. But I feel helpless in the face of this story she's written as if it's already happened.

She takes a breath. A huge breath and in that breath, I try my best.

My best comes out in a growl. "You know how I feel. You know I've opened my heart to you."

She makes a strangled sound but then she seems to steel herself as she says. "I'd have every right to go."

I nod. I can't speak anymore. I feel like she's gutted me. I feel like I'm breaking up like a paper plate left in the surf.

I'm watching her, trying to memorize these last glimpses of intimacy that I'm going to get. And then something shifts in her face and my breath hitches and her next words come tumbling out like they're racing to the finish line.

"But you know what, Nicola? I'm not fucking doing it. I already know who I am. And I know who you are. And maybe I could live without you just fine. But I don't want to. And I'm not putting up with you moping for a month either, so pull those fireworks boxers up like a big boy and get your arms around me like a man."

And I'm so shocked, that I just stare at her stunned for a moment, and she's staring right back at me, biting her lower lip, arms crossed over her chest. I'm being an idiot. I'm just standing here when I could be going to her.

I run up the step and through the door and I sweep her up into my arms, right up so she's hugged in tight to my chest with her bottom under my forearms, and I know that manly men aren't supposed to cry, but I still draw in a shuddering sob of relief as I bury my face into her neck and is she ... is she laughing?

"I can't believe you did that, you ridiculous man."

I stumble us forward so I can set her on the kitchen counter and stand between her legs and the moment my hands are free they find her face.

My eyes close. Holding her is too much. I can't do all the

senses at once. I squeeze my lips together tightly and drag in a long breath full of her and then my fingertips are brushing her cheekbones, my palms moving to cup her face, and I lean in and offer a kiss. I don't take it. My lips are soft, barely there as they touch hers, but I don't have to wait because she leans forward and takes them in hers, and completes our kiss. And I'm not sure I can stay standing when I'm melting like this.

"Who does that?" She murmurs into my hair when the kiss breaks and I rest my forehead against her chest, trying to get my bearings. "Who spends every penny they have on a girl?"

"Not a girl," I murmur. "My wife. My fucking wife gets what she wants."

"Don't put that on me," she argues.

I hear the tremor of fear in her voice so I draw my face up and open my eyes and I growl, "Don't *take* that from me. Don't take away my right to give everything I have to you. You're my heart now. You're my whole life."

She freezes. And I know she's scared. That it's all too much. And then her face shifts again and this time when it does, it shifts from fear to defiance.

"I want to love you, too."

"Then do it," I urge her. "Love me. Stop holding back and just do it. I'm holding nothing back from you."

"Nothing?" she asks, a last note of uncertainty still lingering.

"Ada Ford Petrovic," I say, giving her my most charming smile. "There is not a single sliver of me that isn't yours and there never will be. No matter what you decide to do with your own heart. I do nothing halfway. Certainly not loving you."

And I think that's when she decides, because she says, "I suppose that's an adequate amount of love."

"You're damn right it is," I say into her lips, but if she had more to say, it's lost to my kiss.

Chapter Forty-Three

ADA

HE BOUGHT my family home for me, I think as he kisses me. He cleared all my debts. I'm free.

It should feel like too much. I'm the girl who doesn't like to be given gifts. And it *is* too much. But it is nothing, isn't it, beside the gift of his heart?

Which, apparently, he's just handing over to me, like a laid-back monarch who tosses you the keys to the kingdom and says, "Have a great time. Try not to start a war."

I pull back from his kiss so I can meet his eyes. They're full of bittersweetness and it's so intense that it washes over me and floods me, too. I feel ... strangely powerful ... to be able to affect the moods of Nicola Petrovic, the most impenetrable man I've ever met.

But that power makes me feel soft and vulnerable in a way I never have before, like I'm guarding not just my heart now, but his, too.

I catch my breath and he catches my lips again, trying to tell me with his kiss that he wants to give me everything and I would hope that our kiss is sweet. It tastes like honey and promises to me. Tastes like the very best of everything.

It takes a moment of our lips sliding over each other in reverent caresses before I realize why his every touch is laced with hesitation, lined with bitterness, woven through with strands of longing. In his mind, he's still falling alone.

Oops.

I pull back, breaking our kiss, setting my palm on his broad chest and I catch his bright blue gaze in mine, pushing him back when he tries to lean in for another kiss.

"I have to say something."

He nods, and the bitterness is ascendant now, eclipsing his joy, though it remains glittering around the edges. He stands back a half-step, giving me space, giving me the chance to say what I must.

I take a deep breath and his gaze never leaves mine as I say, "Nicola Petrovic, you are the worst man in the world."

He nods, offering me a regretful half-smile.

"And the best."

His eyebrows shoot up at that.

"And I'm not falling in love with you."

The eyebrows pull down. He doesn't like being toyed with.

So, the rest of my words come out in a gust. "I'm *already* in love with you. Please don't go."

It's like my words have released something inside him. He gasps, and has to pause for a moment to run a hand over his face, as if he can't believe this is true. As if it's everything he'd hoped for.

I can see when he swallows, forcefully, intentionally, like he can force down the emotions that make his hands shake. He pushes a cocky grin onto his face instead, and I love his teasing. I love even more that it hides his seductive vulnerability.

He steps back in between my spread thighs and sets his palms gently on them, leaning in to tease me as he catches my lower lip in his and pulls it back so that I have to follow him to hold onto the kiss. He only lets me go when I'm swaying on the edge of the counter so that I have to grab his upper arms to steady myself. He's chuckling when he speaks, but it's with misty eyes — like he's both amused and overwhelmed all at once.

"I wasn't planning on going anywhere, Ada Ford Petrovic. I was planning to stay. Probably forever."

"Right here?" I ask in mock surprise, patting the counter.

"Well, not *right* there," he admits, smirking. "But close."

"How close?" I like teasing him. It's fun but it feels like more than fun. It feels like every time one of us teases, we put a tiny new thread into what we're weaving together, and I love how the pattern shapes and shifts with our teasing words and glances.

"Let me show you," he says, whispering the words into my ear just before he traces the shell of it with his tongue.

I'm still shivering, little threads of desire curling inside me as he catches my hand, and before I realize what he's doing, he's guiding me to my own bedroom and leading me over the threshold, and then drawing me to the warmth of his chest as he hugs me close.

"Here, then?" I ask.

"Close." He lifts me and lays me out on the bed, following me so that he's on all fours hovering over me, and the heat in his eyes is setting me on fire, right through to the core.

"You're going to live in my bed?" I tease.

"Close." His eyes shutter with desire as he gently strips us both to our skin and presses his body against mine. His whisper sends little shivers down my bare flesh. "I've wanted you since that night in the truck when you cuddled up against me. I can't believe you're mine to hold on to."

"You're late to the party, Nicola," I say, running my fingertips over the roughness of his face. "I've wanted you a lot longer than that."

"You have?" There's wonder in his vulnerability.

"Well, I thought about marrying a dentist instead, but you're so good with your hands."

He laughs and kisses my neck and then slides his lips down my collarbone and between my breasts, down my belly, and right to where he can position himself between my legs. I tangle my fingers in his hair and meet his eyes as he honors me with his adoring kisses.

"You don't have to do this," I murmur. "It seems so one-sided."

He pauses and looks up at me, eyes soft with tenderness. "Oh, I thought I was being clear. This is where I'm staying."

And my answering laugh turns to a helpless moan as he shows me how very good he is at staying, and how good I am at coming, apparently, when I have his soft lips and clever tongue all over me.

When I'm swirling out into a thousand colors and sensations, it's then that he crawls back up me, sliding his warm skin across my sensitive body until every bit of me seems to be sparking and popping like bad wires bundled together. When his mouth reaches mine, I curl my arms around him and hold him close. I don't want him to leave. Not ever. I just want him to stay with me.

I don't realize I've said it aloud until he whispers with his accent so thick that I can hardly understand him, "I will stay, of course, I will stay."

I flip him under me so I can sit up on top of him and straddle his hips. His eyelashes flutter closed and his lips part as if the pleasure of seeing me on top of him is almost too much. His deep groan as I take him inside me makes me tremble. It makes me feel like, for once in my life, I've done something perfectly. I want this to last forever.

I skim my hands over his skin, delighting in every murmur of happiness he makes, learning what makes the corners of his mouth hitch and the air gust from his lungs, and as I pick up my pace, I lean in to catch his lips with tiny kisses. Each one is a promise of more.

He whispers something in Serbian, something that sounds molten on his lips.

"What is that?" I ask, gasping the question between sucked-in breaths. "You've said that before."

His moan is half chuckle. "I said, 'You're like fire in my veins.'"

"There was more to it last time."

"Yes," he says, leaning in to kiss me softly on one shoulder and then the other, one breast, then the other as his calloused fingers skim lightly over my waist. "Last time I called you a terrible hot vixen."

I laugh then and catch his lips in mine before I ask, "And I'm not that, anymore?"

"You're not terrible," he says and his eyes are wide, pupils huge and dark. "But you *are* incredibly hot."

His hands come up to cradle my face and his eyes shut, his expression turning to something almost pained right before he presses his forehead to mine and comes for me and I'm so touched by this softness, this sweet tenderness, that I come along with him and we're one in that sweetness, that furious mad love that shakes us and tears us apart before stitching us back together as one thing instead of two.

I think maybe I'll do this every day for the rest of my life. I mean why not? And I think Nicola will want to, too.

After all, this is what love is, right? That's what everyone says it is. The little moments of the day shared together. And if those little moments can be doing the dishes and smiling over breakfast, why can't they also be those breathless moments right after you've had mind-blowing sex?

I get to pick my minutes and I'm picking these ones.

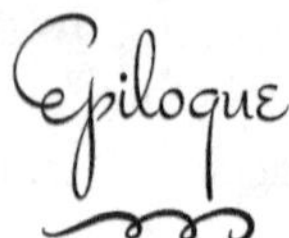

Epilogue

NICOLA

The Silver Bullet is done. It's gleaming in the sunshine and I both — at the very same time — love what we've made, while also seeing every tiny detail that didn't quite come out perfectly.

I'm not pleased with the fit of the oil filter. We had to get a really short one to screw into place to avoid the placement of the engine mount and I wish we'd set the mount back just a little more to avoid having to jimmy the filter so much. There's a spot in the paint that didn't buff out as well as I'd hoped for and it makes me frown every time I see it. The whole car is like that — mostly perfect, but I and I alone, can see the little imperfections, and they make my back itch between my shoulder blades.

"She's lovely," Adam Boomhower says, clapping a hand on my shoulder roughly. He's grinning ear to ear, which I'm realizing is pretty standard Adam.

We're all here at the beginning of the trail to Mikey Hunt's family claim up in the woods. I think Adam wanted to film at the actual cabin, but one look at the so-called road into the woods and he changed his mind. There's no way he's bringing that sweet shiny paint job through all those scratching branches and deep potholes. For which, I am enormously grateful.

We're filming a special episode of Married by Design. It's the episode where we finally reveal the finished product to Mikey Hunt and everyone involved has a huge party. He thinks he's coming to help Tanner plan a restoration for the old cabin, so he's bound to be surprised when his best buddy Adam gives him this truck and reveals that they've already restored his cabin to a degree that it's utterly unrecognizable — or it is to me, since I only ever saw it squished under a tree in the rain. I'm not complaining, though. Without that squashed cabin, I wouldn't have spent one of the best nights of my life in a leaky truck cab.

I smile as I look up to see Ada fussing with her upholstery job. It's gorgeous cream tuck-and-roll leather but it's not the tuck-and-roll that I'm admiring.

"She really is lovely," I agree and I don't mean the truck, though yes, anyone with eyes can see it's an instant classic. Even if we really should have used a Ford original color like I tried to tell Ada.

Adam laughs, catching where my eyes are. "Young love, am I right, Pops?"

He and my father-in-law share a knowing look. Yeah, laugh it up you two. Marvin is laughing, too, and really, I should resent this cluster of old men who took it on themselves to decide my life for me. But right beside Marvin is my dad — mom still can't leave Cedar Ridge — and he's smiling happily while Marvin offers him a drink.

How can you be mad at people who decided to help your family? In their own crazy way, yes. For their own inexplicable reasons. But they did.

And now I get to stay married to the love of my life, *and* see my parents settled, *and* see my business booming. Booming. Ha.

Gracie and Tanner are in the other open-sided tent pouring

over the numbers excitedly. Two million people are watching this reunion live, waiting for the moment that Jasper leads his dad up here to "discover" the truck and all of us. And we have nearly half that number already subscribed on the brand new BOOM Motorsports streaming service. When Ada and I rebuild that gorgeous barn find Adam sent us, who knows how many more people will want to see it?

Yeah, that mix-up was on Adam, too. He couldn't have just put it in his name, could he? He had to put it in mine. When I told him about how much trouble it put me in, he'd just laughed.

"Usually it's me who ends up in that kind of a jam," he said easily before showing me pictures of a six-wheel-drive tank-like vehicle he has Tanner building at the BOOM shop.

"It's going to be unreal," I agreed when I'd seen the pictures. Just like my life now, completely unreal.

And I couldn't be happier.

"What do you think of the old girl now that she's complete?" Adam asks me, nudging me with an elbow. He's messing with some fireworks he has set up. I don't even want to know what they cost him. Like everything else he curates, they're likely top-of-the-line and require a professional to operate them, but will have to make do with Adam Boomhower.

"I think it's perfectly adequate," I say.

They all think that's a joke, laughing like I said the punch-line, but it's only Ada who catches my eyes and lifts a single eyebrow from under her aviators. She knows I mean exactly what I said.

She saunters over to me and pulls me to the side so that we're half hidden by trees. I can hear the crunch of gravel and everyone scrambling. We're seconds from the huge reveal. But I can't pull myself away from her embrace. I never can. I live for her touches. Crave all her kisses.

"Why can nothing ever be perfect enough for you, Nicola Petrovic?" she scolds, frowning.

I steal her frown like I always do. It tastes just like pineapple. I'm a complete addict.

"You're mistaken, Ada Ford Petrovic," I whisper. "And I think you know you are. I think you know exactly what I consider to be perfect."

I lean in and catch her lips for a second kiss. I don't mind pushing my luck. It turns out I'm just about the luckiest guy around.

"Pineapple?" she suggests when I'm done.

I lean in close so I can whisper in her ear, "Certainly that is perfect. But also terrible, hot vixens."

And her laugh is still ringing in the air when the cheer goes up and Adam lets loose the fireworks. Because of course he does.

And I steal one more kiss. Because of course I do.

I'm always fighting for her - for her love, her respect, her happiness.

Even when it's an uphill battle.

Bonus Scene

HAVEN'T HAD ENOUGH OF NICOLA AND ADA?

You'll want this exclusive bonus scene available only to my subscribers.

Get it here.

Or at www.alicedukeauthor.com

Dear Reader

You don't need to be an adrenaline junkie or obsessed with swoonable romance, but it will help!

Join us in cheering on these adorable couples. We're smitten with them and we're certain you'll love their spark and sizzle just like we do!

Each of Alice Duke's books is a stand-alone romantic comedy ready for you to savor, but they all share one thing in common: unforgettable characters, falling in love like only they can.

So, come join us to thrill at the sizzle and swoon at the heat!

PLAY STUPID GAMES, WIN STUPID PRIZES

Gracie's always been her daddy's girl and when your daddy is Big Daddy Boom, popular vlogger in the hopped up world of off-road wheeling, that comes with a lot of visibility. Gracies' dad has high expectations, even now when she's twenty-two, freshly graduated and running his biggest marketing campaign ever.

But when Gracie'sdad tells the world in a live video that she's single and he's going to pick her next boyfriend ... and hopefully the heir to his profitable online empire, all hell breaks loose, all of rural America shows up at their door, and Gracie is starting to think that not only will this be the end of her family, it might be the end of her freedom forever.

Jasper has been secretly in love with Gracie since they were kids. But with Gracie in the crosshairs of every redneck, gearhead, and rebel int he lower forty-eight, the job of winning her heart becomes a lot more difficult. Especially when Gracie comes to him with a proposal: pretend to be her husband to drive her suitors away and she'll set him up with his own online empire to rival her father's.

Jasper doesn't care about the fame and fortune. He's not here to play stupid games. But he does want the ultimate prize -- Gracie's heart -- and he'll do anything to get it.

Alice Duke

COME FOR THE SIZZLE. STAY FOR THE SMITTEN.

Alice Duke is someone who is always falling in love: with fresh ideas, with mouthwatering foods, with beguiling books — and now with vivid characters and their romances on the page. Come fall in love along with her, again and again.

www.alicedukeauthor.com